THE MAKING OF A BANK ROBBER

Eddie Watkins was 16 when he pulled his first robbery. The place was a local grocery store, and Eddie's accomplice was his cousin Jo. At 18, Jo was a stunning blonde with a body that had developed long before its time. She went into the store ahead of Eddie and bought two cans of beans.

Eddie put a carton of milk in front of one of the two clerks, then asked for a pouch of chewing tobacco. As the clerk turned away, he whipped out his pistol.

"Make one sound and your heads come off," he said.

While the clerks stuffed the cash into a paper bag, Eddie grabbed Jo and told them, "You creeps yell and this little lady gets blown away."

It was all so easy. With the bag of money in one hand and Jo's arm in the other, Eddie hustled out to the car and drove away. All the way down the street they listened for sirens, but there weren't any. Eddie pulled off his hat and Jo threw her arms around him.

It was 1934. The 46-year career of Fast Eddie Watkins had begun!

FAST
EDDIE

Neil F. Bayne and Wes Sarginson

LEISURE BOOKS 　**NEW YORK CITY**

ACKNOWLEDGEMENTS:
For Marti, Desiree, Renee and Scot
&
Mom
Sgt. Al Ferrone L.A.P.D
Judge Clinton Devaux
Dan Gleason
And a special thanks to Eddie Watkins who made it
all possible.

A LEISURE BOOK

Published by

Dorchester Publishing Co., Inc.
New York City

Printed in the United States of America

ONE

June 6, 1980. Lodi, Ohio. 9:57 A.M.

The crowd moves in like rubes to a carnival mid-way freak show. Cars are parked all along Route 86. The police have put up barricades and are pushing the crowd back. SWAT teams from the state patrol keep their deadly vigil and wait for just one signal. FBI agents meet in clusters and, like exterminators looking down their steel-blue barrels, wait for a signal.

A man in blue bib overalls standing in the crowd says to his wife, "I 'member he robbed a bank in Cleveland in two minutes flat."

A man pushing against him for a look says, "He robbed them *all* in two minutes. Why do you think they call him 'Fast Eddie'?"

Another man says, "Hell, he's so fast he could sneak a lamb chop out of a wolf's mouth."

Around Ohio they still talk about Fast Eddie Watkins the way people from the Ozarks country in

Missouri used to talk about Jesse James. While the official statement called him a public enemy, many of the folks around Ohio call him a legend. Fast Eddie Watkins to them was practically a romantic hero, a man who beat the machines and computers of a modern, impersonal world that they themselves didn't really understand and didn't always particularly care for. One of a vanishing breed of lone bandit in the tradition of Willie "the Actor" Sutton, Fast Eddie was beloved by the public as an ingenious master-of-disguise bank robber who, during a forty-five-year career, never once hurt anybody. His daring escapades and antisocial genius had prompted 72-point headlines in newspapers and had sparked the imaginations of the people who read them.

Fast Eddie Watkins had fan clubs and his own business manager; he even had a 45-rpm record produced about him. He was the only man who made the FBI's "Ten Most Wanted Men" list and Dun & Bradstreet's list of up-and-coming business executives at the same time.

Now, people were crowding in for a glimpse of Fast Eddie himself as he held police at bay. He was not the dashing young bandit any more, but a balding sixty-two-year-old, baggy-pants rebel who, nonetheless, had pulled off an ingenious escape from the Atlanta Federal Penitentiary while recovering from a triple-heart-bypass operation. A sixty-two-year-old legend escaping like that gave some of the old folks around Ohio, who are struggling to get

6

by on pensions, something to cheer about.

"Gotta admit," said one elderly man in the crowd, "the old boy kept 'em hoppin'." And he had. The FBI had maintained a month-long search, while Eddie toured the country. But now, just Interstate 71, it looked as if "the old boy" had again run out of time.

A man in a pickup truck takes a folding chair out of the back and sits down to watch the show. The crowd grows. The highway is cluttered with traffic. People are coming in like sharks who have smelled blood.

An FBI officer calls out through a bullhorn for Eddie to surrender. Eddie calls back an obscenity, and the crowd loves it. Always a master of improvisation, Eddie Watkins, seemingly out of options, has decided to hold *himself* hostage. He has a gun cocked and pointed to his head as he leans against the open door of his 1972 Mercury, which is resting halfway in a ditch.

He takes a long drag from a fresh cigarette and calls to the federal man on the bullhorn, "If you want my ass, you come get it!" He laughs, amused at the deadly serious yet comically absurd situation he has created. "But when you do come and get me, my brains will be splattered all over *your* asses."

It's a bold bluff but the only card Eddie Watkins has left. He doesn't want to go back to prison. He has spent more than thirty years of his life behind the gray walls and steel bars of America's best—and worst—jails.

As he stands sweating it out under the midday sun, he watches the cigarette smoke drift away and his thoughts go back to a freezing night in a boxcar, when he was eleven years old.

As the freight train crawled along like a black caterpillar inching its way across white carpet, the huge snowdrifts caused the old locomotive to chug in a way that sounded to him as if the train were taking its last breaths. The door of the boxcar was slightly ajar, and the wind and snow had laid a blanket of pure white through the 24-inch opening.

Young Eddie Watkins opened his eyes, anticipating the evening lights in the city of Cleveland. He was startled by a shadowy figure across the forty feet of emptiness on the other side of the car. The fellow stowaway rose, yawned and walked across the empty car toward him, bumping the steel wall as the train bucked against the impact of heavy snowdrifts.

Eddie crouched in the corner. As the man moved toward him, Eddie smelled the familiar blast of alcohol on the man's breath. The man stopped and peered at him. "Damn," he mumbled, "only a kid."

Eddie rubbed his eyes and noticed the bundle of burlap in the man's arms. The smell of cheap wine crowded in.

"Hey, boy, you cold?"

Eddie reared back into the protection of the corner of the car. "What you want?"

"I asked you if you was cold. Damn snow is whippin' in here."

8

Eddie said nothing.

"I asked you was you cold."

Finally Eddie said, "No, I guess I'm not."

"No, you guess you ain't? What kinda answer is that?"

Eddie pulled his jacket tightly around his skinny frame.

"Bullshit," the man said angrily, and Eddie jerked back in instinctive fear.

Defiantly he said, "Mister, I *said* I was okay, didn't I?"

"You don't have to get tough, you little prick. You wanna ride these damn rails, boy, you best know what you're doin'. Hell, you'll find your skinny ass froze some mornin'. Here, wrap up in these burlaps." The man dropped some burlaps down on Eddie. "Hold the wind out."

Now, fifty years later, Eddie's thoughts go back to that miserable day on that freezing freight. While Eddie locks his thoughts on the incident in the boxcar, the FBI and police officers across the road are talking strategy. Earlier in the day a bulletin had come from the Cleveland office of the FBI, saying that the driver of a 1972 Mercury Cougar which had been spotted was none other than the notorious Eddie Watkins, better known to the banking community as "Fast Eddie." The FBI memo had described him as "a bank robber, an escaped prisoner, a woman-crazy, two-gun-carrying thug who likes roast pork with rice."

Eddie could understand their ire at his having escaped and his carrying two guns; he could make peace with their description of him as a "thug," and he could certainly understand their fascination with his fascination with women. But he couldn't quite figure why they included the bit about the roast pork with rice. Perhaps, he thought, they were going to stake out every hash house and diner and staff it with agents, so when anyone came in and ordered roast pork with rice they'd spring out and yell, "Freeze!" Or, he mused, maybe they were simply trying to distinguish him from all of the other escaped prisoners who also were carrying two guns and were woman crazy, but did *not* like roast pork with rice.

But Eddie's mind keeps drifting back to that boxcar in 1929. The thought of roast pork reminds him of how hungry he was as the train chugged up the grade toward the first glimpse of Cleveland. Only three days before he had been in California. The smell of alcohol on the hobo's breath reminded him of leaving for the train, with his father lying on a sofa dead drunk. Eddie had been forced to hustle the streets of Los Angeles, selling shoelaces, collecting pop bottles, carrying beer up six flights of tenement stairs to the local drunks; later helping pimps to hustle their whores, and then stealing to survive and to take care of his father. While other kids his age were still dressed in knickers, white, starched-collared shirts and smart caps, Eddie was already hustling the streets. He knew where the hookers hung out, he knew the corners where he could make a buck, and he had spent many a day and night carrying his old man back from the corner saloon, as people gawked and sniggered.

It hadn't always been that bad, when his mother and father were married. As he rode along on the freight he imagined her beautiful face. His father had always been on the booze; thus he had never been able to hold a job long. His mother finally couldn't take it any more and the marriage ended. Eddie's brother, Robert, had gone to live with Aunt Belle. He and Robert had always been close, but Aunt Belle didn't have room for both boys. Eddie went to California with his father.

The memories of his horrible life in California were soothed by the thought that the next day he would see Robert, who now was probably snuggled in a warm bed with clean sheets, in a home where somebody loved him.

While Eddie plays the boxcar scene over in his mind, FBI agents, police and highway patrolmen are waiting for instructions. Paul Burke, an FBI agent who had been following Eddie's career and trying to put an end to it for nearly twenty-five years, had been summoned and was flying in from Pittsburgh. The agents and officers who were waiting were simply trying to contain Eddie until Burke arrived. In a sense Burke and Fast Eddie were old friends, and Burke will try to reason with him.

Captain David Brent of the Ohio State Highway Patrol kneels next to FBI Agent Bill Rush. It has been close to two hours since the police forced the car off the road. Now camera crews begin rolling into the area. Captain Brent doesn't like the three-ring circus that he sees unfolding.

"We're the laughing stock of the world right now, I imagine," Brent says. "I wish this thing would end."

Agent Rush tells Captain Brent that senior officers of the FBI are on their way, and that they should wait.

One police officer says to another, "Look at that old bastard. He's grinning over there. He thinks it's a big joke."

Actually, Eddie was smiling because he was thinking back to seeing his mother that day in 1929. He had jumped off the train as it entered the Cleveland station, dodged the railroad detectives and trudged through the cold wet snow to find his mother. He tried to eat his last peanut-butter-and-jelly sandwich as he walked along, slushing through the snow, but the bread was frozen and he had to throw it away. He had fashioned a makeshift overcoat out of one of the burlap bags and he walked until he heard the trolley car clang. He paid his two cents for the ride and rode until he saw the familiar turn onto Euclid Avenue. He remembered many a day of shopping on that street, and as he saw the Christmas lights and the Salvation Army Santas ringing their bells, he felt both lonely and warm at the same time.

He got off the trolley and walked through the slush until he saw the huge sign that read "May

Company Department Store." He took off his burlap wrap, folded it neatly and placed it into the paper sack he carried.

The store was filled with shoppers and Christmas music. He rode the elevator up to the floor that said "Women's Apparel" and got out. His eyes searched from clerk to clerk and then finally he stopped when he heard the familiar voice.

"Now, Mrs. Clanton, if this is not what you really want, just bring it back and I'll be glad to help you find something different." She placed the article in a bag. "You have a good holiday now and it was nice seeing you again."

It was her, all right. Eddie walked up as she turned and went behind the counter, her back to the register. Her light brown hair was fastened neatly with a bow. She turned and said, "Can I help—" Then her eyes opened wide. "Eddie, what are you doing here?" She put her hands to her face. "Eddie!"

Eddie smiled. "Hi, Ma. Thought I'd surprise you, you know?"

"Oh, Eddie, let me look at you." She came from behind the counter. "Oh, Eddie." She hugged him. "How on earth did you get here?"

"On a train."

"Oh, you look so tired. It must have been a long ride." Her eyes filled with tears.

He held back the emotion from his own voice. "I've waited a long time to see you." He clutched her around the waist.

"Me too, son."

"And Pa—"

She put her finger to his mouth. "Eddie, please, we'll talk about your father later." She looked up at the clock. "I won't be getting off for about another two hours." She walked around the counter. "Why don't you go over to the house and wait till I get off? Then we'll talk. You know, Eddie, I've remarried." There was a short silence. "You remember Mr. Barnes?" She looked at him anxiously.

"You mean the conductor?" He walked toward the counter.

"Yes, the conductor. And we are doing really well."

Eddie toyed with his cap. "He's going to be at home now?"

"No. He's working and doesn't get home till after midnight. So you go over to the house and wait for me and I'll be home around nine-fifteen."

Eddie nodded.

"Then we can get something to eat and get you warmed up," she said. "Is that the only jacket you have?"

Eddie raised the bag. "No, Ma, I got another one in this bag."

"Well, you make sure you put it on." She came around the counter and kissed him. "Don't forget to put the jacket on—and I'll be home very soon."

As Eddie left the store, he felt warm inside—so warm that he didn't need the jacket. He was home now, with his mother. He had been anxious because of what happened the year before, when he rode the bus from Los Angeles to Cleveland in the hope of staying with her then. But she had met him at the bus station and, with tears in her eyes, explained that things were so bad she couldn't keep him. She put him right back on the bus for California.

On the trolley ride to the house he passed his old grammar school and the church his mother used to take him to. He got off the trolley at his street and walked down it slowly. Finally, there it was—home. The house had new paint, but nothing else had changed. He tried the knob but the door was locked. He realized that he had forgotten to get the key. The windows were too high to reach, so he wrapped the burlap around him and, as the temperature dropped, he sat down and waited and waited.

Two hours later his mother came home. Snow had partially covered Eddie. She dropped her purse and pulled back the burlap. "Eddie, are you okay? What are you doing out here?"

Eddie shook the snow from himself. His lips were blue. "You forgot to give me the key."

"Oh my God." She took the key from her bag. "You must be frozen. Where are your hands?" She felt his sides.

"Under here," he said.

She got him in by the fire and pulled off his jacket. He hugged her and said, "I'm not cold, Ma, when I'm with you."

The house was pretty much the way Eddie had remembered it in his lonely Los Angeles daydreams of home. In the corner sat his dad's rocker. He glanced around and the time on the old grandfather clock startled him. It was nine-thirty.

"Eddie, now get those clothes off and let me find something for you to put on," his mother said. She came back with the small woolen robe that he had left behind. She hugged him and told him to run a tub of hot water and to be sure to wash behind his ears. As he told her again how good it was to be home, she turned to hide the tear that was slipping out of the corner of one eye.

She fixed the stew that he had liked so well and as they sat there talking about the warm weather in California and he told her about his trip, she suddenly said, "Now listen, Eddie." She hesitated. "You know I love you, but you know—well, I'm remarried now and—" She got up, walked to the window and turned away from him. Snow was whipping against the pane. Eddie went to her and hugged her.

"You crying?" he asked.

"I've missed you so," she said. "I get to see your brother quite often, but I do miss you." She fondled his hair. "What have you done to your beautiful hair?"

"You like it? Even had the barber put some of that lilac-smelling stuff on it. Cost me two cents extra, but I figured you'd like it."

He started to ask her why she was crying, but before he could she reminded him of how late it was. She fixed him a spot on the sofa. "In the morning we'll talk about a lot of things," she said.

She put a clean white sheet and a blanket down on the sofa, fixing him a bed, then tucked him in and kissed him. "Sleep good, my son."

Some time later that night he could hear loud voices in the house. He rose slowly from the sofa and walked toward the stairway. He could hear his mother and her new husband arguing.

"I'm not going to stay in this house if that boy stays here." Eddie could hear the man's stern, gruff voice echoing down the stairway and hitting his ears like a slap. As he stood there he felt devastated.

"I don't care," the stern voice said. "This was discussed before we got married. You'll have to make a decision, it's either him or me. I'm not going to discuss it any further."

Moments later, after Eddie laid down again, he felt a nudge on his shoulder. He pretended he was asleep, hoping that, like the ostrich, he could hide his head away and when he pulled it back out everything would be okay.

"We have to talk for a minute, Eddie."

"No, Ma, we don't."

"I guess you heard." Her voice sounded drained. She reached down for him and he pulled the covers around his head. She pulled his hand from under the sheet and put a fifty-cent piece in his hand. "I guess you'll be asleep when I leave for work in the morning. I'm sorry, Eddie. I had it so hard, so hard. Such bad times . . . with your papa. This man . . . . he's been good to me and—"

She looked at him. He had turned his head away. "Eddie, say something."

He said nothing. She reached over to try to kiss him and he pulled back.

"I understand, Eddie."

"No, you don't."

He pulled the covers back over his head until he heard her going softly up the stairs. As he sat there full of loneliness and feeling a terrible rejection, he could hear the man's voice upstairs.

The voice was saying, "You get it all straightened out?"

When everything was very quiet, he got up and searched around for his clothes, then slipped the fifty cents into his pocket and took one last look up the dark stairs. As he trudged through the snow and headed for the trolley stop, he took one last longing look at the house.

He waited out the night in the bitter cold of an old railroad car that was sitting on a spur. When the morning sun woke him, he pulled off the pieces of old newspaper and burlap with which he had protected himself against the bleak cold. It had stopped snowing, but he could barely see out over the high drifts. As he shook from the cold, he peered out of a half-broken window of the old railroad car. He watched as trains slowly puffed in and out of the rail yard and, finally, he eased out of the car and inched his way to a fence. He waited for a freight to come along and block the yard shack's view of the fence, so the railroad detectives wouldn't be able to spot him. When a freight finally came by he sprang like a cat, climbed the wire fence and dropped into the snow. He could hear the voices of the yard dicks as they walked along checking the open cars. They were laughing about some old wino they had caught the night before, and Eddie wondered if it was the one who'd been in the car with him.

He finally spotted an open boxcar that bore the sign "California Fruitgrowers' Association." Knowing it would be heading west, he darted across the two sets of track between him and the open box-car. With a leap he grabbed the metal steps, climbed to the top of them and jumped inside. He moved to a corner of the car and carefully searched it in the half darkness until he was sure he was alone. He pulled some of the old newspapers from his jacket and laid them in the corner. The wind eased off and the sun was warming things up. That and the fact that he was alone in the boxcar were about the only good things he could think of right then.

He lay there covered with the burlap for a long, long time before he finally heard a chug and felt the couplings jerk as the train began to move. As it rolled along he looked through the door crack at Cleveland as it went the other way. Why did the people there have homes and love and all of those nice things, and he didn't?

He felt the bitterness build inside him as the train got up steam, and he didn't know whether to cry or kick something. As the train picked up speed he re-solved that nobody was ever going to turn him away like that again. Someday he was going to be somebody. He'd show them all—his mother, the new husband, and maybe the whole city of Cleveland. Maybe the whole big world.

And then, as he took some small solace from the fact that he'd made it safely onto the train, he laughed to himself about how he'd outfoxed the detectives. Being able to clear the fence and make it all the way to the boxcar without those detectives seeing him—now *that* was exciting!

TWO

Life in America changed dramatically after 1929. The stock market crashed, the breadlines came, and many of the executives who didn't jump out of office windows to their deaths ended up on street corners inspiring songs like "Brother, Can You Spare a Dime?"

Prohibition had given the organized crime element a powerful economic base. The 1930's spawned many a renegade bandit: Pretty Boy Floyd, Clyde Barrow and Bonnie Parker, and John Dillinger, to name just a few.

Foreclosures on farms and homes became commonplace in the 1930's. Between 1929 and 1934 the world saw Herbert Hoover—the man who had fed the starving nations of Europe but could no longer feed his own people—fall from popularity and power. The world saw J. Edgar Hoover and his "G-Men" come to power. Between 1929 and 1934, Franklin Roosevelt became President, Hitler was elected Chancellor of Germany, Prohibition was repealed in the United States and liquor was flowing again. Roosevelt made some powerful federal moves to shore up the banking industry—which helped the banks and also opened a whole new frontier for those who came armed with pistols and machine guns to make unscheduled withdrawals.

In 1934 Eddie Watkins was sixteen years old. He had gone back to Los Angeles to hustle the streets and survive as best he could. His father's drinking problem got no better, only worse. His mother never came to rescue him from his unsavory existence, so he pressed on the only way he knew how.

By 1934 Eddie Watkins had moved in with an aunt in Los Angeles. That year a lot of people were living with relatives, and it was certainly no disgrace for a sixteen-year-old boy to do so. In Eddie's case, however, it was quite a temptation.

This particular aunt had an eighteen-year-old daughter named Josephine. "Jo," as she was known to every girl watcher in that particular part of Los Angeles, had long, flowing blonde hair and a body that had developed long before its time. At eighteen Jo was generally considered to be a hot number, and Eddie was street wise enough to realize she had been around and knew how to use that body. In fact he was informed enough to know that she frequently did.

Eddie had tried to talk Josephine into his bed from time to time since he had moved in, but she always refused. And then one night, as he was sitting on his bed wondering what to do, he saw Jo walk toward the bathroom door, her young bottom swaying in the flimsy but tight nightgown. He could picture her looking in the mirror and combing her long hair. Then suddenly she came out, opened his door and walked toward his bed. The darkness of her nipples showed through the nightgown. As she got close to the bed, he reached slowly and lightly for her thigh. She laughed.

"You're not going to learn sex with me, Eddie," she said.

She sat down on the bed and he felt himself getting aroused. And he knew she knew it. "What did you do today, Eddie? Rob pop bottles?" she teased.

"I did okay," he said, and reached over and put his hand on her shoulder.

She left his hand there for a moment, then picked it lightly off her shoulder and placed it down on the bed. "Eddie, what's a sixteen-year-old boy going to do for me? I can't think what on earth it could be."

"You'd be surprised," he said.

She giggled. "Eddie, I'm sure you're sure about your rags-to-riches dreams . . . but me, I want to live nice."

"I don't blame you there, Jo. I'm going to have nice things too."

"Doing what, picking up bottles? All of that hustling you do?"

"I'll have big money," Eddie said.

"Yeah, well, it's nice to dream."

"You watch."

"Yeah, right, I'll watch."

"You don't think so, do you?"

"You're just a kid."

"So are you."

She held her arms outstretched and he could see her nipples. "Do I *look* like a kid, Eddie?"

He knew how much she was enjoying the feeling of control over him, being the tease she was.

"So you want money?" he said.

"That's right."

"Big money?"

"Why shouldn't I have it?" Then she turned and started for her room.

"Hold on, Jo. I've got something to show you."

She grinned. "I'll bet. Is that a banana in your pocket?"

"What are you talking about?"

"Eddie, big girls like me know what those things are."

"What are you talking about?"

"You have a hard on, Eddie. I know what a hard on is. Poor boy gets hot, doesn't he?"

Eddie got up and walked toward the dresser. "I'll show you something hot." He reached under some clothing and took out a brown paper bag.

"What's in there?" she said. "Your lunch?"

"Maybe both our lunches." Eddie sat back on the bed.

"You going to show me what you have to show me? What do you have there?"

Eddie grinned. "Now who's excited?" He opened the bag and eased out a .45 Colt revolver with an eight-inch barrel. "A person can get anything with this baby. No more two-bit shoplifting." He held the gun proudly.

"Gee, where did you get it?"

"Somewhere."

"Loaded?"

"Not yet." Eddie opened the breach and she reached for the gun.

"Let me look at it," she said. She began rubbing the cold steel against her breasts and she knew that excited Eddie. "You know," she said, "maybe—just maybe—you can afford somebody like me. Maybe you can."

Eddie noticed her nipples getting hard through her gown. She watched him and stared at his pants. She kept caressing the pistol and finally began licking the eight-inch barrel.

"Give me that thing," Eddie said, and she turned away.

"Just think, Eddie. If everything works out— well, who knows." She reached over and put her hand on the bulge in his pants. "Who knows? Maybe I'll be licking something else pretty soon."

She pulled her hand away and he tried to pull it back.

"I said if everything works out, Eddie." She laughed as she walked out of the room.

It took him a long time to get to sleep that night.

The next day, a single light lit up the dingy basement. In one corner was the table and the mirror. Eddie sat on a wooden Borden's Milk box. The wax, makeup and cotton were on the table. He was startled as the door screeched open.

"That you, Jo?"

"It's me, Eddie."

"You got the car?"

She backed up in disbelief. "That you, Eddie?"

"No, I'm the czar of Russia." He laughed. "Looks good, eh?"

"God, Eddie, they'll never recognize you. Maybe I ought to let you do my makeup." She put her hands on his shoulders. "You're pretty sharp for a kid."

He pushed her away angrily.

"Don't get mad, Eddie."

"Don't call a man with a loaded gun 'kid,' " he said. "You just make sure you have enough gas in that car. Did you change the plates?"

"Sure did. Picked them up from an old junker down by the railroad yard." She played with his hair. "You proud of me?"

They could hear footsteps above. Eddie turned off the light and Jo's breathing seemed loud in the darkness. "It's Momma," Jo said. They listened as her footsteps diasppeared up the stairs of the house.

Eddie switched the light back on. "Where did you tell her we were going?"

"Soda shop." She put her leg up on the box and fixed her stocking. Eddie looked down. He was getting aroused again, and Jo knew it.

"How do I look?" Eddie said.

"*I'd* never recognize you."

They walked up the street to where the old Ford

was parked. Eddie had a hard time with the clutch at first, but after a few blocks he was doing fine.

"Eddie, you sure you don't want me to drive?"

"I've been driving all my life."

"You're jerking this thing like a jackass being hit with a two by four."

"I've got everything under control."

As he drove, his eyes scanned every inch of Jo's body. Her skirt was pulled up, exposing her long slim legs. As he got closer to the robbery destination, Eddie suddenly wondered about his father. It had been a couple of years since he had even seen him. He wondered about his mother and brother back in Cleveland. The only contact he'd had since the 1929 boxcar ride was a couple of birthday cards.

The Friday-evening traffic was light as he made the last turn onto the boulevard. He pulled his cap down and glanced in the mirror. He looked older, much older than sixteen. The bright lights from the blinking signs bounced off the windshield.

And suddenly there it was, the grocery store. Eddie had cased it for the past two weekends and noticed that every Friday night customers came in to pay their weekly bills. He'd seen a lot of cash in the register the week before, and only two clerks on duty.

Jo was to go in, pick up something and go to the counter when she saw Eddie take some milk. Then they would wait until no other customers were in the store. He handed her some money.

"What should I buy?"

"Oh, just get a couple of cans of baked beans."

"I don't like baked beans," she said.

"Pick up . . . pick up douche powder, then."

"What?"

"I don't care. It doesn't matter. Just pretend you don't know me. You're going to be a hostage."

She reached for his pants. "Maybe you aren't too young."

"Cut that shit."

Eddie pulled the gun from his belt. He was nervous, but his hand was steady. His watch said 9:20.

As he walked into the store he pulled up the lapels of his overcoat. There was only one customer besides Jo in the store. She nodded and he headed down the aisle toward the icebox. He picked up a quart bottle of milk and turned when he heard the tinkle of the bell. The last customer was leaving. Jo moved to the counter and put two cans of beans in front of one of the clerks.

"This be all, ma'am?"

"No. Let me have a pack of Lucky Strikes."

Eddie put the milk down in front of the other clerk, then asked for a pouch of chewing tobacco. As the clerk turned, Eddie whipped out the pistol. The other clerk saw it too.

"Listen, assholes, make one sound and your heads come off."

Jo jumped back.

"You too, sister." He added to the clerks, "Get a paper bag and keep your hands down." He waved the gun. "All the bills—into the bag."

The smaller clerk said, "Don't shoot. Please."

He emptied the drawer and Eddie waved the gun to signal the other clerk to do the same. The clerks handed the bags to Eddie. He motioned to Jo. "Get your ass over here, sister."

He grabbed her by the arm. "You creeps yell and this little lady will get her tits blown right off."

He took her with him to the car, which was hidden from the clerks' view. Quickly he cranked the car and made a U-turn, and they were away. All the way down the street they listened for sirens. Nothing. He pulled off his hat and she reached over and hugged him.

It was his first big robbery, and even more exciting than dodging railroad detectives. More profitable, too.

That night he counted the money. A hundred . . . two hundred . . . three hundred . . . nearly three hundred and fifty dollars. He was into the big money. That was almost as much money as some people made from their jobs in six months.

Suddenly the door opened and Jo came in and stood there in her white nightgown. He could see the outline of her body. She walked toward the money on the floor and stood in the middle of it, spreading the bills around with her feet.

"We're rich," she said.

"Well, not rich yet." He grabbed her hand and she came to him easily now. "There's more out there."

That excited her. He ran his hand through her hair

and she came to him, her breasts pushing hard against his naked chest. He kissed her neck, then her ear, slowly, and he could feel her nipples harden against his skin. He rolled her over and looked at her. "Put the light out."

Only the full moon now lit the room. Slowly he began to lower her gown. He kissed her breasts and she pulled his head down toward her stomach. She moved excitedly. Suddenly she laughed.

"Eddie!"

"What the hell's the matter?"

"I never did pay for those baked beans."

"Send a check in the morning."

Her body arched up and he could feel her wetness. He moved easily onto her body as her legs opened wide. She moaned and then both bodies moved in perfect rhythm.

Eddie had conquered two challenges that night.

For the next two months they hit several more grocery stores and some laundry outlets. But Eddie quickly grew tired of the nickle-and-dime grocery-store holdups. Why take a risk for two hundred when you holdups. Why take a risk for two hundred when you can take a risk for two thousand? he asked himself. He'd had all he wanted of Jo, who was content to stay in the same house with her newfound money and her mother. Eddie made sure she had plenty of money, and that the break was clean and smooth. He didn't want her to have any reason to blow the whistle on him.

Now he had a score to settle with the city of Cleveland.

Edward Owen Watkins ("Fast Eddie"), aged nineteen, at the beginning of his career.

Eddie at the age of twenty-six.

Note used by Fast Eddie during an Indianapolis, Indiana robbery.

Do Not so
Much As Move
A Finger or you
ARE Dead

Eddie enjoying the good life at the Dunes Hotel in Las Vegas, May 1965.

Later that same year, Eddie and friend relax in Eddie's San Francisco apartment.

A hidden camera records Eddie's request for cash at the Society National Bank in Cleveland, Ohio.

Bills in hand, he waits for the rest of his "withdrawal."

The transaction completed, Eddie smiles his thanks . . .

. . . then sprints for the exit.

Fast Eddie is famous for enjoying the company of beautiful women like Karen Rosen, his constant companion for many years.

"MUG" SHOW-UP FOLDER

Eddie's the one in the upper right hand corner.

FBI's 10 Most Wanted Men

A woman-crazy bank robber, a trigger-happy bad-check artist and a beatnik sculptor who allegedly killed his wife and infant daughter are included on the FBI's current list of 10 Most Wanted Men. This list gets scant coverage from American newspapers and TV news broadcasts.

The ENQUIRER, as a public service, is publishing a description of the men and their crimes and reproducing their photographs. If you have information regarding any of these men, please contact the local office of the FBI or your local police.

JAMES RINGROSE

Trigger-happy and allegedly a bad-check artist, known by dozens of aliases, including "The Ring." He and accomplices are believed to have passed fraudulent checks and advanced thousands of dollars throughout the U.S. Is an excellent auto mechanic who likes to rebuild stock cars and attend auto races. Soft-spoken and highly intelligent. Speaks fluent Spanish. Likes sailing and motorcycling. Smokes. Wears "Ivy League" clothes. Fired at police officers in alleged escape and is an alleged user of narcotics. Worked as farm worker, electronics worker and tractor driver. Height, 6 feet 1 inch, weight, 160 lbs, hair, brown; eyes, blue. Known as John David Baldwin, John J. Baxter.

CHESTER COLLINS

Attempted murder. Poet, actor, painter and playwright, hatchet-wielding prison escapee. Was attack with a razor-sharp hatchet on his girl friend who was in her company. Reported to have a violent uncontrollable temper, especially when drinking. Usually travels alone as friends are scared of him. Scar in center of forehead and scar on right ear which causes ear to stick out. Conservative dresser, likes books, records, dancing and good cars. Worked as farm worker, cook, dishwasher. Height, 5 feet 8½ inches, weight, 176 lbs, hair, black, eyes, dark brown.

EDWARD WATKINS

Armed bank robber. Known as "woman crazy" Allegedly ringleader in several bank robberies, he carries two loaded revolvers in two bank bags. Allegedly threatened, at gunpoint, to use any employee as an alarm for "target practice." Is reportedly a young striptease dancer, Kathleen Marie Rosen. Both are believed to be using elaborate disguises. He wears dyed beard, a toupee and horn-rimmed glasses. She wears wigs. He likes gambling with dice. Drinks highballs, smokes cigarettes and boasts of his exploits. Height, 5 feet 10 inches, weight, 185 lbs, eyes, brown. Scar on right cheek, right arm.

restaurants is a good cook, fond of preparing roast pork with rice.

EDWARD MAPS

Allegedly killed wife and infant daughter. Firearms expert, college graduate, artist and sculptor. Firemen attempted to extinguish blaze in Maps' home, found his infant daughter dead of smoke inhalation and his 22-year-old wife dying of a fractured skull and cerebral hemorrhage. Ten fires had been set in the home and the gas oven was turned on. Maps goes barefoot in summer and without socks in winter. Has worked as a dishwasher, elevator operator, farm worker. Sloppy dresser, was discharged from Marine Corps of "ladies' man" with reputation for "sponging" off women. Suspicious. Often wears full beard and mustache. Height, 5 feet 8 inches, weight, 170 lbs, hair, brown, gray; eyes, brown. Maps is also known as "Eddie."

The Big Time: Fast Eddie makes the "Ten Most Wanted" list.

ALSON WAHRLICH

Allegedly kidnapped and molested 6-year-old girl. Schizophrenic paranoid and sexual deviate with a history of antisocial behavior, according to prison psychologist. A close relative calls him destructive, untruthful and cruel. Reportedly has mental blackouts. Has tattoo of a heart and the name "Cindy" on his left arm. Worked as truck driver, ranch worker, dishwasher, house trailer repairman, hospital orderly, insurance salesman and ice cream truck vendor. Occasionally drinks beer, is very interested in guns and likes traveling by car. Besides pistol he reportedly always carries, he's believed to carry surgical scalpel in trousers pocket. Height, 5 feet 2 inches; weight, 140 lbs.; hair, brown; eyes, blue. Also known as Thomas Jefferson Clark.

LYNWOOD MEARES

Escaped con, bank robber with a 35-year criminal record. Reportedly boasts of his ability to crack safes. Describes himself as the "old master." Above-average IQ. Drinks moderately, preferring wine. Gambles slightly, favors poker. Enjoys swimming, hunting, fishing, dancing, movies, TV and attends most sporting events. Married and divorced twice, he reportedly considers himself a "ladies' man." Has been employed as a salesman, grocery store manager, elevator construction worker, farmer, millwright, cook, electrician, general laborer and operator of an appliance store. Height, 6 feet 2 inches; weight, 200 lbs.; hair, brown, receding; eyes, blue. Meares is also known as Irwin Linwood Mears, Lin Mears, Linwood Irvin.

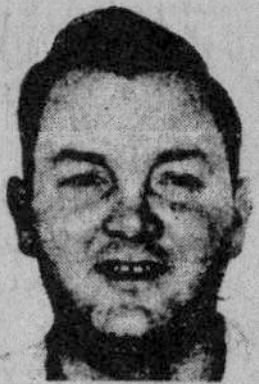

DONALD SMELLEY

Alleged armed robber, who claims he will not be captured alive. Uses disguises, false eyebrows and moustaches, dyed hair and cosmetics, and has possibly had plastic surgery performed on his face to change appearance. Heavily tattooed, with a heart with names "Don" and "Billie" on right forearm, hypodermic syringe on left forearm, twin pigs on his lower left leg, paratrooper insignia on right arm, nude woman on lower right leg. Allegedly used narcotics. Gambler, attends dog races. Plays pool and poker. Associates with prostitutes. Described as heavy drinker and "loud mouth." Dresses neatly. Speaks Spanish slightly. Height, 6 feet 2 inches; weight 210 lbs.; hair, brown, receding; eyes, blue. Uses many aliases.

JOHN CLOUSER

Insane escapee from mental hospital. Ex-policeman, he was arrested by police department which formerly employed him and was convicted of participation in the robbery, kidnapping and beating of two men. Hair may be dyed black. Has worn beard, wig and moustache. Tattoo of panther on right shoulder, heart pierced by arrow on right shoulder. Wears jewelry. Considers self a "ladies' man." Said to be a braggart, a "mama's boy" and sadist. Likes to start fights when drinking and would not hesitate to beat victim to death. Likes poker, steaks, watching football and baseball games and drinking beer, bourbon and whiskey. Sings and plays guitar. Associates with homosexuals. Expert pistol shot and proficient in judo and karate. Height, 5 feet 9 inches; weight, 200 lbs.; hair, blond; eyes, blue. Also known as Chuck A. Williams.

ROBERT LEWING

Alleged bank robber. Believed accompanied by 18-year-old girl. Quiet nature, lives modestly, simple tastes. Drinks beer in moderation. Usually dresses in work or sports clothes. Scar between eyes, on lip and on upper arm, one from wrist to elbow of left arm. Left hand and arm are partially deformed. Tip of left middle finger is partially amputated. Tattoos on inside of right forearm are woman's head and flowers. Has worked as chauffeur, cook, painter, seaman, welder and oilfield roughneck. Is believed to be armed with a .22 caliber automatic pistol and a .32 caliber revolver and had been reported as saying that he won't be taken alive. Height, 6 feet; weight, 145 lbs.; hair, blond, graying; eyes, blue. Lewing is also known as Ralph Johnson, Ben Van Lewing, Bob Lewing, Ralph Terry, "Cotton" and "Slim."

G. EDMONDSON

Armed robber and escapee from penitentiary. Highly intelligent and not reluctant to use pistol or rifle he usually carries. A reputed braggart and chronic liar, he began his armed robbery career at 17 while in the Navy when he robbed a bank of $4,146 cash. After seizing the loot at pistol point, he forced bank employees to lie face down on the floor and bound their hands behind their backs with adhesive tape. A skilled computer operator, draftsman and civil engineer. Speaks fluent German, lives expensively, dresses neatly. Enjoys movies, plays, operas, ballet, stereo music, hunting, fishing, card playing and reading books, especially on law and engineering. May be wearing dark glasses and have a mustache. Height, 5 feet 11 inches; weight, 140 lbs.; hair, brown; eyes, blue. Also known as Alex Gadsdorff and Phillip D. Kinney.

Nov

The FBI circulated this photograph of Eddie, accompanied by the following information:

LA 91-16365
EDWARD OWEN WATKINS
FUGITIVE; FAMILY S & L, 1746 S. La Cienega, LA, CA., 7/7/75, and three other small S & L's in Los Angeles area 7/30, 8/27, and 9/24. All robberies one man take over and .357 Ruger with 6 1/2" barrel displayed.
EDWARD OWEN WATKINS described as: born 4/10/19, 5' 10", 180, grey hair, may be dyed black, brown eyes, 1/2" scar right cheek; scar right arm. ARMED AND DANGEROUS; ESCAPE RISK.

Any info, contact SA W. F. STOVALL, FBI, LA, 477-6565.

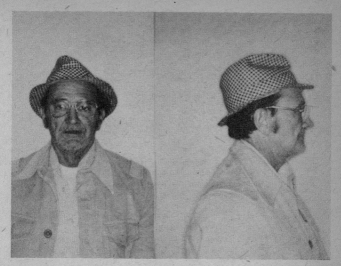

Fast Eddie in 1980, the year he escaped from the U.S. Penetentiary in Atlanta, Georgia.

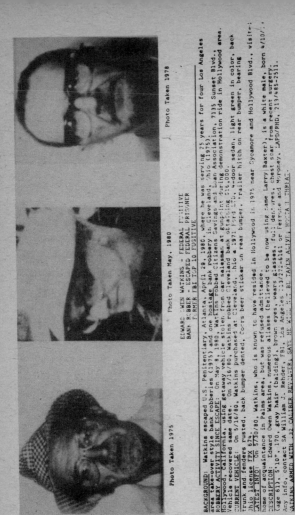

Photo Taken 1975 | Photo Taken May, 1980 | Photo Taken 1978

EDWARD OWEN WATKINS - FEDERAL FUGITIVE
BANK ROBBER - ESCAPED FEDERAL PRISONER
FORMER FBI TOP 10 FUGITIVE

BACKGROUND: Watkins escaped U.S. Penitentiary, Atlanta, April 29, 1980, where he was serving 75 years for four Los Angeles area take-over style bank robberies (1975) and one hostage bank robbery in Cleveland, Ohio (1975).

ROBBERY ACTIVITY SINCE ESCAPE: On May 8, 1980, Watkins robbed Citizens Savings and Loan Association, 7135 Sunset Blvd., Hollywood, California, using getaway vehicle stolen from car salesman, a gun, demonstration ride in Hollywood area. Vehicle recovered same date. On 5/16/80, Watkins robbed Oceanside Savings, totaling $16,000.

CURRENT VEHICLE: On 5/16/80, Watkins purchased a 1971 Ford LTD, 4-door sedan, light green in color, back trunk and fenders rusted, back bumper dented, Coors beer sticker on rear bumper, trailer hitch on rear bumper, bearing Ohio license FPX 670.

LATEST INFO: On 5/29/80, Watkins, who is known to have resided in Hollywood in 1975 near Sycamore and Hollywood Blvd., visited home of acquaintance in Palms area, but was refused admittance.

DESCRIPTION: Edward Owen Watkins, numerous aliases (believed to be now using name Larry Baxter), is a white male, born 4/10/..., (age 61), 5 10", 170, gray hair (balding), brown eyes, wears glasses, full dentures, chest scar from recent surgery.

Any info, contact SA William J. Render, FBI, Los Angeles 213/272-6161 or Ferrare and Moroney, LAPD/PHD, 213/485-2511.

WATKINS ARMED WITH .22 CALIBER REVOLVER, SAYS HE WILL N T BE TAKEN ALIVE, HOOKA THREAT.

Three of the many faces of Eddie Watson.

At Eddie's "last stand" (so far) in Lodi, Ohio, police riddled his getaway car with bullets, but Eddie emerged unscathed except for a finger wound.

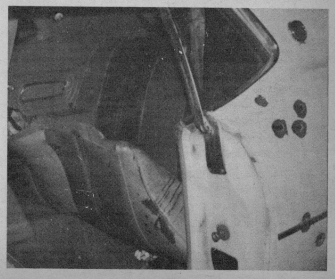

THREE

It was about four in the afternoon when the Los Angeles bus rolled into Cleveland that day late in 1934. The route into town ran past the railroad yard and the water tower that still read "Welcome to Cleveland," except the paint had peeled since 1929.

He did not go to Mays Department Store this time. He did not attempt to see his mother or his brother. He didn't want his presence too widely known. Besides, he didn't want to see people who didn't want him. This time he wasn't a shivering little kid in a burlap wrap, and this time he would take more than a pitiful fifty-cent handout home with him.

"Cleveland," he said to himself as the bus rolled into the station, "you are mine."

He had two thousand dollars tucked into his jacket pocket as he walked up and down the street searching for "Room for Rent" signs. Finally he saw a suitable-looking place.

The old woman who answered the bell inspected him closely. Seeing his bag, she said, "You come about the room?"

Eddie tipped his hat. "Yes, ma'am."

"Four dollars a week," she growled. "First week in advance. No loud radios, no drinking, no fighting, no women. Bathroom's not to be occupied for more than five minutes at a time. Rules are rules. You have to keep your room clean, too. How old are you?"

"Twenty-one," he lied. "You need to see my birth certificate?"

"No. You want the room or not?"

"Can I see it first?"

"Don't you trust me?"

"Sure," Eddie said. "I'd like to see where I'm going to live, though."

The old lady moved up the stairs like a cat, winding around each corner without stopping. He had trouble keeping up with her. His room was on the fourth floor, Room 409. There was a brass bed in the middle of the room. It wasn't a fancy place, but it was clean. From the window he could see the old smokestacks puffing.

"Want it or not? I'm not going to stand here while you look out the window."

Eddie reached into his pocket and slid a bill from his roll with some difficulty. He did not want her to see how much money he had. "I'll take it."

"You sure you got the money?"

Finally he managed to pull out a five-dollar bill.

"I don't have no change," she said. "Come by later and I'll give you your change and a receipt."

He flopped down on the bed and the door opened again. "Here's your key," she said. Then, with a knowing look, she shook her head and said, "Twenty-one, huh?"

The phony identification had cost Eddie twenty dollars, but now he could legally buy a car and move around as an adult.

From his window he could see the Standard Bank of Cleveland, and he said to himself, "That's where I'll start my banking business."

He laid back down on the bed and didn't wake until honking horns and the sounds of morning shook him. It was 9:00 A.M.

The teller at the Standard Bank of Cleveland was a pleasant woman of about forty. As he stood there, he realized how much he disliked bankers. All he wanted was their money. And he wanted to beat them—to outsmart them, to outwit them, to show them that he was just a little quicker, a little smarter, a little better prepared.

The teller handed him change for a fifty. Eddie scouted the bank as she counted. There were three tellers and a manager.

The bank was on a corner at a crossroad where four streets came together. This would provide alternate escape routes. Down one street was an office building with a parking lot full of cars. After scouting out the lot, Eddie went to a used car place and purchased a 1933 Chevrolet four door for $300. Then he timed the route from the bank to his rooming house. Three minutes.

Since his room was on the fourth floor, it would be hard to get out of the building unnoticed in his disguise. But there was a toolshed near the house, and he set up his makeup stand there.

In all humility he knew he was a true artist with makeup. He widened his nose by shoving cotton up into it, made a small scar on the side of his nose with wax, made his cheeks puffier to make him look heavier, and put a slight touch of gray into his sideburns, which would show from under his hat. The secret of disguise, he had decided, was not to overdo it. Subtlety was the key.

He drove to the parking lot across from the bank and parked his car, then checked the end row looking for a car with keys in the ignition. He found a gray Ford coupe.

At 10:00 A.M. that day he pulled the gray Ford into the customer parking area of the Standard Bank of Cleveland. Leaving the keys in the ignition, he went into the bank to make his withdrawal.

He looked at the tellers working behind their cages. He had nothing against these people. They hadn't done anything to him. It was strictly business, and he didn't want to hurt them. The best way to pull off the robbery without having to hurt anyone—or, even more important, without being hurt—was to establish control and keep it. He had decided that if he put up a bold bluff in the beginning, his sincerity wouldn't be tested.

Eddie walked over to the manager's desk, looking every bit the businessman. He glanced at the name plate and said, "Mr. Troy?"

The manager looked up. "Yes. Have a seat, have a seat."

Eddie sat down in the leather chair. He had timed his move perfectly; there were no customers in the bank.

"Can I help you?"

"As a matter of fact, yes," Eddie said. He eased the pistol from his belt. "Listen very carefully. Under this desk I have a gun pointed at you. One move and I'll put a bullet right through your balls and you'll be dead before you can blink."

Mr. Troy removed his glasses. He was shaking. "I have a wife and children."

"I don't want your fucking wife and children, I want your fucking money. Now when I stop talking you get up and walk behind the tellers' cage. Advise your clerks what is happening. No screaming, no panic—just get them packing the money in the bag. Only bills, no change. Have I made myself clear?"

Mr. Troy nodded. He moved swifly around his desk.

"One outburst," Eddie said, "and you're dead. Please remember that."

Mr. Troy wiped his face with his handkerchief and quickly and efficiently went about his task. He brought back the money. "It's all there; I swear that's all of it."

"Now get behind the counter and order everybody to lie on the floor. The first one who gets up, his head comes off. And that, Mr. Troy, is a fact."

Troy and the tellers did as they were told. The whole operation had taken only a couple of minutes. Eddie walked calmly out of the bank and nonchalantly got into the coupe and started it. He drove down the street into the office parking lot, put the coupe back in the space from which he'd taken it, and drove away in his own car. In three minutes he was back at the rooming house. He slipped unnoticed into the toolshed, cleaned off his makeup, washed the gray from his sideburns, took the cotton out of his nose, stuffed the makeup kit into a paper bag, and went to his room.

As he was counting his money he heard a siren wailing. He listened. The siren faded. He'd done it. He'd pulled off his first bank job.

The take came to a little over three thousand, five hundred dollars. In the Thirties, during the Great Depression, people who were lucky enough to be working at all might be making ten to fifteen dollars a week. Eddie had taken in, in two minutes, what it took most people six or seven years to earn.

He flipped a money parcel into the air, laughing triumphantly.

He thought about Mr. Troy. It wasn't Mr. Troy's money he had taken. He tried to imagine the banker's family. Mr. Troy was probably a good father; he probably had a nice family. His efficiency had impressed Eddie; he was probably very good at his job and Eddie hoped he kept his job. Mr. Troy would have a lot of exciting things to talk about with his family when he got home that night.

Eddie didn't have a real family, but the money made him feel warm, comfortable, at ease, at peace. The bank was to be congratulated on having an efficient man like Mr. Troy as its manager—someone who would follow instructions. He hoped there were more banks with managers like that. It would make the bank-robbing business a much easier and more lucrative profession.

Eddie listened to the radio that night and read the paper the next morning. The description Mr. Troy had given was that the bandit was a man in his early thirties, with graying hair and a scar on his nose, weighing approximately 175 to 180 pounds. Eddie was seventeen and weighed barely 160. The disguise had been perfect.

Although he had enough money to live comfortably for a long time, he wasn't through with Cleveland yet. He felt that he had a large score to settle with the city. His childhood, that train ride in the boxcar, those flimsy burlaps, that freezing cold, and that lonely middle-of-the-night exit from his mother's house were burned deep into his heart. The debt was not yet paid.

Wagerers bet to make money. Gamblers bet for the thrill. Eddie had the philosophy of a gambler, not a wagerer. He wanted all they had, and *that* might not be enough. The satisfaction of outwitting the powerful filled his half-empty heart.

Eddie Watkins, the mysterious bank robber to police and banking officials, the abandoned son to his mother, the pleasant and likable young man to others he met along the way, went on a spree of banditry that lasted a year and a half and frustrated banking officials and Ohio police.

But the law has time on its side.

Although Eddie became a suspect of sorts in several bank robberies, he was not apprehended or indicted for any of them. Edward O. Watkins had something in common with J.P. Morgan—banking was his specialty.

At age nineteen, after the year and a half spree of successful bank robberies, Eddie decided to dabble outside his field of expertise. He robbed a small grocery store that had a large sum of cash on hand. In the middle of the stickup, a policeman walking his beat looked in and saw what was happening. He went in with his gun drawn and Eddie surrendered without a struggle.

Eddie was off to the Ohio State Penitentiary to do a three and a half year stretch before he was paroled. It was the first of many stretches Fast Eddie Watkins would do in an adult life that was divided between prison sentences, paroles, escapes, bank robberies, and grabbing pieces of love and the good life when he could.

FOUR

June 6, 1980. Lodi, Ohio. 11:38 A.M.

"How many years that guy spend in prison?" one police officer asks another, as he rubs the barrel of his 12-gauge shotgun.

"I don't know. Ask the FBI guy. He's worked on this case for twenty-somethin' years."

"I couldn't do no time," the first officer said.

"Me neither. Not a day."

"Maybe a day."

"Yeah, a day. Maybe."

As they talk, Eddie Watkins reaches in the car and police guns cock and aim. Eddie still has the pistol to his head. He doesn't come out of the car with a weapon, just a Polaroid camera. He aims the camera at the policemen and the crowd and begins snapping pictures. He examines each picture and nods or shrugs his critique at each one as he watches it develop. After several pictures, he yells to the police.

"I'm documenting police brutality," he yells, then snaps another picture. "Maybe I'll set up a souvenir stand." He snaps another. "Or maybe you can all have keepsake pictures of Eddie Watkins' last day on earth."

The picture taking entertains both Eddie and the crowd for several minutes. Bored with that, Eddie turns on the radio. An upbeat song comes on and Eddie turns up the volume. He drums his fingers on the top of the car in perfect tempo with the music. He hums along. He gets into the music.

"This is better than the Johnny Carson show," one police officer says, laughing.

A highway patrolman objects, "I don't see the humor in it."

"It is kind of funny, in a way."

"I'd like to dust the old fart."

By now both NBC and CBS have arrived, with cameras and crew. TV reporters from forty-eight miles away, in Cleveland, are now on the scene.

A helicopter whirs closer, carrying Inspector Paul Burke, who has worked on Eddie Watkins' case for over twenty years. Burke has retired, but has been called to the scene to talk to Eddie. The helicopter lands behind the crowd.

A police officer greets Inspector Burke with a firm handshake. "We've blown his tires out," the officer says. "He can't go anywhere. He won't surrender, though." The officer lowers his voice as the chopper blades finally stop. "We've got a situation here, Inspector. He says he's not going to give up.

Says he's going to blow his brains out if we rush him. He claims he can keep us here a week and become a TV star. Well, the cameras are all here and we're looking like idiots."

"The last of the professional bank bandits," Burke mumbles. He is a rugged, hefty man with silver-flecked hair.

"What's that?" the officer says.

"We're dealing with a dinosaur—an anachronism."

Burke knows Fast Eddie Watkins better than almost anyone else. For years the FBI and other law-enforcement authorities tried to catch Eddie Watkins and pin bank robberies on him. Every time Eddie Watkins' "M.O." came up in a bank robbery, J. Edgar Hoover would personally write letters or memos, or call the agents in charge of the areas and chastise them for not having been able to catch Watkins with the goods. Burke himself had enough letters from J. Edgar Hoover practically to qualify as a pen pal.

Each time Eddie got caught it was for dabbling outside his area of expertise—grocery stores, convenience stores, laundries. From 1934, when he robbed his first bank, until many banks later, in 1966, he had never been nabbed for the federal charge of bank robbery.

Finally, in Missoula, Montana, in December of 1966, Fast Eddie was apprehended by federal authorities and convicted of that crime.

Between 1966 and 1980, Burke, who had been

working on nabbing Eddie since 1960, got to know Edward O. Watkins very well. He had actually become like a friend to Eddie, as much as adversaries in such situations can become friends.

Eddie Watkins commanded respect for two basic reasons: first, he was absolutely topnotch in his operations; but more than that, in all of his robberies, in 46 years, he had never hurt one person. There must be, Burke had decided, something somewhere down-deep decent about a person who could go into all of those banks during all of those years, always carrying a firearm, and never hurt anyone.

"You know," Burke tells the officer, "Eddie Watkins had a heart attack in a bank once, and he was holding some people technically hostage. Those people actually saved his life. They liked the guy."

"He's desperate now," the officer says. "Don't you think it might be better to move in and—"

"No!" Burke says. "No guns. He won't use his, we won't use ours."

The officer shrugs.

Burke shakes his head as they move toward the crowd. "You know, he's a talented man. A fabulous painter. His I.Q. tested out at a hundred and thirty-five."

"Why's he rob banks, I wonder?" the officer says.

Burke shrugs. "You know what Willie 'the Actor' Sutton said when they had a psychologist ask him that on the stand in court?"

The officer shakes his head.

"The psychologist said, 'Mr. Sutton, why do you rob banks?' And 'The Actor' answered: 'Because that's where the money is.' "

"I always heard that people steal because they're unloved," the officer says. "They're looking for love."

"Who knows?" Burke says. "It might be true."

"Well, I don't believe that one," the officer says. "I think they steal because they want other people's property."

Burke makes his way to the front of the barricade and asks for the bullhorn. He calls out, "Eddie! Eddie Watkins! This is Paul Burke."

His amplified words echo down the road.

"You remember me?"

Fast Eddie smiles and waves a friendly greeting, the pistol still pointed at his own head. "Hello, Burke," Eddie calls back. "You okay?"

"Yeah. How about you, Eddie?"

"I've seen better days."

Burke pleads to Eddie to forget this whole thing and come on over. Eddie holds his ground and keeps the pistol to his head. Burke does not want to shoot him, but he wonders whether it just might come down to that.

One police officer talks to another. He lights a cigarette with one hand, resting his pump shotgun in the other arm. "Burke, the FBI guy, he says Watkins spent over thirty of the last forty-six years in jail."

"Told you it was over thirty years," the other policeman says. "Can you figure it?"

"I dunno," the first cop says. "You wonder. Maybe they get used to it in there. Maybe they're scared out here. I bet he's seen a lot of stuff come down, all those years in those prisons."

While they talk, one of them notices that Fast Eddie is edging back from the door toward the trunk of the car, with the keys in his hand. As he moves toward the trunk, the SWAT boys notice too, and they ready their weapons. The crowd begins to notice, Burke notices, and suddenly it is so still that you can practically hear the crickets sweat.

FIVE

Indeed, Eddie Watkins did see a lot of things come down during all of his years in prisons. The millions he stole in no way made up for the years he was incarcerated. Eddie was smart, and he found out early that the best way to get by in prison—and the best way to get out again—was to behave. He quickly discovered who would be helpful and who would be harmful in prison. He quickly assessed those with whom he could get along, and those he should avoid.

It was 1936 when Eddie found his first real "home," although it was a poor substitute—the Ohio State Penitentiary. The Ohio State Pen was a stone-gray facility tucked into the middle of Columbus. Traffic moved freely outside the walls. Passersby could look at the high protective walls, the towers and the barbed wire, and quickly read the grave message of the function of the facility.

Eddie Watkins saw right away that the function of the prison system was more to contain and punish than to rehabilitate. Even during those early years, he saw first offenders come in and train for the outside world on outdated equipment—learn welding, or printing, on equipment no longer used in the free world, and be qualified, actually, to do nothing. And he saw many of them come right back to jail, even more bitter than before.

He saw the best and the worst from the criminal world. During one stretch he was in jail with the infamous Chicago gangster "Bugs" Moran. Moran was assigned to the mental "range" in C&D cellhouse. Moran had by luck escaped being mowed down in the St. Valentine's Day Massacre or the other infighting that took the lives of most of the tough, legendary gangsters of the 1920's. But eventually he had been brought down by the sophisticated crime-fighting methods of the federal government.

In Moran, Eddie saw a man who must have thoroughly enjoyed his bloody underworld years. While working in the prison mental ward, Moran frequently tortured patients. He put pillows over their faces when they refused to take their medication; he burned them with cigarettes when they acted up. Luckily, the complaints eventually got to the warden's ears and Moran was demoted to the laundry, where about all the harm he could do was to spit on the dry cleaning.

Eddie learned to keep to himself, yet to get along with those he had to get along with. He was a model prisoner, and in 1940, after three and a half years in the Ohio State Penitentiary, he was paroled.

The problems of the Great Depression had now taken a back seat to the problems of a coming war. Eddie Watkins was a survivor; he was one of the species that could adapt to its environment. The dinosaurs of the world—like the Bugs Morans and the Al Capones—were gradually caught. Eddie Watkins survived his childhood, survived the slums of Los Angeles, had in his own way survived his early rejections, and planned to continue getting by as best he could however the cards were dealt.

The economy picked up with the increased production of a nation readying itself for war. That meant more money in more banks, and it was not long before Eddie went back to doing what he did best—reducing surpluses in those banks. He was back out in the jungle and he was surviving.

Eddie had a thing for Cleveland, and he stayed in the area, getting better and better at his antisocial trade. In faster, out faster. Being on parole, and being a convicted armed robber, he was conservative in the frequency with which he struck at the Cleveland banking community.

On December 7, 1941, the Japanese bombed Pearl Harbor and Roosevelt declared war on Japan and Germany. Convicted felons like Eddie Watkins were not asked to serve, and Eddie continued to make war on the banking community.

In 1942 the tide of World War II began to swing a bit toward the Allied forces. At about the time Jimmy Doolittle was raiding Tokyo, Eddie Watkins was raiding a grocery store in Nashville, Tennessee.

Again he had stepped outside the boundaries of his specialty, and again he was nabbed.

He followed the remainder of World War II from inside the Brushy Mountain prison in Petros, Tennessee. Again a model prisoner, he was paroled in 1945, about the time World War II ended. He was twenty-seven years old.

America had the atom bomb, and once again the city of Cleveland had Edward O. Watkins as a resident. Now a two-time loser, Eddie once again had to be very careful in his vocational dealings. He had always had a knack for charming people, especially females. He loved and left several of them, some of whom were—like his cousin Josephine—simply challenges to be conquered.

Crime-detection methods became more and more sophisticated. Technology and research gave more and more of an advantage to the police and state and federal authorities. No longer could the Bonnie and Clydes, the Dillingers and the Pretty Boy Floyds of the previous decade hit banks and disappear into the next counties for safety. Now there were sophisticated alarm systems in banks. There were airplanes and there was radar and there was a new thing called television to alert the community. This was a challenge that Eddie Watkins accepted. In the late 1940's and early 1950's, he continued to be successful in withdrawing funds from banks.

His disguises were better, his technique had improved. By this time the FBI knew very well that Eddie Watkins was making a mockery of the federal bank-robbing statutes. But they couldn't catch him.

Eddie continued to diversify his exploits, robbing an occasional laundry or grocery concern, almost as if to avoid the boredom of repetition.

In 1950 America went to war again, this time a "police action" in Korea. Eisenhower was elected President in 1952 and, at about the time that Truman left office, Eddie Watkins was again invited to visit his old alma mater, the Ohio State Penitentiary. In 1953 Eddie was arrested for the armed robbery of the Menk Brothers Laundry in Cleveland.

He was 35, in what should have been the prime of his life and the height of his earning power. Instead, he was fast becoming what the FBI would later classify a "public enemy." The FBI hadn't been able to nab him, but he was back on the ice again.

He would remain on ice for twelve years, and would come out with a burning desire to become America's number-one bank robber. He had passed the Point of No Return.

SIX

It was during that twelve-year stint that Eddie met Dr. Samuel Sheppard. The Sam Sheppard murder case caused an upheaval not only in Cleveland, but all around the world, and Dr. Sheppard would end up in the same dormitory with the notorious Fast Eddie Watkins.

About a year after Eddie had been sentenced once again to the Ohio State Penitentiary, thirty-four-year-old Dr. Samuel Sheppard went on trial for the murder of his wife, Marilyn Reese Sheppard, in one of the most sensational murder trials of the twentieth century. It was such a flagrant example of trial by press that the conviction would be overturned and the judgment reversed twelve years later.

On July 4, 1954, Marilyn Sheppard was bludgeoned to death in the home she shared with her husband, Sam, a successful Cleveland osteopath. Twenty-six days later, after an almost daily assault by the Cleveland press, Dr. Sheppard was arrested. He was indicted eighteen days later. His trial began

October 18th and lasted more than a month. The trial began two weeks before a hotly contested election at which the chief prosecutor and the trial judge were both candidates for judgeships. Newsmen were allowed to take over almost the entire courtroom, small as it was, and were allowed to hound Dr. Sheppard and most of the participants continually. Three months before the trial, Sheppard was examined for more than five hours, without legal counsel, in a televised three-day inquest conducted before an audience of several hundred spectators in a gymnasium. Dr. Sheppard was, in effect, apprehended, indicted, tried and convicted by the Cleveland press.

In the courtroom, there were so many reporters so close to Sheppard that he had little or no privacy with his counsel. The movement of reporters within the courtroom frequently caused confusion and disrupted the trial.

The story that Sheppard had pieced together for several local officials was that on the evening of the killing, he and his wife had entertained a neighborhood couple in their home. After dinner, Sheppard dozed off on a couch and Marilyn went to bed. The next thing he recalled was hearing his wife cry out in the early morning hours. He hurried upstairs and in dim light from the hallway saw a "form" standing next to his wife's bed. As he struggled with the "form," he was struck on the back of the neck and rendered unconscious. On regaining his senses, he found himself on the floor next to his wife's bed. He got up, looked at her, took her pulse and "felt that she was gone." He went to his son's room and found him to be unharmed.

Hearing a noise, he hurried downstairs, saw the "form" running out the door, and gave chase down to the lake shore. He grappled with the person until he again lost consciousness. He woke up face down and partially in the water. Going back home, he again checked the pulse on his wife's neck and determined her to be dead. He then called a neighbor, Mayor Houk of Bay Village, who came over and found Sheppard slumped in a easy chair downstairs.

When he asked what happened, Sheppard said, "I don't know, but somebody ought to try to do something for Marilyn."

Upon seeing Marilyn Sheppard's body, the mayor's wife called local police, and also called Sam Sheppard's brother, Dr. Richard Sheppard. He examined Marilyn's body and determined she was dead, and also examined his brother's injuries. After the police arrived, Richard removed Sam to a nearby clinic which the Sheppard family operated.

From the outset, officials focused suspicion on Sheppard. And from the outset, looking to increase circulation, the three Cleveland newspapers enraged the public against the doctor. The massive, pervasive and prejudicial publicity against Sheppard so influenced the people of Cleveland that it became impossible for Sheppard to receive a fair trial. The trial court compounded matters by failing to invoke procedures which would have guaranteed Sheppard's civil rights. The court did nothing to insulate Sheppard nor to control the release of leads, information and gossip to the press by police officers and prosecution witnesses.

Marilyn Sheppard had been pregnant when she was bludgeoned to death, further compounding the heinous and wanton nature of the murder.

The day of the murder, the coroner told his men, "Well, it is evident the doctor did this, so let's go get the confession out of him." Sheppard was asked by police to take a lie detector test, and said he would if it were reliable. Lie detector tests, of course, are not infallible and not admissible in courts of law. Later, as the coroner pushed for a lie detector test, newspaper headlines suggested that Sheppard had refused to take such a test, although he was still considering taking one. The papers also reported that he had refused to take "truth serum."

The editorial inquiry that began shortly after the murder, and continued throughout the trial and conviction nearly six months later, included among its headline assaults: "WHY NO INQUEST? DO IT NOW, DR. GERBER." "WHY ISN'T SAM SHEPPARD IN JAIL?" "QUIT STALLING—BRING HIM IN." "NEW MURDER EVIDENCE IS FOUND, POLICE CLAIM." "BUT WHO WILL SPEAK FOR MARILYN?" "SAM CALLED A 'JEKYLL-HYDE' BY MARILYN, COUSIN TO TESTIFY." (No one, in fact, ever testified to such a thing in court.) " 'BARE-FACED

LIAR,' KERR SAYS OF SAM."

And there was much, much more. The press (TV and radio were just as guilty)—decided to make a Roman holiday of the whole affair, and to be sure that Sam Sheppard was judged and convicted without a fair trial by an impartial jury of his peers.

While in prison Sheppard authored a book concerning the case and his innocence. But nothing did more to generate and reflect the growing public sympathy for Sheppard than the TV series *The Fugutive*. This weekly drama was thinly disguised from the Sheppard case. In the show, a "Dr. Richard Kimball" came home to find a one-armed intruder in his home. He battled unsuccessfully with the intruder and later discovered that his wife had been murdered. "Dr. Kimball" was tried and convicted in a similarly sensationalized trial, and sentenced to death. But while he was being transported to prison there was a train wreck. Dr. Kimball escaped and set out to seek the one-armed man, while running from one "Lieutenant Gerard," a police officer obsessed with finding him.

The TV show brought more and more attention to the Sheppard case as the series became increasingly popular. *The Fugitive* ran for four years, with David Janssen doing a remarkable job in the part. It was so popular that when Janssen was recognized, at a bullfight in Spain, people shouted, "El Fugitivo, El Fugitivo." And when they saw Spanish police nearby they actually urged Janssen to flee. Episodes of the show were viewed around the world in several dubbed languages.

Sheppard was convicted in December of 1954 of second-degree murder and sentenced to life imprisonment at the Ohio State Penitentiary. He had been successful and financially very well off, he had been sleeping in a warm bed while Eddie Watkins was riding a cold freight train to Cleveland in 1929. He had lived a comfortable childhood while Eddie Watkins was hustling in the slums of Los Angeles, and while Sheppard was in college Eddie was serving time for his first armed-robbery conviction.

Yet these two, from entirely different backgrounds, suddenly had much in common, being thrown together in the same dormitory. Sheppard perceived Eddie's intelligence immediately and they became good friends.

The doctor continued to fight for his exoneration, and others on the outside continued to battle for him as well. He would speak to Eddie often about the case, and bitterly about his wife.

If Sheppard were not an odd person before he went to prison, he certainly became one while there. He walked around constantly with the Bible in his hand. He rarely talked with any of his fellow inmates. To Eddie, he often referred to his deceased wife as "that bitch."

The two men met when Eddie was a clerk in the warden's office and Sam was assigned to the clinic. Sam was later relieved of his job for taking more drugs than he prescribed.

One day newspapers reported that a man confessed to the murder of Marilyn Sheppard. "Yes, yes," Sheppard said when he saw the man's newspaper photo. "I *remember* that face. I *saw* that man around the area several times. Yes, yes, I know that was him. . . . Sure, it all makes sense now. That's *him. That's* the man."

While Sam tried to convince himself, the man who had been arrested in Florida and had confessed was found out to be a chronic confessor to crimes; he had confessed to many murders which he could not have done. He had not even been in the Cleveland area at the time of Marilyn's murder. The police released him as a kook.

When the man was discovered to be just another weirdo with a guilt complex, Sam refused to discuss the matter with Eddie. At this point Eddie began to doubt that Sheppard was indeed innocent. Perhaps, he conceded, Sheppard was at the point of grabbing anything to clear himself—even a crazy man who went around confessing to things.

By 1965 nine years had passssed since the Marilyn Sheppard murder. *The Fugitive* was into the second year of a four-year run, and Sheppard's lawyers were fighting harder than ever for an appeal.

By the way Sheppard had talked about his wife and about the case, Eddie got the impression that Dr. Sam was putting on one of the greatest acts of all time. Although Sheppard never actually told Eddie that he had killed Marilyn Sheppard, Eddie began to suspect that he had, by reading the innuendos—the way he acted, the way he talked.

But he also gave him the benefit of the doubt, because, after all, he had been persecuted, subjected to a three-ring circus, and carted off to prison. He had begun to take drugs heavily, and perhaps, Eddie decided, Dr. Sam was not operating with a sharpened scalpel.

As Sheppard's appeal became more and more of a possibility, Sam became more and more talkative. Then one day he was unusually silent. Eddie tried to talk with him in the mess area but Sam's mind was far away. Sam read his Bible and wouldn't speak.

Finally, in their cell, after a very long silence, Eddie said, "You know, if I had to live my life over I'd make sure that on the days I was arrested I would have stayed home in bed." He filled a washbasin. "I've lived a lousy life."

Sam's eyes finally lit up. "In all, I've lived a fairly *good* life, Eddie." He thought for a moment. "The only thing I'd change would be I'd have divorced that bitch—or better yet, I'd never have married her."

"Yeah," Eddie said, "I guess divorce would have solved all your problems."

"Only thing is," Sam said, "I would've ended up a pauper and that bitch would have grabbed everything I had."

Eddie cautioned him, "The walls have ears."

"Fuck it," Sam said angrily. "She won in the end anyway. I ended up broke as it is."

"And in prison, too," Eddie said.

Sam sat up in his bunk. "She screwed up my life

when she was alive, but I never figured she could screw it up when she was dead. Well, maybe you *can't* win 'em all. Maybe you really can't."

At that point Eddie was sure Dr. Sam had killed his wife. Certainly he was not the loving husband he had publicly purported to be. At least he didn't seem to be unhappy about his wife's no longer being among the living—except for the fact that he was in prison because of it. Eddie figured an innocent man would never say such things about his deceased wife—although drugs and ten years in prison could do strange things to the mind. He decided to give Sam the benefit of the doubt, but deep down he would always be convinced that the doctor did the deed.

One day not long after the conversation, when Eddie was working at his desk in Psychological Services, a lifer named David Walton entered the office. "You hear the latest, Eddie?"

"What's that?"

"Sam won his court case. The judge ordered his release on an appeal bond."

Eddie was elated for his friend. He banged the counter. "No shit!"

"You know," Walton said, "some guys really do get away with murder."

F. Lee Bailey had worked very hard for Sheppard's release. The U.S. Supreme Court affirmed the undeviating rule that Mr. Justice Holmes had expressed more than a half century before in *Patterson vs. Colorado*. "The theory of our system is that the conclusions to be reached in a case will be induced only by evidence and argument in open court, and not by any outside influence, whether of private talk or public print."

In its opinion, the high court wrote of the Sheppard case, "With his life at stake, it is not requiring too much that the petitioner be tried in an atmosphere undisturbed by so huge a wave of public passion."

Amid overwhelming public approval, Sam Sheppard was released. He and Eddie said their goodbys that day in the dormitory.

"That's right," Sam said, "they gave me the green light on the bond." He grabbed Eddie's hand.

Eddie pumped his arm excitedly. "Great, Sam. I'm glad for you. When you think you'll be leaving?"

"This afternoon, maybe tomorrow," Sam said. His face was lit up with a color Eddie had never seen before. He talked fast, excitedly.

"Well, Sam, you finally beat those mothers."

"Those motherfuckers," Sam emphasized. "I've got them right where it hurts, by the nuts." He sat down on the cot. "They thought they had me and I was beginning to believe that I'd fucked up somewhere along the line." He smiled broadly.

"So, Sam, you finally made it. You know, I never thought you would."

Sam looked him in the eyes. "Neither did the Cleveland cops, the press, the goddam prosecutor, the coroner . . . or the assholes who run *this* place."

Sam jumped to his feet. "The secret is *fight, fight, fight*. Never give up, never back down, and then you fuck up *their* minds. They don't know whether you're guilty or not."

"Well, Sam," Eddie said, reaching for Sam's hand again, "I'm glad that you finally won. Wish I could do the same."

Sam patted Eddie on the shoulder. "Well, maybe you will. How many years you been in here now? Ten?"

"Twelve," Eddie said, "I'm beginning to feel like a piece of the decor."

They both laughed. Whether or not Sam had killed his wife didn't concern Eddie as much as the fact that Sam was a good guy. He had been good to Eddie, and even those who didn't get close to him considered him a good guy, a helpful person. Eddie was not Sam's ultimate judge.

"I might not see you later, so I want to say goodby now, Eddie," Sam said. "I want you to call me when you get out. I'll have a hot number all lined up for you."

"After twelve years," Eddie said, "I'd settle for a mule or a warm sheep."

Eddie was sure they would not get together when he got out. After all, Sam was going back to his own world, and it was entirely different from Eddie's. When Eddie woke up the next morning Sam Sheppard would be gone.

The previous night Sam had said, "I guess I'm going to have to start all over. Who knows—hell, I might even get married again."

Eddie said, "In that case, I'll make your bunk warm."

Sheppard did not laugh. He didn't even smile at that one.

And when he left he did not take his Bible.

When Sam Sheppard was released he went on several talk shows, wrote another book and got national press attention. But the drugs had gotten to him. He built a successful practice again, but soon abandoned it to become, of all things, a professional wrestler. Soon afterward he died of an overdose of drugs.

Sam Sheppard had beaten the system. He was tried again for the murder and found not guilty. The case still continues to remain a mystery, stuffed away in the police files and left only to curious historians.

After Sam's release, Eddie thought about how nice it must be to have people fighting for you on the outside the way Sam had. Eddie's parole hearing came up about six months after Sam was released, and, although Eddie didn't realize it, there *was* somebody fighting for him on the outside. It was not Sam Sheppard. It was not Eddie's family. It was, in fact, someone with very strange motives—someone he didn't even know.

SEVEN

When Eddie's parole hearing came up, it came as a total surprise to him that he was being paroled at the behest of a total stranger. A man named Johnny Clark, who owned the Able Window Washing Company in Cleveland, had agreed to give Eddie a job. Who, Eddie wondered, was this benevolent stranger? A freelance missionary? The Good Samaritan? A man with an angle?

Whatever his purpose, Eddie thought, God bless Johnny Clark and the Able Window Washing Company. Twelve years had passed—twelve years and six months, to be exact—since Eddie had been sentenced to ten-to-twenty-five in the Ohio pen. It was twelve years cut out of his life, twelve years when he could have been enjoying life instead of sojourning in the confines of the gray walls of the stone-cold cage known as the Ohio State Penitentiary. Many things had passed. Eisenhower had left office, Kennedy and Camelot had come and tragically gone, the old war in Korea had been replaced by a new one in Vietnam. It was the same old jungle out there, it simply had a new coat of paint. Kids were dancing to something called "rock 'n' roll." Eddie Watkins was twelve years older. He had spent twelve years on ice—cold, lonely, without purpose years.

On a chilly morning, January 14, 1965, Eddie walked out of prison a free man again, his debt to society paid, but owing a debt to a mysterious philanthropist he was anxious to meet.

As he left the prison gates, he stared at the passing automobiles the way Tarzan must have stared at the Empire State Building on his "New York Adventure." Things looked very different. One thin Eddie had noticed about inmates who kept coming back to prison was that many of them were afraid of the outside world when they went back into it. The humdrum conditioning of a prison became a way of life; adjustments were required when one left it. Ex-convicts weren't easily accepted, and, of course, were rarely trusted by free worlders. They stood, basically, in the very back of the opportunity line. Those who wanted to reform had a rough battle to fight.

Although the wind was whipping and snow was blowing, Eddie felt warm inside, excited. He pulled up the lapels of his overcoat to protect himself from the cold, then reached up and grabbed a snowflake.

So this is freedom, he thought. He'd almost forgotten how it felt. An elderly woman walked past him, battling the wind that was in her face. Eddie tipped his hat. "Morning, ma'am." She managed a smile and went on her way, fighting the cold with each step, with nowhere to hide from its icy blast.

Eddie watched as a new Cadillac pulled away from the curb in front of him. *What a beauty!* As he carried his secondhand satchel toward the Greyhound Bus Depot, he watched children on their way to school. Something deep inside him longed to be one of those children, they who looked so happy, so secure, so far from the hard realities of life. He wondered who they were, where they lived, what kinds of dreams they had in their little heads. The happy looks on their faces made Eddie feel good inside, but sad at the same time.

As Eddie made his way toward the bus depot, he breathed in the air deeply. Exhaust fumes and all, it felt good to be outside again. In spite of the freezing cold, freedom was absolutely divine. He was forty-seven years old and he was free again. Oh, how he had dreamed about this day. Even in its best moments, life behind those walls was misery.

Near the bus depot, Eddie watched three pretty girls walking by—probably on their way to work. The wind whipped the girls' coats momentarily open and he noticed their short skirts. He smiled. That was the miniskirt he had heard about. He approved wholeheartedly.

"Will that be one way or round trip?" the ticket agent said.

"One way. That's all I need."

The bus would be leaving in twenty minutes. There was no time to have that big meal he had promised himself, so he got a hot dog, then made a very important phone call. He spoke in whispers. The voice whispered back what he had wanted to hear: "I'll get the money off to you at Western Union right away. It'll be waiting in Cleveland."

When he boarded the bus he smelled the long-lost odor of perfume. How sweet that smell was, and how he had missed it! He longed to hear soft sweet voices again, to have soft warm skin against his, to wake in the morning with someone pretty next to him. He spotted an attractive, darkhaired young woman sitting by herself.

"Anyone sitting here?" he asked. As she glanced up from her magazine, he got a good look at her piercing eyes. She was young, probably early twenties, and she had an olive skin that indicated she might be an Indian. She invited him to sit. As the bus left the station, Eddie tried to make conversation. "Hope that snow doesn't cause us any problems."

She smiled. "I don't think it will."

"Where you headed, miss?"

"Cleveland." She didn't look up.

"What a coincidence. So am I."

Eddie had realized from his early days that there was something intimate about riding a bus. There was nothing to do but look out the window or read, and after a while, everybody talked to everybody. People shared secrets on buses that they wouldn't confess to priests.

By and by they began to talk. Her name was Cheeta, and she was indeed an Indian, fresh off an

Oklahoma reservation, headed for a waitress job in Cleveland. She was only twenty years old. Eddie told her that he was a salesman and was headed back to his Cleveland office.

"Never been to Cleveland?" he said, then placed a pillow behind her head. She smiled again.

"No," she said, "but I hear there's opportunity there."

"I've certainly found plenty," he said. "I've been there most of my life and I'll help you find a place to stay and—well, I'd like to show you the town."

"I'd like that," she said. "I don't really know a soul."

They talked all the way to Cleveland, and when the bus rolled its last mile off the exit ramp down Euclid Avenue, Eddie thought of his childhood and his mother and Mays Department Store. He began to wonder why he had come back. After all, there were many cities with much more sunshine. He had many bad memories here. What was there for him in Cleveland?

She was impressed with the size of the town. Eddie suggested they get something to eat, and as they waited for a cab she slipped her hand onto Eddie's arm and Eddie's blood surged. She asked him many questions about Cleveland as they rode in the cab, and what thirteen years had done to change the city, Eddie talked around or faked.

He thought about the girl and saw himself in her face: 1929, riding a boxcar, all alone in the city with no one to turn to. Even if he didn't get any love from this girl in return, or if he didn't even get a fast fling, he wanted to make some sort of gesture. She got a room and Eddie paid for it; then they headed for dinner, running through the cold like two kids chasing balloons. Eddie felt good again.

As he sat there with Cheeta the loneliness dwindled with the flickering table candle that glowed around her face. If somebody had just been kind to him thirty-six years ago, he thought, maybe his life would've been a whole lot different. They talked on about her future, about her parents, the Indian situation, and her new job, and finally it was time to leave. The weather was getting worse; snowbanks had formed outside along the building.

They hurried back to her hotel and Eddie did not want to leave, but he didn't want to make a fool of himself, either. He walked up to the room with her and, as she went in and surveyed the room, he said, "I suppose it's time for me to go."

She stopped smiling. "You have to?"

"Not yet, I guess."

"Please stay a while."

Eddie felt warm inside. He did not want to go back out into the cold streets alone.

"I'm all alone in this town. You're a nice man. I really—" She hesitated. "Would you like to stay here with me tonight?" She seemed to feel awkward saying it, but she got the words out and Eddie was ecstatic.

"Yeah." He paused. "I really would, Cheeta, I really would."

She came to him and kissed him tenderly and he held her close. As she pushed her warm body against his, Eddie had a dark prison thought: he hoped nobody had put saltpeter in his steak.

The bed was clean smelling, fresh. As she slowly removed her coat, dress and underwear, Eddie felt his blood pressure surge. He looked at her young body, her flat stomach. She was perfect; she reminded him of the first issue of *Playboy* that he had seen in prison. He reached over gently and fondled her neck, then moved down to her breasts. He kissed her very, very tenderly and she moaned softly.

Then she said, "You're a very gentle man."

"What makes you say that?"

"I can tell," she said. "Indians are tuned in to people. I sense a lot of gentleness and a lot of goodness coming from you."

Eddie was anxious to continue, but he was also anxious to hear more. "A lot of people don't feel the same way you do, Cheeta."

She hugged him and kissed his neck, then looked at him. "I know you have a lot of goodness in you. I feel that—that—" She hesitated.

"What? You feel what?"

"Forgive me for being too personal," she said, "but I get the feeling that you've never really been loved."

Eddie resented it, her reaching through his defenses, but at the same time welcomed it. "Not for quite a while, I can assure you straight out."

"I can feel that you want to be loved."

"Everybody does, don't they?"

"Yes," she said, and then the talking stopped.

For Eddie, the next two hours were like being in heaven. It was one of the finest physical experiences he had ever had, but this young girl gave him emotional comfort as well. After she finally went to sleep, he stroked her hair gently. He wanted to remember her just that way forever.

He had his appointment with Johnny Clark the next morning, and he got up early. She went back to sleep after they had said a sleepy goodby. Eddie slipped two twenty-dollar bills out of his pocket and left them on the dresser. She would need the money to get started. He was never to see her again, as it turned out. He realized there was no place in this young girl's life for a man like him, and, he was sure, no place in his life for a girl like her. She would meet somebody young, somebody who would care about her, somebody who would deserve a good soul like her. Perhaps she'd get the house, the picket fence, the station wagon. At least he hoped it would turn out that way.

Eddie pulled his overcoat lapels tight around his neck to protect himself from the cold as he headed out of hotel for his meeting with the mysterious Johnny Clark.

EIGHT

The sun had begun to melt the top snow when Eddie got out of the cab in front of the Able Window Washing Company offices. Up on the second floor was the office of a man to whom Eddie owed a great favor. Without the promise of a job to the parole board, Eddie would still be sitting in the pen in Columbus.

As he walked up the stairs he could smell the scent of Cheeta's perfume on his coat.

Johnny Clark was a cherubic, balding man who was dressed in a tattered sweater and dungarees. He smiled and offered a handshake. "Don't tell me . . . *you're* Eddie Watkins?" Before Eddie had a chance to answer, Johnny said, "Figured you'd be here last night—but then, the weather and all. How are you?"

"A little bewildered, actually."

"Have a seat, Eddie." Johnny got an old wooden chair from the corner.

"I really don't *have* a job for you, Eddie."

Eddie was puzzled.

Johnny continued, "Now, don't get excited. I heard the word about your parole coming up and I knew you couldn't get paroled without a job. I called the board and told them I'd give you one."

"But—"

"Look, Eddie, I've hit the skids in this business and I barely have enough work to justify the other two men on the payroll. I hope you're not mad."

"Mad?"

"Look, I can give you a place to live and—"

"Hell, Johnny, how can I be *mad?* I'd still be in jail if you hadn't done what you did."

"The only thing we have to make sure of is that you and I are the only ones who know about this," Johnny said.

"Well, you don't have to worry about it from *my* end," Eddie said. He wanted to ask Johnny why he'd done this, but he decided not to. Better to wait and figure it out later. After all, he was out.

Eddie's Las Vegas friend had been holding some money for him, and had sent it directly to Able Window Washing rather than through Western Union. The letter had arrived that morning, special delivery. Eddie put the fat envelope in his coat pocket. He knew it contained five thousand dollars in fifties and hundreds. Johnny introduced Eddie to the other two employees and told them that Eddie would be working with them for a while.

When they had left, Johnny said, "I talked to the parole officer this morning and he said he wanted you and me to come over and talk with him. We'd

84

better get it over with."

They rode to the parole officer's office in Johnny's beatup Plymouth. The heater didn't work right and Eddie's feet were numb by the time they got there. The parole office was on the fifth floor of the courthouse building. Questions about Johnny's angle ran through Eddie's puzzled mind as they rode the elevator to the fifth floor.

"Did you ever notice something, Eddie?" Johnny said. Then he answered his own question. "Everything that has to do with the law is built in stone gray."

The parole officer was a young man, in his late twenties, a psychologist who was fairly new to the parole system. "How does it feel to be a free man now, Mr. Watkins?"

"Eddie is going to be just fine, Mr. Howard," Johnny said.

"It's great to be out," Eddie said. "I'll never be able to thank Johnny, and you, enough, for the chance you've given me."

"Well, Mr. Clark has definitely done you a service, and I know you are aware that there are a few regulations you must obey."

"Yes, sir," Eddie said.

"Regulations call for you to be at home no later than midnight." He looked at Eddie for his reaction. Eddie nodded. "You are required to report monthly and you must request permission to change your job or residence. You will not leave the country, nor buy anything on credit. And no drinking, no shacking up with any ladies." Eddie listened with secret amusement to the last two regulations. He had already broken parole.

"We will need," Mr. Howard continued, "a monthly report of your earnings and savings. You know, Eddie, the bets around here are that you will be back in jail in a month." He rose from his desk, extending his hand, and said, "Let's prove them all wrong."

"I hope we will," Eddie said.

The parole officer was a likable fellow, though a little young, a little inexperienced, especially in this field of work—no matter how many degrees he had on his wall. He looked even younger than his years, and Eddie had a sad thought about prison—how many times he had seen young fellows like this one come there. Young, naive, bewildered kids—first offenders, many times. The rabble among the lifers took quick advantage of kids like that. They gang raped them, made basket cases out of them, sometimes even murdered them. A kid like this wouldn't have a chance in the joint.

As they rode down in the elevator, Johnny said, "Shit, Eddie, how you gonna do all those things? Saint Peter couldn't stick to those rules."

Maybe I'll have to join the priesthood," Eddie said.

Johnny laughed. "Make sure it's the monks."

Eddie wanted to see an old friend and he and Johnny decided to meet later, back at the office. He took a city bus over to the home of an old girlfriend.

Her name was Virginia and she had offered to sponsor him for his parole, but the parole board had refused. They had felt that having a parolee living with a woman who was still technically married to a city fireman would not be in the best interests of all concerned. Eddie lunched with Virginia and spent the rest of the day with her. He bought some clothes and, at about five o'clock, went back to the office.

He and Johnny had coffee and talked. Johnny told Eddie his life story. He was unhappily married but stayed in the situation because he had four children and didn't want to put them in the middle of a divorce. He was deeply in debt and about to lose his business. He had begun to drink heavily, "to kill the pain," he said. "To kill the pain of life as it is, and to conjure up daydreams of life as it *should* be."

They talked on until dark. Johnny gave Eddie the key to an apartment that was in the back of Johnny's office. "If you take a broad in," Johnny said, "put the chain on the front door so I won't accidentally walk in on you. Sometimes I use the bed."

Eddie grinned. "If you do, just leave the girl in the bed, and I won't mind at all."

The living space was an absolute dump. It was one large room with a bed, a stove, a refrigerator, a sink and two old chairs. The bathroom was in the basement, and there was no shower or tub. His old cell in Columbus had been better than this. But it was the best Johnny could do, for whatever reason he did it, and Eddie was nonetheless touched and grateful.

Eddie couldn't see staying in that apartment for long; it was too depressing.

As he left, Johnny offered Eddie some money. "I know you're low on cash," he said, "just getting out of prison and all."

Eddie pushed the money back. "No, Johnny. I'm okay. I have a decent amount of savings. You've done more than enough already."

For the next few days Eddie moved around town enjoying himself. Johnny agreed to cover him with the parole officer by making him a sales manager. That way he could excuse Eddie's being away from the office; he was out getting new business. Eddie would get some business cards printed and would give Johnny ninety dollars a week to deposit in the bank, and Johnny would give him a ninety-dollar paycheck every week. Eddie bought a car in Johnny's name and registered it as a company vehicle. He had convinced Johnny that he needed to live in his own apartment, and had a telephone extension of the business number put in the apartment to cover himself with the parole officer.

Eddie had saved, from his robberies, more than $30,000 and had hidden it in markers in Las Vegas, through a friend who worked at a casino. The money had been there for thirteen years—on ice, just like Eddie. It amounted to less than $3,000 a year to compensate for the loss of nearly thirteen years of freedom.

Eddie began to make up, as best he could, for those thirteen years—hitting the night spots, buying new clothes and driving the two-year-old Cadillac which was in Johnny's name.

Johnny said he was trying to work something out financially, so that Eddie could really put his wits into the job of sales manager. Eddie didn't want to go back to prison again, shave in cold sulfur water or drink gritty prison coffee. He never again wanted to be awakened by a guard's shaking the bars for a head count; never again wanted to go through the shakedowns, or eat bread and water in the hole. The money helped him push those prison thoughts into some half-conscious corner of his mind.

Eddie was hanging out at the Gay 90's Bar at 12th and Chester. He soon met the owner, a woman named Mary. Mary had been a looker in her day, but at forty she had begun the fastfade, and Eddie liked them young. He met a hooker named Cathy Ann, a blond, slinky, classy type who knew all the answers. He always tried to score with Cathy Ann without paying the regular fare. He would buy her drinks and dinners, but just when he thought he would get the chance to climb into bed with her, she always found some excuse to leave. That made him more determined, and he went through five thousand dollars trying to score with the fifty-dollar hooker. But he was having a good time.

Johnny Clark had never moved through the fast life the way Eddie had. Johnny was fascinated by the nighttime scene and began to hang out with Eddie at the Gay 90's, or the Roxy Bar at 9th and Chester. He had had a falling out with his wife and was sleeping in Eddie's apartment. His wife was a strict Catholic who believed that sex was only for conceiving babies. Johnny was always trying to prove his sexual prowess with other women, but he always failed. Guilt would make his sword droop every time he got close to battle. Eddie found a hooker for him, but Johnny couldn't go through with it and he didn't pay her. Eddie was in another room with another girl, and Johnny's hooker came in screaming about how he wouldn't pay her. Johnny denied it, but Eddie knew it was just Johnny's way of creating a scene so he wouldn't have to attempt to have sex.

Johnny's guilt with women, and his problems with his wife, made Eddie feel even sorrier for him. After all, Johnny had enough problems as it was.

One night the two men were sitting around the office. Eddie was telling Johnny all about his criminal past.

Johnny said, "I used to have a bank in Akron as a customer. We'd get there before the bank opened and it made me sick to watch people carrying around trays full of money while we were washing windows. Sometimes I sent new crews to the bank and it always surprised me that the bank let them in without asking for identification. All it took to get in was my name on a truck and, *bang,* that was it."

Eddie didn't like the direction of the conversation.

Then Johnny said, "I don't think I could rob a bank." His hand was shaking as he put down the coffee cup. "I'd be scared shitless. But . . . I'll tell you, Eddie, right now I don't even know where I'm gonna get my next truck payment." Eddie didn't answer, and Johnny said, "Ever rob any banks in Cleveland, Eddie?"

"Did a polar bear ever piss on the ice?" Eddie said.

Then Eddie was sure of what he had suspected but didn't want to believe: Johnny Clark had gotten him out of prison so Eddie could teach him how to rob banks.

"Eddie, just one robbery would get me out of this mess. I could pay off my truck, get rid of some bills—"

"Johnny, it's a lot harder than you think. And risky. You could—"

But Johnny wasn't listening. "I've been thinking a lot about it, Ed. I just don't think I'd have the nerve."

"Most people don't—and for good reason. You could get caught, you could get hurt."

Johnny pleaded with Eddie to teach him the way to do it, but Eddie knew his benefactor would botch it by himself. That night Eddie lay awake for a long time thinking. He thought about Johnny and his pitiful situation, his terrible life, and he thought about the favor he owed the man who had gotten him out of prison. Johnny was determined; there was no talking him out of it.

Finally Eddie said to himself, "Shit! Shit! Shit!"

The next day they planned the robbery.

It was to be just a one-time thing; then Johnny

was going to pay off his debts and go back to washing windows. But Eddie knew Johnny couldn't pull it off. If he got caught, even if Eddie wasn't with him, the parole board would see the connection and pull Eddie right back into prison for the rest of his twenty-five-year sentence. Now Eddie was in the position of having to rob a bank to stay out of prison.

The plan was that Eddie would use Johnny only to stand by the door with a gun. They would split the take down the middle but Eddie would run the show. He would do the talking, and there would be no shooting, only threats. Eddie would pick the bank, one that fit all of his requirements.

The next day Eddie drove around looking for the right bank. He drove out to Lorain Avenue and Detroit Avenue, then down Madison and all of the main drags. He finally found a bank that he liked and he went inside and changed a twenty-dollar bill. He looked the place over, locating the exits and searching for back-room offices. Eddie liked his banks to have big, airy main business rooms and no employees in back rooms. That day he found several banks which would do. He wrote down the addresses, made notes about the number of employees, access streets and escape routes. He went over the list several times, narrowed it down and then went back for a second look at the banks he liked best.

What he finally decided was the ideal bank was one on a corner, with five male employees including the manager. It wasn't a big bank and wouldn't have as much money as some, but there were fewer risks. That was especially important, since Johnny was going to be involved.

The escape route was perfect. Driving north one block, then turning right one block, you came to a factory parking lot. There they could stash one of Johnny's trucks and drive off looking like a couple of window washers.

Once Eddie had picked the bank he didn't want to wait; he didn't want to give the nervous Johnny Clark too much time to think about the robbery. They hot-wired a late-model Oldsmobile, drove the stolen car to an apartment complex and left it there, then took a cab to pick up Eddie's car and drive to the bank for one more look. Driving the escape route one more time, Eddie watched for alternate routes in case something were to foul up the original plan. On his way back he bought pistols at a store where they didn't care about permits; he got two .38 revolvers. Then he went back to the office.

He told Johnny, "Okay, I've picked out the bank."

"You're kidding," Johnny said, reaching for a half-empty liquor bottle on his desk.

"Kidding?" Eddie said. "Kidding? I just spent a *week* preparing for the dam thing. No, I am not—repeat, *not*—kidding."

"I can't go through with it Eddie."

Eddie was burning. It was just like sex—Johnny couldn't go through with it.

93

"Screw it," Eddie said, "I'll do it myself,"

"Can I watch?" Johnny said.

"Watch? Watch? Jesus, Johnny, this isn't a puppet show. For god's sake, I thought you wanted to do this."

"I can't. I'm scared." He sat there looking like a big, pathetic Saint Bernard dog.

"Then I'll do it alone. I've gone this far, I might as well finish."

"Well, could I just park the car down from the bank and watch maybe from there?"

For some reason Eddie said yes. Johnny would pull up a block from the bank, on Detroit Avenue, and sit in his car reading a newspaper. Eddie felt very foolish, as if he were a TV actor performing for Johnny's amusement.

That night Eddie couldn't go to sleep. It wasn't like robbing a bank when he was a kid; he was forty-seven years old. He could go to prison for the rest of his life. He made a pot of coffee and thought about it, then finally said, "Screw it," and laid out his clothes and guns.

He set a chunk of beeswax on the stove to soften it for his disguise. Thinking about all those years in prison, he made up his mind that though he didn't intend ever to hurt anyone in a bank, he might shoot it out with the police. He would not let them take him alive.

Early that morning he caught a cab to Johnny's office. Johnny handed him the truck keys, cautioned him to be careful, and said—as if to provide

94

comfort—"I'll be watching."

Back at the apartment, Eddie worked up his disguise. He broke off a piece of the beeswax and chewed it. He molded some modeling clay into a round disk about the size of a dime, shaped it down even smaller, touched some iodine to it for color and put some hair from his head on it for effect. He rubbed some spirit gum on the clay and stuck it on the side of his nose. Now he had a mole on his nose. He took the chunk of wax out of his mouth and shaped it, then shoved it up his nose to spread his nostrils. Then he used spray dye to make gray streaks in his hair. Then he removed his bottom plate, put on dark glasses and a hat, shoved both guns in his belt, grabbed a paper bag and was ready for the bank.

He parked the truck in the factory lot, put the keys under the floor mat, and walked toward the bank. It was exactly 9:37. He strolled past the bank once to count the employees, then walked on to the stolen Olds, parked nearby. He left the motor running. As he headed for the door of the bank he was nervous, sweating; he could feel the sweat trickling down the back of his neck. It was February and he was sweating. He hesitated, looked back at the car, and for an instant thought about just driving off. But he did not.

He walked into the bank and went over to the manager's desk. He introduced himself to the manager with a phony name.

"Sir," he said to the manager, "I have a slight

money problem that I feel sure you can solve." He glanced around quickly.

The manager said, "Well, I'll do my best." He smiled.

Eddie said, "I'm sure you will. In my pocket I have a gun. My hand is on that gun. It is pointed directly at you. Please look at my belt. You will see another gun there. If you cause any disturbance whatsoever I will blow your fucking brains out. Understand?"

"Yes . . . sir," the bank manager said. He started to rise from his chair.

"Sit back down," Eddie warned. "I haven't finished. I'm going to give you a paper bag; go directly behind the tellers' cages and put all the money in it. I'll be watching closely. If you press an alarm button, you will die. Understood?"

The banker nodded.

"One final word," Eddie said. "You are to make damn sure nobody, but *nobody,* touches any alarms. If the cops come before I leave, I'm going to have to kill you."

The manager pleaded, "No one will set off the alarm."

Eddie handed him the bag and walked behind him toward the tellers' cages. He knew the manager was nervous, but he felt just as nervous.

When they got to the counter, Eddie took his gun out of his pocket. "This is a stickup," he said. "No hands in the air. Stay away from the counter. Don't so much as brush it or I'll blow you to hell." Everyone froze while Eddie moved to the end of the counter where he could watch everyone. There was one customer in the bank; he was as still as petrified wood.

"Let's go, let's go. Fill the goddam bag." They moved quickly. Less than a minute had passed. "No silver. Leave nothing in the drawers. If I find anything in the drawers—"

The manager was filling the bag so fast that he kept dropping the money. When he had filled it he put it on the counter next to Eddie.

"Okay, everybody hit the floor," Eddie barked. "Don't raise your heads for five minutes."

Eddie grabbed the money and walked out. He was on his way in the stolen Olds when he remembered he'd forgotten to hit the safe. He scolded himself, "Hell of a bank robber I am." Fighting the urge to drive fast, he went one block north and one east, then stopped at the curb, jumped out and walked to the truck. He removed the jacket and shirt, put on a hard hat and drove off. As he moved east on Detroit Avenue he heard the distant sirens. He drove on casually, just another window washer in a panel truck.

Back at the office, he pulled off the mole and took the wax out of his nose. He wiped the dye from his hair with a wet towel. It was all over. He was shaking as the adrenalin from fear and anticipation spilled out of his system like dammed-up water. He wrapped the bag of money in a newspaper, caught a cab and headed for his apartment. When he got there Johnny was waiting.

"Ed, I was scared to death," Johnny said. "I saw you go into the bank, but I didn't see you come out." He wrung his hands. "Then the cops came roaring up and I was sure you were nabbed. I walked up to the Central National and saw the car was gone, so I knew you were gone, too. Those cops!" Johnny got up and slapped the table. "Why, they didn't know *what* they were doing." He laughed. "They ran around looking behind bushes and in parked cars. It looked like a damn cops and robbers movie from a Saturday double feature." Johnny kept walking around like a excited kid and talking on and on about how slick Eddie was.

"Keep you voice down, Johnny. You're going to tell the whole neighborhood."

"How much you get? How much you get?"

"Don't know," Eddie said. "But I blew it. I forgot to hit the safe."

"I looked at my watch when you went in and then again when the police came. Took eight minutes, Eddie. How long were you in there?"

"No more than three," Eddie said. "That means it took the cops three minutes to get there after the alarm sounded." He had always worked on two minutes maximum in the banks, in case someone tripped an alarm.

This had been a fool's errand. He had netted just five thousand dollars from the robbery. It was hardly worth the risk.

"Johnny," Eddie said, "You ever been to Las

Vegas?"

"No," Johnny said. "Never."

"How would you like to go?"

"Wow! We gonna go there?"

"You're gonna go there. I have to stay because of the parole officer."

"Why should I go by myself? That doesn't make sense—if you can't go."

Eddie explained that all tellers have a few bills in their cash drawers that can be traced, and the best place to launder money was Las Vegas. "It's simple," he said. "You just go buy chips at the tables for cash. Then you turn them in at the cashier's window for money—clean money. Hit one casino after another until all the money is clean. Then catch a plane back."

"Hell, yes, I'll go."

Eddie had laundered money in Vegas in the old days, and had been keeping it there in markers.

They bought Johnny's ticket at the airport with clean money, and Eddie gave him some extra cash for cab rides and pocket change until he could turn the hot money into clean money. He warned Johnny not to get drunk, not to gamble, and to come back with the money quickly. Then Eddie went to the Roxy Bar at 9th and Chester for a night of celebration.

Eddie and Johnny had spread the word around the bars that Johnny owned a big window washing company and Eddie was sales manager. That was good cover for spending the kind of money they had been throwing around on liquor and ladies.

That night, after buying several splits of champagne for a tall, lanky girl by the name of Shirley, Eddie said, "Shirley, it's silly, me buying you splits of champagne at thirty bucks a pop and you sitting there for a quarter of the take. You know I want to get in your pants, so what's the price? A hundred? Two hundred? Is that your range?"

"What about my boyfriend?" she asked. "He's a cop—and a jealous one, too."

"I don't care if he's the President. Name your price and we'll go to my place."

She wanted four hundred. Eddie laughed. "Sorry, baby, I don't want to buy, just rent. I could go on Euclid and get it for twenty bucks."

"Not like me you can't," she teased.

And she was right.

After all, Eddie figured, it was just money, just filthy lucre. Easy come, easy go.

Johnny didn't come back from Vegas when he was supposed to and Eddie figured he was out there drunk and gambling away Eddie's money. Johnny seemed to be a man who couldn't handle temptation—a fool. And if he got drunk and started talking, Eddie would be as good as back in jail.

The night after Johnny was supposed to get back, Eddie checked the office, he still wasn't there in the morning, he wasn't there by noon, and again, at six o'clock, still no Johnny. At ten o'clock that night the phone rang. It was Johnny.

"Eddie, boy, you wouldn't believe this town. It's fantastic."

"Johnny, I've been there. You're supposed to be back in Cleveland. Come on, this is business. Are you drunk, Johnny? Have you blown all the money?"

"I haven't even had a drink," Johnny lied. "And I'm five hundred ahead at blackjack."

"Johnny, goddamit, you're not supposed to be gambling. You got a job to do and you're blowing it. Johnny, goddamit, please get your ass back to Cleveland now. Cash your chips and come back. What about our business—did you finish it?"

"Oh, yeah, Eddie. In thirty minutes. I'll come back, but Eddie, we gotta come to Vegas again,"

"Okay, Johnny, but just get back here, okay?"

Eddie knew that Johnny was a sap, and that made him a sap for counting on a sap. Poor Johnny, he had never had a hundred bucks just to blow on a crap table. All he had was a nagging wife and a stack of overdue bills.

Eddie had the aggravating thought that Johnny was drunk and all the money would be gone when he got back.

NINE

Six hours later Eddie was awakened by a knock on the door. It was Johnny, bubbling over about Las Vegas and how great it was.

"Do you have the money?" Eddie said.

"Yeah. Got it all changed out."

"But did you bring it back?"

"Sure. Oh, hell, yes. Don't worry about it."

Eddie counted it. Johnny was five hundred short. As he was explaining the missing five hundred, Eddie counted out a thousand dollars and tossed it over to him.

"What's that for?"

"I owe you a debt," Eddie said. "Maybe this will kind of even us up. Maybe you can pay some of those back bills with it, get all squared around."

Johnny looked at him affectionately, "Geez, thanks. I—"

"Don't say anything, Johnny. Hell, let's go celebrate."

They went to the Roxy Bar and Johnny paid the bills, then ended up going home with one of the girls. But Eddie had the feeling it would be another dry run for Johnny. In spite of spending most of his youth in prison, Eddie felt a whole lot sorrier for Johnny than he did for himself. Johnny had a pathetic life. But he did have some wonderful children; Eddie liked them. He had sort of adopted them and they had adopted him, like an uncle. He talked to them, took them to the zoo, joked with them, counseled them. They were great kids; if Johnny had nothing else going for him, he had those kids.

The next day Eddie went by the hotel where Cheeta had gone, but of course she was no longer there. He couldn't remember where she said she was going to work, so he had no way of looking her up. He wondered how she was doing, if she had met anybody nice. He was very wistful, very pensive and reflective that day. He didn't feel like doing much of anything except stare out the window and think.

Eddie had found out that his mother, Bessie McMahon, was living in South San Gabriel, California. He had seen very little of her since he left in 1929 in a cold boxcar. He had seen her last just before he went to prison in 1953. He told Johnny he was going to California, and if the parole officer buzzed around he should call him quickly so he could catch the next plane back to Cleveland.

Although time had begun to age his mother, Eddie could still see the signs of beauty that he had preserved in his mind when he was a scared, confused, unwanted child. She greeted him warmly, although the first few minutes were very awkward for both of them. But after a little while they began to relax and talk.

"You look very good," she said. "Eddie, you must be doing well."

He handed her a business card.

"Oh, my," she said, "a sales manager. You should be very good at that."

Eddie told her about all the money he was making, supposedly legitimately, about the window washing business, his friends and his new Cadillac. She was impressed and it was a lovely visit and a lovely weekend. The weather was gorgeous, the sun was warm, the countryside was beautiful. Everything was simply great.

The day he left he brought his mother a bouquet of flowers. They said their goodbys and he felt as if somehow within himself he had made peace with his childhood, and was beginning to understand that his mother did what she had to do in those days. But when he went back to the kitchen to put his coffee cup in the sink, he noticed that she'd tossed the bouquet of flowers into the trash can.

TEN

When he got back to Cleveland, Eddie decided he would hit one more bank. After all, he'd already broken parole in every possible way, including robbing a bank. Perhaps one more big job, he thought, would give him the financial edge he needed. And it would make up for a lot of lost years and a lot of hurt. Maybe after one more score he could start over in a new life.

But it would have to be a big haul.

He made an excuse to get out of town by himself for a day. He visited his parole officer and then headed for Indianapolis. That was March 8, 1965.

He found a bank that looked good—the Union Federal Savings and Loan, Maple Road Branch. It was a true plum. The only drawback was that it had only female employees, six in all. Eddie knew that women seemed to have more nerve in such situations than men, especially when it came to tripping alarm buttons. Perhaps, he thought, they just hated to lose a dollar, whether it was theirs or somebody else's.

He decided that he must take the bank quickly—"western style," just in and out. So it wouldn't really matter whether someone hit the alarm. He was going to be in, out and gone in a flash. He didn't even bother to steal a car for this one. He stole some plates for his own car in case someone were to see him drive off.

It was the location of the bank that made it easy: far enough away from the mainstream, with plenty of alternate escape routes. He spent the night in a motel thirty miles out of town, and was on hand when the sun peeked over the skyline and the bank opened. The six women were there on time—eight o'clock. Eddie waited in the car, smoking cigarettes, to give them time to get the safe open.

Then he walked into the bank with his gun drawn. "Everybody hit the floor," he screamed. "This is a stickup."

They dropped fast. He figured one of them probably tripped the alarm, but he was quickly across the counter and filling a big pillowcase with cash from the safe. He scooped out the big bills in each cash drawer and was back over the counter in less than sixty seconds.

As he reached the door he yelled, "Anybody so much as poke a nose out this door and I'll blow it off."

He was in the car and on the highway before he even heard a faint siren. He was thirty miles away, with the license plates changed, before thirty minutes had gone by. And he was in Cleveland, with a smile on his face and $14,000 taped to the back of his commode, before dinner time.

It was a lightning fast robbery, and he had that feeling of excitment again, the way it was back in '29 when he'd outsmarted the train detectives. Eddie Watkins had won.

Within twenty-four hours after the time of the robbery, Eddie was back in Las Vegas and home again with the laundered money.

Johnny had gone through the money that Eddie had given him and Eddie gave him another fifteen hundred. But once again Johnny found a way to squander it. He was a dilemma. He had all the mannerisms of a loser; he had been down so long that he didn't seem to to recognize up. After he blew the fifteen hundred he started to bug Eddie about another bank job.

"Man," Johnny lamented, "I'm in debt over my head. I'm about to lose my trucks. I owe four months' rent on the house and the office. I gotta scrape like hell to buy groceries and pay doctor bills. And you're spending money like there's no tomorrow."

Eddie picked at his teeth with a swizzle stick. "Maybe there isn't, Johnny. Maybe there isn't." Then he said, "What about those twelve and a half years in prison? What about coming out of a bank waiting for a bullet to cut me down? Besides, Johnny, I gave you a thousand and you blew it in one night. I gave you fifteen hundred and God knows where that went. You could've paid some bills."

Johnny bowed his head. "I did," he said softly. "I did. I'm really in the tank, Eddie. I don't know—maybe I'd be better off . . . dead."

Eddie patted him on the shoulder. "You don't want to think that way."

Johnny went on and on about the situation in his home, the fact that his wife wouldn't have sex with him unless she was prepared to get pregnant again, and how if he could make just one score. . . .

Eddie laid it on the line. "It takes guts to rob a bank. One screwup and you're finished—no more family, no more freedom, just a jail cell or a bullet. I have to be selfish, Johnny. I can't afford to let you be the cause of my getting caught."

Johnny looked at him pleadingly. "Eddie, goddamit, I'm desperate. I can do it. I'll do just what you tell me. I did you a favor once, Eddie. Now I need one real bad. You can't say no."

Johnny was right; Eddie couldn't say no. So, finally, he told Johnny he'd find a bank outside Cleveland—a big one—and he told Johnny that he didn't want any suggestions on how to do the job; they would do it Eddie's way.

Johnny agreed.

The next day Eddie went back to Columbus to pick out a bank. When he'd been in the Ohio pen he'd often read of bank robberies being pulled off in that town. And the newspapers had come out with an article entitled "Bank Robbers Beware," which explained how the Columbus police had a foolproof system to beat them. The artist in Eddie came out and he accepted the challenge. "Forewarned," he said to himself, "is forearmed."

He was worried that he might walk into a bank and find that one of the customers was a prison guard, and he would be recognized. Then he would be on the run and wanted again; the cover he had worked so hard to build would be blown. So he cased a bank that was a long way from the penitentiary, in a fairly wealthy area where he figured a prison guard couldn't afford to live.

Back in Cleveland he sent Johnny to a gun shop on Pearl Road to buy a shotgun and Colt .45. "Why such big guns?" Johnny asked. "Expecting trouble?"

"The bigger the guns, the quicker the tellers do what you ask," Eddie said. "A shotgun and a colt are about as big a request as you can make."

Eddie sawed off part of the shotgun barrel and part of the stock. Now he could attach a leather belt, slip it over his shoulder and conceal it inside an overcoat.

On the ride to Columbus Eddie thought about what he had to lose. He enjoyed Johnny's kids and Johnny adored them. Eddie didn't want to see them fatherless.

At a motel on the outskirts, they went over the bank's layout. If ever there was a bank perfect for robbing it was this one. The floor was wide open and everyone could be seen from the entrance. There were eight employees and two clear getaway roads, both with access to the interstate. They could be on their way to Cleveland within two minutes of leaving the bank.

Eddie bought a used Ford, using an alias and paying cash. He got the dealer to put on temporary plates and said he would be back the next morning for his new tags. He left the car in a parking spot near the bank. In the morning, before they hit the bank, he would unlock the car and put the key in the ignition.

Johnny picked up Eddie in the Cadillac and they went to a drugstore. There they bought temporary hair dye—one can of black and one can of gray—two pairs of dark glasses and a bottle of iodine. At a grocery store they bought some beeswax, then went to a shop for two hats.

Back at the motel, Johnny was nervous enough to be sick. He had a bottle of liquor but Eddie made him toss it out. No drunk, trigger-happy rookies were going to be in a bank with him. Johnny did a lot of tossing and turning that night and Eddie was wondering what thoughts were going through his head. In Johnny's place, Eddie knew, he'd be thinking about the kids, though he wouldn't lose an ounce of sleep over Johnny's witch of a wife.

It was March 19, 1965, a cool, crisp morning, and Eddie was up bright and early. He let Johnny sleep, though, and when Johnny woke his face looked like death. He complained over breakfast that he couldn't sleep, and he complained after breakfast that he couldn't eat. Eddie ate a hearty meal. If he were to get caught, he didn't want to starve while he waited for the paperwork to be processed. If he were to go to jail it wouldn't be on an empty stomach.

On their way back to the room from breakfast, Johnny said, "Couldn't we wait a day, maybe take another look, hit it tomorrow?" His eyes were underlined with deep circles and his forehead showed immense strain.

"Stay in the room if you want," Eddie said. "I'm going through with it."

Johhny sighed. He was going through with it too.

Eddie put beeswax between his upper teeth and gums to make them protrude. He engineered the makeup job for both men, and it was superb, with just enough noticeable details to make the teller give a completely erroneous description. To each other, Eddie and Johnny looked as different as total strangers.

They checked out the getaway car and put the key in the ignition, then waited in Eddie's Cadillac for the employees to arrive for work. While they waited a police car cruised by and Johnny got scared. But Eddie calmed him down.

When the eighth employee went into the bank, Eddie suggested that they kill a little more time in a restaurant near where they were parked. They could still watch the bank from the restaurant.

At 9:30 Eddie walked in the front door of the Ohio Savings Bank while Johnny drove the Ford into the bank's parking lot. Eddie filled out a deposit slip while he waited for Johnny to come in the front door. When Johnny appeared, Eddie walked to the bank manager's desk and shook hands with him, a Mr. Hofstetter.

Mr. Hofstetter looked up at Eddie. "What can I do for you?"

"There is a gun in my lefthand pocket," Eddie said. "It is pointed straight at your fucking heart. One wrong move and you die."

Mr. Hofstetter clasped his hands together to keep them from shaking.

Eddie saw in Hofstetter's eyes what he wanted to see—fear. Everything was okay. "Do you see that man near the door?" He pointed toward Johnny.

"Yes."

"He has a sawed-off shotgun. One wrong move and he'll cut half of your employees into little pieces. Don't press any buttons. If the cops arrive before I'm finished I'll kill you. Is that clear? If you don't want to die you better make goddamn sure *no one* pushes the alarm button."

The bank manager had broken into a sweat. "I don't want any trouble."

"That's up to you," Eddie said. "Give me all the money in the safe."

"It's on a time lock. It doesn't open until the bank closes."

"I think you're lying," Eddie said. "I'm going to ask one of the tellers. If she says different, I'm going to kill you. So now is your last chance to tell me the truth."

"I'm telling you the truth. I swear it."

Eddie pulled the .45 from his belt and told everybody to move to the center of the lobby. He moved to the counter and hollered, "Okay, Bill."

Johnny raised the shotgun.

Eddie yelled, "Anybody so much as moves a finger and I'll blow it off."

As Johnny watched the customers, a young teller of about nineteen asked if she could help Eddie with the money from the cages. As she took all of the money from the drawers, Eddie noticed that the bag wouldn't be big enough. When it was full, the girl offered to get another and she filled that too. She seemed to enjoy stuffing the money into those bags, and she would have, Eddie thought, made a pretty good partner. She even emptied the head teller's safe into the second bag. She knew where the money was and got it all.

All of this took little more than a minute. Eddie was a little worried about Johnny; he hoped he wouldn't get nervous and pull the trigger. Johnny would probably kill half the people in the place with that scattergun, Eddie concluded.

As he checked the drawers he found two blocks of wood in each one, with money between them.

"Oh, my God," the girl said. "I forgot about those. That's the hundreds."

Eddie told the girl to open the safe.

"I can't. It won't open till closing."

The manager had told the truth.

Eddie ordered everybody to the floor and told

them not to get up for five minutes. He hopped over the counter and followed Johnny out the door. Johnny drove slowly out of the parking lot and up the street to the grocery store where the Cadillac was parked. They switched cars quickly and they could hear the wailing of sirens. But they were on the freeway heading for Cleveland before the police ever got to the bank. Eddie made Johnny stay on the floor, even though Johnny wanted to sit up and count the cash.

They cleaned off their makeup along the side of the road and tossed everything into a garbage can. Johnny had done everything as he was supposed to and Eddie was relieved about that. He was on the verge of messing in his pants, but Eddie wasn't worried, and he stayed within the speed limit. The police were looking for two men in an old Ford, not one man in a Cadillac.

Back in Cleveland, they counted the haul at Eddie's apartment.

"Jesus, Eddie." Johnny's eyes were wide as silver dollars. "Look at it all."

Each pack of twenties had $2,000. Eddie pulled the wooden blocks off the hundreds and watched them drop onto the table. They started splitting the money. When they had counted it and divided it, they each had over $15,000.

"Here, old buddy," Eddie said. "Fifteen grand. Now you can pay all your bills." Eddie felt good inside as Johnny stared at the money. He was close to tears.

"Eddie, I don't know what to say. It's more damn money than I've ever had in my life."

They went to Vegas the next day, but this time it was a pleasure as well as a business trip. On the flight out, Johnny talked about buying a new truck, new clothes, presents for his wife and toys for his kids.

The warm Las Vegas sun felt good, and Eddie was anxious to get to the crap tables. At the hotel, they took separate rooms. Eddie intended to find himself a lady, and he didn't want Johnny's hangups to interfere.

Eddie didn't play much on the tables until after he'd laundered the money. He put $13,000 in the hotel safe and took two thousand to the tables.

The excitement of the crowd, the beautiful women, the stickmen hollering out the points on craps and urging on the bets, the girls in skimpy outfits serving drinks on the house, the chips falling, the screams of the winners and the moans of the losers—it was all like a drug to Eddie. He made passes at the tables with the dice, and passes at every goodlooking girl who came by. He did better with the dice, and was almost two thousand up when Johnny finally showed up. Johnny was drunk and he said he was ahead, but Eddie didn't believe it.

Eddie handed a bellhop twenty dollars and asked him to find some girls and some liquor. The bellhop delivered two beautiful young women who were dancers in one of the casino shows and were turning tricks on the side. Their price was fifty dollars a half hour.

After the first half hour Johnny suggested a swap, and Eddie took the tall brunette to his room. She had large breasts, big and firm, and she started kissing him all over. He returned the favor. Quickly his body was wrapped in hers and they were rocking the bed springs.

At the end of the half hour there was a rap on the door. It was Johnny's girl, the blonde, asking to speak with the other girl. She said, "All this guy wants to do is sit on the end of the bed with a limp pecker and talk about his goddamn frigid wife. Shit. Is he some kind of freak?"

Eddie shrugged.

Eddie kept the brunette for another half hour, and when it was time to switch, Johnny didn't want to. He wanted to keep the blonde there and talk about his wife and his wife's sexual problems.

Eddie decided that Johnny could fuck up a one-car funeral.

That next morning Eddie went out and bought a $500 gray-silk Italian suit and a silk shirt and tie to match. It was the most expensive suit he had ever owned and he felt good in it. He went back to the crap tables, where his luck continued. He won $1,200, enough to pay for the whole trip.

Johnny claimed he had broken even, but Eddie suspected the worst. Later he found out the truth—Johnny had dropped ten thousand dollars at the tables.

These had been two of the finest and happiest

days of Eddie's life. He could feel the glamour ooz-ing off him from the bubbling, sizzling neon of Las Vegas. As the plane took off, he could see the huge sign of the Dunes Hotel beckoning him to hurry back.

Back in Cleveland, Eddie sold his Cadillac to Johnny for two thousand dollars, which was a lot less than he could have made. But he still felt be-holden to Johnny. Eddie bought a brand new red Cadillac convertible with all the options and it was truly a beauty.

Eddie decided that on the day he finished his pa-role he would hit enough banks to retire. And he wondered what he would do when he had the money. Suddenly an old feeling of loneliness flashed within him. The bar girls and the hookers were fine, for fun and for filling empty moments. But something deep inside him wanted a more meaningful relationship.

His luck was good, he was on a roll, and as he was leaving his apartment he heard a young girl's voice call out, "Eddie."

He didn't turn around at first, because he had been such a loner around his apartment building he didn't figure anyone knew him by name. The girl's voice called out again, and this time Eddie turned around.

He liked what he saw. He liked it very much.

ELEVEN

June 6, 1980. Lodi, Ohio. 1:58 P.M.

Eddie had held himself hostage, successfully, for nearly six hours now. The SWAT men were getting anxious simply to blow his head off and be done with it. The TV cameras were on the scene; they had just seen him toss the money into the air and had seen the animals start scrambling for it.

FBI agent Burke did not want to have to kill Eddie, but he had a dilemma on his shoulders. Eddie had refused to surrender. Finally, Agent Burke brought somebody to the front of the crowd.

"Eddie," he yelled through the bullhorn, "somebody here wants to talk to you."

"Sure," Eddie yelled, "I have nothing better to do. But I think I'm supposed to have tea with

118

the queen at three."

The woman stepped to the front of the crowd, and Eddie squinted. My God, it was Karen. Karen Rosen.

"Eddie, it's me," she called.

"How the hell are you?" Eddie called back. He waved to her, but kept the pistol flush against his head and cocked.

"I'm okay," she called back. "My feet are a little sore. I don't think these shoes fit."

He laughed to himself. She hadn't changed a bit. Here he was with a gun to his head, with half the state police force and the FBI around, SWAT exterminators with fingers to the trigger, and she's complaining about tight shoes. She was the same nut that she had always been. He wondered where they had found her. Eddie wasn't even sure how old Karen was now. It was 1965 when he first met her, when she called his name in front of the apartment building that day. That was fifteen years before, and Eddie figured it up. She was nineteen then, so now she had to be thirty-four.

"Well, you should definitely do something about those shoes, honey," he yelled. "Did you come to talk to me about your shoes, Karen? Because I can't really help you with them right now."

"Oh, no Eddie. They wanted me to come talk with you."

"About what?"

"About giving yourself up," she said.

"I can't do that."

"Well, hon, I wish you would."

"Why? So I can go back to prison?"

She had to think about that one. "I guess so. And so you won't die, Eddie. I don't want you to die."

"Well, eventually I'm going to anyhow. I'd just as soon you didn't stick around to watch it."

They talked back and forth for a while, and then Burke said something to her and took the bullhorn. It was obvious Eddie's mind was made up. But it was still a Mexican standoff of sorts, and they would wait a little longer.

Karen waved goodby and Eddie waved back. Karen was married now, older, but just as crazy. Eddie thought back to that first day he met her in front of the apartment house. That meeting would take them all across the country and into some wild adventures. Eddie lit a cigarette with one hand and tried to remember her just as she had been then, on the day he first met her.

The girl had called him by name and said she wanted a ride. She had auburn-red hair and was a real looker, but she couldn't have been over nineteen—which was fine with Eddie. Young women made his blood move faster. She lived in the downstairs apartment and had seen his name on the mailbox.

She was never home in the daytime and he

was never home at night, she explained; that was the reason they'd never seen each other.

Her name was Karen Rosen and she needed to go to the store to pick up a few things. Eddie agreed to go with her to shop, since he had nothing in particular to do that day.

He was disappointed to hear that she was married, but she immediately told him she wasn't getting along at all with her husband and planned to leave him. That rang Eddie's bell. Before the afternoon was over Eddie asked her if she'd ever been to Las Vegas.

"No," she said, "but I'll go someday."

"What about tomorrow?" Eddie said.

"I'll be packed and ready to go."

"What's your husband going to say?"

"I'll tell him I'm going to spend a few days with a girlfriend. I do it often. He doesn't mind."

Before they got back from shopping, they had decided not to delay the trip. Karen went home, packed and left her husband a note, and they were off on the 6:15 flight.

They got to know each other a little better on the flight. She had worked as a stripper and a go-go dancer at downtown clubs. Eddie wondered what kind of husband would let her pull these kinds of deals on him, and what kind of woman she must be. But, since he was the beneficiary of her easygoing ways, he wasn't going to moralize.

Halfway to the Dunes, Eddie stopped the airport limo driver at a car-rental place and rented a Cadillac. He had brought along $5,000 to have fun for the weekend.

As they stepped up to the hotel desk to register, Eddie could hear the sounds of action—stickmen calling out numbers and urging on bets, the clicking wheels of slot machines and most of them came up with "Sorry, better luck next time" thumps, and the sirens going off when someone hit a jackpot, exciting the players who weren't winning.

Eddie wanted to go back down to the tables and start playing right away. But almost as soon as the bellhop closed the door, Karen moved in and started playing around with Eddie. She pulled up her dress slowly as she sat on the bed, exposing her smooth thighs. Her legs were in perfect shape from all the years she had been a dancer.

He had always had to pay for women this nice, and here she was making all the moves, talking off her clothes and his too. She dropped her dress and it fell to the carpet; then she slowly took off her bra and began rubbing every part of her body on every part of his. She was as hot as a torch as she pressed, pushed and stroked. Quickly he was inside her and quickly he forgot about the gambling tables. Finally their heavy breathing stopped and they lay still in each other's arms.

This was the life Eddie had missed. This was the life that he wished he had lived. The pleasurable experiences of life had been diminished for him by the hard struggle of survival in the jungle. He wished he could turn back time, return to his childhood again and change things. He believed that he was smart enough to be a success in the world without robbing banks. But he was a creature of habit. The fact was that he could not turn back time, could not change the way he had lived and the things he had done.

A forty-seven-year-old ex-con in the marketplace? Who would want him, and how could he make it to the top? He realized then and there, as Karen lay in his arms, that the only way he could make it was to get all of the money he could, enough to protect him from the hazards of life, and start his own business. He wanted to set up Karen like a queen, his queen. To do that he knew he would have to rob banks.

He thought of his mother tossing the flowers in the trash can, and he realized what he had realized many times before. He had tried to push it into the corner of his mind, but it kept coming back like an unwanted house guest: he was alone in the world.

Eddie blew his $5,000 fun money at the tables, but it was a good weekend. He had figured a woman tossing dice would bring good luck, yet Karen couldn't hit a point. For a moment on the flight home he considered that she might be a bad luck "black cat," but he shook off that thought.

As it turned out, he should have listened to that little voice inside him.

TWELVE

The following weeks were magnificent. Karen lived downstairs, but every morning when her husband left for work she would be up the steps and into Eddie's bed.

In those few weeks Eddie found out that Karen had to make a great effort just to tell the simplest truth. She would lie even if it was handier to tell the truth. Even when he asked her the time he began to wonder whether she wasn't shading it five minutes just to keep her hand in.

But she wasn't a malicious liar, just a habitual one. And she was not particularly good at it. Sometimes she would tell two more bad lies just to cover a first inept one.

He also knew that whatever it was Karen would ultimately do with her life, she would not become a great rocket scientist or a renowned philosopher. She just didn't have it in the belfry. She was not much of a mental challenge, not one of those people who made you think.

To fill the voids, Eddie began playing around

with a waitress named Cookie, trying to impress her with money, leaving big tips. After a short time she began to accept rides home from him, to a very posh high-rise building that she obviously couldn't afford on her salary. But she would never let him past the door.

One night he was sitting in the bar where she worked and every time she came to talk to him, two intoxicated patrons would call her over. The last straw was when one of them said, in a voice that he made sure Eddie could hear, "Stay with us, honey. Screw that faggot over there. He's just a queer."

Eddie saw the bluff in the man, and figured he would teach this bully a little lesson. He grabbed a beer bottle and busted it on the table, and, before the guy could move, had the jagged bottleneck at the drunk's throat.

"What was that word you used, fuck face?"

The fellow whined and pleaded, and quickly left the bar.

Just as Eddie was thinking that he shouldn't have made such a scene, the blue eyed Cookie became very warm to him. She was not upset at all; she was almost turned on by the violence. She told him that she would get off at two and if he waited tonight he would get inside her door.

At her apartment, she explained that three years before, when she was eighteen, she had met a man of retirement age who wanted to see her once in a while. The man visited her occasionally and paid her rent in exhange, with one strict clause in the verbal agreement: no other male visitors. The man didn't want any trouble with boyfriends.

"Why do you work if he takes care of you?" Eddie said.

"He just pays the rent, nothing more. Why? Why do you ask that?"

There was a strange look in her eyes, one that Eddie mistook for lust.

He spent the night in that lovely apartment, and made the boast that he could take care of her better than her present benefactor did. He said that it wouldn't be much trouble to run the old fellow off. But when he left there he realized hat he didn't want to be involved in paying Cookie's bills. He didn't want to buy the cow, he just wanted the milk.

Sometimes when he talked to Cookie, her eyes would get a very far-off glaze and she would say strange things. He put it down to her being kooky and offbeat.

But one night as they lay there, after they had made love, Eddie felt a sharp pain in his neck that felt like a bug bite. When the pain became sharper, Cookie said, " Don't move or I'll kill you."

Eddie froze. "Is that a knife?"

She said. "Did you mean that about running daddy off and paying the rent?"

She had just asked him one of those "damned if you do and damned if you don't" questions, and he didn't know how he should answer it.

"What are you talking about?"

"You know what I'm talking about." She pushed

the knife a bit harder against his neck and drew a trickle of blood. "You threatened to run daddy off."

"Baby," he pleaded, "I was just joking. You know, playing around. Hell, I wouldn't do anything to hurt your daddy." Eddie held his breath.

"Well, I don't believe you. You were going to hurt my daddy."

"I was just kidding," Eddie said. "Hell, I like the idea of his paying the rent. He's been doing it for years. Why should I want to stop him? I can't afford to pay it. If you think that of me, if that's all I mean to you, I'll leave and won't come back."

He waited; no answer. The knife was against his jugular vein.

Finally Eddie said, "You've hurt my feelings, you know that."

He could feel the blood trickling down his chest. He felt for an instant that she was going to kill him, but he did not dare make a move for the knife without the risk that she would slash his jugular.

And then, after what seemed like ages, he felt the pressure from the knife ease a little.

"You're not lying to me?" she said.

Eddie rolled quickly out of the bed, jumped up and grabbed a chair. He held the chair with one hand like a lion tamer holding back the cats, and quickly put on his pants with the other hand. All the while he kept talking.

"You dumb bitch. You'd spend the rest of your life in jail."

In the dim light he could see her eyes go far away again. She smiled strangely, a half smile that he had seen a few times before.

"No, I wouldn't go to jail. I'd cut up your body and run it down the garbage disposal. The only problem would be getting those great big bones down it."

She talked as if she were talking about dumping hamburger down the disposal.

As he put on his shirt, she said, "Why are you leaving?"

"Why?" Eddie said. "Look, just stay in that goddam bed until I'm gone or I'm liable to knock your brains out with this chair."

She started at him with the bread knife but, as Eddie drew back the chair, she backed off. He was gone in a flash, wiping the blood off his throat as he went down the stairs. It was at this point that he decided Karen wasn't such a bad bet after all.

THIRTEEN

By this time Johnny had all but quit working and was going to hell in a bottle. He was too tired to work with his men and they were barely doing their job. Johnny told Eddie he hadn't paid off his trucks yet, and justified that by saying he didn't want to create suspicion by spending too freely. But he'd brought the payments up to date.

And then the quesiton, "Eddie, can we do another job?"

"I thought you were finished after just one, that you were going to straighten out your life." Eddie was angry. He thought about Johnny's kids, and he knew that Johnny was neglecting them in favor of licking his wounds with the bottle. "Why don't you sober up and be a father to your kids, goddamit?"

"I'm going to, Eddie."

"When? When they're grown up and you've drunk yourself into the gutters of life? When they have to drag you home from saloons and clean up your puke?"

"Aw, come on, Eddie."

"Fuck you, Johnny. Goddamit, why don't you wise up?"

"Eddie," Johnny pleaded, "I've got all those wild hairs out of my system. I promise I won't blow the money this time. One more job and I'll be the father I used to be. I'll be out of debt and I'll straighten up my life. You'll see."

Eddie gave in. He wanted to find an easy bank for Johnny, and while he was figuring it out he went to St. Louis by himself and pulled off a job. It was a clean, smooth, patented Fast Eddie bank job. In, out, wham. Just like that he had $27,000 that he hid in shoeboxes under his sofa.

He decided that business was business, and he agreed to pull off another job with Johnny, but Johnny would only get a third. Johnny agreed that it was a fair deal. On April 16, 1965, they hit the Central National branch at Detroit and Mars in Lakewood, just outside of Cleveland. Eddie wore a scar that he had picked up at Jean's Funny House on East 9th, and the scar looked very true to life.

Once again Johnny was a physical and emotional wreck and wanted to put it off. But they hit the bank as planned and the job was fast and clean, and they were quickly away with more than $20,000. Eddie paid Johnny his $7,000 from his stash of laundered money, to save another trip to Vegas.

Two of the packs of big bills from the Central National job were brand new and no doubt marked. So Eddie boiled a pot of coffee and tossed the bills in, then rubbed dirt on the money after it was stained. Finally he baked it a very low temperature and presto, he had old money that would be easier to pass.

A few days later he took forty thousand dollars from the past two jobs to Vegas for the final laundering job. He took another $5,000 for fun at the crap tables.

It was on this trip that Eddie discovered a new way to launder and stash stolen money. At a pay window a man in front of him asked the cashier to hold fifteen thousand dollars for him in the form of a marker. Eddie had been worried about robbers coming into his apartment and finding his money; this was a way of keeping the money safe. He would get markers at the big casinos and take them to the safety deposit box, and his money would be safe from burglars.

Afer all, in his profession he could not rob from one bank and then go deposit cash in another.

Eddie left ten thousand at the Stardust, another ten at the Riviera, nine thousand at the Sahara and ten more at the Dunes. On his next trip back he would bring the thirty thousand he had stashed behind the toilet and in shoeboxes.

But before leaving he hit the tables and started getting lucky. The dice were hot and he rode a streak that put him in an all-night game and ten thousand ahead by nine in the morning. By noon he was twenty grand to the good.

He finally took his winnings and picked up a marker for half the amount; another ten thousand he put in the safe for gambling money. He wasn't going to let some hooker roll him for that. When you win big the word gets out fast.

The next morning he came to his senses and hustled back to Cleveland to check in with his parole officer. He left Las Vegas with $59,000 in markers that would be safe as long as he wanted to leave it there.

When he went back he found out in the news stories that a police car had been just three blocks from the bank and had seen the getaway car. The police had given chase but the getaway car had crossed the Mars Avenue railroad tracks and a freight train had interceded and blocked the road. He read that the Cleveland police had chastised the Lakewood cops for not having notified them immediately so they could block the getaway car farther ahead.

Eddie hadn't even known that the police were giving chase.

His days in Cleveland were fast drawing to a close.

FOURTEEN

The weather began to turn to spring and Johnny's business was picking up. He had paid some bills and hired a new man, who turned out to be an ex-con named Al Marks, to work for him. Al was on parole from the New Mexico state pen, and after a while he got fed up with the low pay of a window washer and began being very friendly toward Eddie. Eddie knew it was almost impossible to fool an ex-con who'd served as much time as Al. He was afraid Al would soon get the idea that it was Eddie who was responsible for the barrage of bank robberies in the area.

One night Eddie was talking to him at a bar and Al asked about the possibility of making a big score. Eddie said that he wasn't into anything at the present time, that he had a few bucks stashed away from the old days, but that if he heard anything he would let Al know.

Eddie kept a book that rated the banks and contained all the information necessary for him to pull off a robbery.

Al began to press Eddie and Eddie knew it was just a matter of time before Al figured things out. So he checked Al out with an ex-con who had served time in New Mexico, and he said that Al was okay.

It was then that Eddie made a big mistake. He invited Al to come along on a bank job for a third of the take. Al agreed, and he got the car for the getaway and took care of the stolen plates. Maybe it wouldn't be so bad with a pro like Al, Eddie reasoned. He would be a big improvement over Johnny, at least.

But before they could hit a bank, as he left his apartment, the building manager asked Eddie if that was his green Ford parked in the back lot. Eddie explained that it belonged to a friend who was out of town for a few days.

He went back to the apartment to get a couple of cans of beer, one for himself and one for the manager. When he walked back out he saw the manager talking to a policeman in a cruiser car. He heard the manager tell the police that it was all a mistake, that he had handled it and probably shouldn't have called them.

But the police car drove around the back, where the Ford was parked. Eddie panicked and took off on foot, as fast as he could, for Johnny's house three blocks away.

If the cops had taken down the license number and started getting nosey, they could connect Eddie to the car through the manager. There were still money and guns in Eddie's apartment, and if they found those it was back to the big house for Eddie Watkins.

Johnny was frightened half to death and Eddie calmed him down. "There's nobody who can link you to anything, except for me," Eddie said. "I'm blowing town now. I can't take a chance of being picked up."

Eddie went to St. Louis on a bus, wondering whether the police were staking out his apartment. He called Johnny when he got to St. Louis and Johnny was calm. He said he didn't think there was anything to it. He'd checked out the apartment and there were no cops, and the green Ford was still there. Nobody had come by the office asking questions. Just to make sure, Eddie asked him to go by the apartment to check things out. He would call back in two hours, and if Johnny wasn't there, Eddie would know that something was wrong and he would bolt for parts unknown.

The two hours seemed like days to Eddie. But when he called, Johnny was there and said the situation was calm. He said that he had gone up to the apartment and had knocked on the door, and Eddie would never guess who was there.

"Who?" Eddie said.

"Al Marks."

"What?"

"He said you were supposed to meet him there, and when he got there your door was cracked, so he just walked in and had been waiting on you ever since."

Eddie remembered that he hadn't closed his door when he'd walked out to take the manager a beer. Eddie hoped that Al didn't decide to search his apartment for money, and he caught the next flight back to Cleveland. When he got back to his apartment everything was in order.

He found out later that it had been a false alarm. He had linked the manager's questions about the Ford to the police car that had come by, but actually the two were unrelated. There had been a domestic quarrel at the apartments and the manager had called the police because of that, but it had been straightened out before they arrived.

Nonetheless, Eddie decided it was time to get a different apartment. It should be something more luxurious, and maybe he'd move Karen in. She was about ready to leave her husband.

The green Ford was useless now, and Al had to get another car; the Ford and the plates would be hot. Anyway, the apartment manager had seen the car and sometimes papers publish pictures of get-away cars.

They made their plans to rob a bank, and on the morning of the job—May 26, 1965—Al was there at six in the morning waking Eddie up. Either he was on the ball or desperate for a dollar.

Eddie had told Al nothing about the job, not even what bank it would be. Al's job was the same as Johnny's had been—just stand by the door and guard it.

They wore dark glasses and disguises into the

Cleveland Trust Bank, Madison Avenue branch. At exactly 10 a.m. they walked in and Eddie went to the manager's desk, while Al headed for the counter to fill out a withdrawal slip.

When Eddie told the manager he had a gun pointed at him, the manager smiled. "No kidding?" he said. "You're not serious."

"Very serious," Eddie said. "I'll blow your head off."

"Well, I'm a sonofabitch," the manager said, still smiling. "I can't believe it."

He really didn't believe it.

Eddie pointed to Al, who gave him a nod, but the manager was still grinning. He wasn't a bit frightened.

"Goddamit, mister, your life's in my hands. Move."

Finally the manager moved, but he was very calm, almost nonchalant—much calmer than Eddie and Al. He told his tellers, "Girls, we are being robbed by these two gentlemen. Please cooperate. Just stand still and do as you're told and none of us will be hurt." He was still smiling. He calmly filled up Eddie's bag with cash, very deliberately, even though Eddie and Al had guns drawn.

Al walked over to a telephone operator and jerked a phone out of her hand, then fired a shot with the .38 into the wall and told her that if she tried anything the next one would go into her head. Eddie was doing a fast burn. The goddam James Gang, he thought. Eddie had never fired a shot in a bank in his life. He wanted to walk over and slug Al, but there wasn't time. After the shot, however, the manager worked faster. They had emptied the drawers and were headed for the safe when a Brinks truck pulled up and two armed guards got out.

Eddie grabbed the bag, tossed it to Al and told him to get the car cranked. The guards were waiting for traffic to clear so they could cross the street. Eddie kept the bank employees covered till Al pulled the car up. The manager followed Eddie out and yelled to the Brinks guards as Al and Eddie pulled away. The guards broke for their truck but had to make a U-turn. Al gunned the car and the truck gave chase. Eddie gave directions, as he knew the alternate getaway routes, and they highballed it for the spot where the window-washing truck was stashed. After a few turns down sidestreets they lost the Brinks guards, made it back to the truck and hurried away toward safety. They could hear sirens wailing in their direction, closing in faster and faster. But they were safe in the truck, and they drove calmly down the Cleveland streets.

When they got back to the apartment Eddie grabbed Al and gave him hell about firing the gun. All it did, Eddie told him, was cause a lot of noise. Al was bigger than Eddie, but he was afraid of Eddie and intimidated by him.

Nevertheless, Eddie was impressed by Al's calmness in the bank, his attention to details and his reliability. He would just have to straighten things out about this gun-shooting business. Al hadn't even made the tires screech, when they had to take off in a hurry at the bank.

The take was only a little over ten thousand, but Eddie gave Al half, in clean money. Al was excited: Eddie knew that this was probably more money than he'd ever had at one time. He would see to it that Al's next payday was bigger.

Eddie Watkins had passed the point of no return as a bank robber. The big money had gotten to him. He loved the luxuries of life too much to give them up. He was still excited by the robberies, and he decided that if he were going to rob one bank he might as well rob them all. Thus he would get enough money in a short time to retire.

Eddie got a new apartment and Karen moved in soon after. They rented it under Karen's stage name as a dancer and stripper.

Things were good. The parole officer told Eddie that since he'd gotten such glowing reports from his employer about how much new business Eddie had brought in, and since Eddie had been promoted to sales manager, he would no longer have to report each week. All he would have to do was check in every now and then and report any change in job or address.

Eddie figured there would be no stopping him and his bright new partner, Al. But he was wrong— very wrong.

Karen got a job as a dancer at a club downtown and they spent most of their days going out to restaurants. She didn't cook well enough for them to stay home for lunch. Her idea of a homecooked meal was a TV dinner.

Johnny was on the outs with his wife and living at the office. The sad thing was that he loved his wife, in spite of her Victorian hangups.

Johnny finally started dating a girl named Helen, who was a big improvement over his wife, in spite of the fact that when Johnny brought her over she called her boyfriend from Eddie's apartment and the boyfriend came banging on the door looking for her. Eddie had to pull a pistol to get rid of him, since he was about twice the size of the side of a house.

Spending money on Helen made Johnny broke again, and Johnny again was able to find a soft touch in Eddie. He still felt that he owed Johnny, no matter what. He agreed to find a three-man bank where Johnny might do some good. It was in the Collinwood district of Cleveland. Al would be the backup man and Johnny could more or less be third base.

Al had gone out of town with some woman he'd met, so Eddie set the date of June 20th to rob the bank, with or without Al.

The police were dumbfounded by the robberies, because the same "M.O." had shown up on many of them in the past six months. Eddie, however, had a good cover and had kept the original apartment as an address. As far as anyone knew, Eddie wasn't living high on the hog.

Karen did not know that Eddie was a bank robber. She was not the quickest mind in the meadow, but just the same Eddie told her a story that would stop her from asking questions. The tale was about his having an ex-wife who wanted alimony; that was the reason for the apartment being in Karen's name, and for all of the secrecy.

The three-man bank had sixteen employees. It was out on Waterloo Road, where a police cruiser made rounds once an hour.

To buy a used car for the robbery, Eddie told Karen that he had a daughter and wanted to surprise her with a new car for her birthday. He gave Karen cash to buy the car and a phony name—which he said was his daughter's last name, from her stepfather—to register the car for purchase.

She bought the car, and on June 20th Al still wasn't back in town.

Eddie and Johnny decided to pull off the job by themselves. Things went wrong almost from the moment they entered the bank. A drive-in teller spun her chair around, saw Eddie's drawn gun at the manager's desk and tripped the alarm. Eddie knew he had only seconds to do his thing, or a fifty-thousand-dollar job would be up in smoke and he would be very dead or very in jail.

Johnny held a shotgun while Eddie jumped the counter like a Hollywood stunt man and began cleaning out the drawers. He had ordered the employees to lie on the floor. Within a minute the two men were outside and into the car, listening to the police sirens get closer and closer. Eddie broke out the back window in case he had to shoot at the police cars. The two men were just turning the first corner when the first police car pulled up in front of the bank. The three blocks to the car-switch site was the longest distance Eddie had ever traveled.

He had expected Johnny to panic, but he didn't. He remained calm the entire three blocks.

They lucked out and made it back to the truck. They had tried a three-man job with two men, and it was only Eddie's great speed that had got them out of the bank in time to get away. If he had stopped to wipe his brow, if he had hesitated just once, they might still have been in the bank when the police arrived.

But Eddie had been sure that an alarm was tripped by the woman at the drive-in window. He had operated on his instincts—instincts that had been sharpened over the years, during a lot of years and a lot of robberies. But never again would he rate a bank as a three-man job and then hit it with two.

Since they hadn't gotten to the safe, the take was only about five thousand dollars. Eddie gave Johnny half.

They found out that Al was in jail, that he had gotten drunk, kicked in a filling station, taken the keys to a parked car and passed out in the car in the filling station parking lot.

Johnny went down to bail him out before they started running fingerprints that would trace him as being an ex-con, and start grilling things out of him.

They paid his $500 bond with cash and got him out before he could be nailed as a parole violator. Eddie advised Al to leave town, but Al said he needed a stake. Was there a three-man bank still on Eddie's charted list?

It was important to get Al out of town monied, because if he were caught around Cleveland the law would certainly grant him immunity from prosecution to tell them all about Eddie. Eddie knew it and Al knew he knew it.

They hid Al out in Eddie's apartment for a couple of days while Eddie cased a few banks. Something with a lot of cash and little risk was what he wanted. Eddie had always worked alone as a young man because he knew the risk of having partners. You had to make sure they were taken care of before you could feel safe.

In 1965 you could get a very nice car for a thousand dollars, and Eddie gave Johnny the money to buy one. Eddie told Al that he was leaving town, too, after this job, because he didn't want Al hanging around deciding that one wasn't enough.

He wanted Al out and far away after this one because he knew that somewhere along the line Al was going to get caught.

Eddie had made the unfortunate mistake of surrounding himself with amateurs, fools and losers, and the chickens were coming home to roost.

The night before the robbery, Eddie got Johnny and Al together and told them that if either of them blew this job he would personally kill him. Eddie had made up his mind that Al was going to be out of town on the first available plane after the bank job, and that he was going to inform Johnny that Johnny was no longer in the banking business.

That next morning, instead of being worried about the job, Eddie was daydreaming about pretty girls and picnics. All the way to the bank he thought about taking Karen on a picnic. He used to dream about those things when he was locked up in jail, especially on lonely Sundays.

This particular bank covered nearly an entire city block. There were thirty employees in plain sight. They would have to take it Western style—hit and run. When they parked the car behind the rear door of the Cuyahoga Savings and Loan on the morning of July 9, 1965, there were at least fifty customers inside the bank.

Johnny was his usual bundle of nerves, and when Al walked over to the manager's desk and informed him this was a robbery, Eddie drew both guns and hollered out, "This is a stickup. Anybody moves, they die."

Johnny raised his shotgun and blocked the front door. Eddie blocked the back door. Al had 120 seconds in which to clean out the vault. They had positioned themselves so that anyone whom Eddie couldn't see, Johnny could. The customers were frightened but didn't panic.

After thirty seconds, Eddie knew that the alarm had been tripped for at least twenty seconds.

Within 45 seconds, Al was filling the bags from

the vault. Eddie moved around, keeping an eye on the crowd and watching Al.

He looked at his watch. Twenty safe seconds left. He watched the crowd and glanced at the ticking second hand. Ten seconds ticked off. Eddie looked around and yelled to Al, "Come on, Jack, let's get out of here."

As Eddie backed toward the door he yelled, "Anyone moves, I'll use them for target practice."

Al had a bulging pillowcase full of big cash. They moved quickly to the car and nobody followed them from the bank. They headed east a block, turned south a block, made another turn and whipped the car over to the curb. They walked on foot to the Kinsman Avenue supermarket parking lot and got Johnny's truck. Eddie and Al got in the back and covered themselves up with canvas; Johnny drove slowly away.

After a few seconds they felt the truck turn, and Johnny yelled, "Shit, shit!"

"What's the matter?" Eddie called out.

"I turned the wrong way," Johnny said. "I'm heading right for the bank."

Two ways to turn—right or left—and Johnny turns the wrong way.

They drove within a half block of the bank and Eddie could hear the screaming sirens and his own heart beating throught the wail. They drove on and after five minutes Eddie got up from under the canvas. They had made it.

Johnny gulped hard when he saw a police car

parked across the street from his office. "Oh, holy mother of God." But Eddie knew there was a bookie joint across the street and sometimes the police would stop there for their payoffs.

They carried the money upstairs in the canvas while Al waited in the truck. Upstairs, from the window, they could see the police officers leaving the bookie joint. When they drove away, Johnny went down and got Al. Then they came back upstairs, where Eddie had the money spread out on the floor in a gigantic pile.

"Merry Christmas," Eddie yelled. "Christmas in July."

The take was nearly $50,000. The next day they would read that just after the robbery a Brinks truck delivered another $100,000—but no matter.

It was time to get Al out of town. He wanted to pick up his girlfriend, but Eddie wouldn't let him. Eddie told him to leave his clothes and that hunk of junk he called a car and head for Vegas. After explaining to Al how to launder his share of the money, he took Al to the airport—with instructions to buy a flight bag to carry his money in and wished him a fond farewell.

There was one thing that Eddie knew about fools: You can never trust them. If something can be screwed up they will find new and creative ways to do it.

Eddie would realize later that what he should have done was wait at the airport and personally escort Al to his plane, then watch the plane take off.

He did not. Instead he headed back to his apartment, with one intermediate stop to buy a new color TV set for the living room. They were to deliver the set that night.

Eddie would never get to watch one minute of programming on that set.

FIFTEEN

When Eddie got home that afternoon, he took Karen out to eat at an Italian restaurant on Clark just off West 25th Street. Johnny brought his girlfriend, Toni, and it would be Johnny and Eddie's last nice evening together.

At 5:45 the next morning, Eddie answered his phone. It was Johnny and he was in a panic.

"Eddie, we're in big trouble." His voice quivered.

"What the hell—"

"Al," Johnny said.

"Al?"

"Al's in jail, Eddie."

"What? How do you—"

Eddie jumped out of bed, wide awake from that bit of news.

"It's on the front page of the morning paper— about how the cops caught him and they think he might be one of the robbers on yesterday's job."

"Oh, shit."

"What are we gonna do, Eddie?"

"Get your ass over here, fast."

Eddie raced for the front door and grabbed the paper. Sure enough, there was Al's picture staring right at him from the paper. He'd been picked up just after midnight on a drunk driving charge. Eddie hit the wall with his fist. Dammit, he thought, that idiot. He read further. The police had shaken down his car and found packs of twenty-dollar bills under the seat with fresh Cuyahoga Savings and Loan wrappers on them.

Eddie would find out later that Al had left the airport in a cab and went back to the home of his girlfriend, whose name was Maureen. She worked at a downtown bar. He spent the night trying to talk her into leaving town with him and she kept refusing. He had flashed money around the bar, bought drinks for the house and announced he was going to marry Maureen.

After making a total fool of himself, and being asked to leave the bar, he went back and got his car and the police caught him on Euclid Avenue—not far from the department store where Eddie had gone to find his mother, thirty-six years before on a cold, horrible day.

It was only a matter of time before Al cracked; Eddie knew that. He would be plea bargaining for probation, using Eddie and Johnny as bait. He had figured Al for a fool, but not as big a fool as Al had proved to be with his stunt the night before.

Johnny was there before Eddie had finished reading the paper; Karen was still asleep. They went to Eddie's Clifton Avenue apartment. Eddie got his money from there and sat down with Johnny. He gave Johnny some clean money and instructed him carefully.

"Johnny, I've got to get out of town. But you'll be safe if you do what I say. You don't have a record, so it's Al's word against yours. Don't crack. Don't take any lie detector tests. Get a good lawyer and, if they lean on you, say it could have been me—I was missing from work that day."

Eddie knew that if Johnny toughed it out there was no way they would get a conviction on him. But with his own record, he'd be back in jail in a flash and would probably never get out. His word wouldn't be any better than Al's. Eddie would do time and Al would go free; Eddie was certain of that. He knew that Johnny was weak and might crack under pressure. But there was nothing Eddie could do about that.

He told Johnny that he was heading for Florida, although he was planning to go in an entirely different direction.

Johnny said he would go with him.

"No way," Eddie said. "The heat's on and we have a better chance making it alone. They'd have both our descriptions and they'd spot us in a second."

"Then I'm gonna go to Canada," Johnny said. "I'll send money to my family." He buried his face in his hands and began to sob. "I'll never see my kids again."

Eddie put a comforting arm on Johnny's shoulder. "That's why you'd better stay, Johnny, and try to beat the rap. You're the business man with no record who befriended two ex-cons and they went bad on you. Play that up for sympathy. If they catch me I'll stick to that story. Hell, you'll come out a martyr and a hero, and Al will look like a rat for trying to use his old boss who helped him when he was down."

Johnny nodded and wiped the tears from his face.

"If you get caught," Eddie said, "don't cop out. Make them prove you did something. If they offer you a deal, don't take it. Police don't offer deals unless their cases are shaky."

They said their goodbys and Eddie felt sad about Johnny's situation. He had his own problems, but as he watched Johnny walk out to his car, it aroused a piercing emotion inside him. The poor fellow was on his own now in a world where he was a stranger.

Johnny was in the jungle.

When Eddie reached his other apartment, Karen was at the kitchen table drinking coffee.

"I got some bad news," Eddie said. Karen looked up. "Remember the car you bought for my daughter?"

Karen nodded. She was still half asleep.

"Well, my ex-wife traced it and she has a warrant for nonsupport. I either leave town or go to jail. I've got to go."

"Where?"

"You stay here. The rent's paid three months in advance. I'll give you a couple of thousand."

"But where are you going to go, Eddie? I want to go with you."

Eddie tried to convince her to stay, but there was no doing it, and he couldn't waste any more time. He expected the police to break in any minute to his old apartment and dragnets to go up.

While Karen grabbed her clothes, Eddie started pulling money from under sofas, out of shoeboxes, behind the commode. Normally he would have expected a lot of questions about it, but not from Karen. She was like Alice in Wonderland, she never needed explanations. She simply got up in morning and went to bed at night. A hurricane could tear down the building and she would just shrug, not wonder long about what happened, and move on to the next place.

As Eddie stuffed the thousands and thousands of dollars into a bag, she said, "What about your clothes?"

She would never ask about the money.

For Eddie, the dream of getting enough cash to retire had gone up in smoke when Al was caught. Before he had never had anything to lose, never any possessions. Now there were all those nice things he'd acquired; he had to leave them behind. That apartment was the first place where he had really felt at home since he was a little boy. Now he had to leave and he felt, for the first time, a true sense of loss.

He drove the Cadillac, which was in Johnny's name, out onto the interstate toward Chicago. Johnny could claim Eddie had stolen his car, and Eddie knew the police wouldn't be looking for it yet—even if Al had already blown the whistle—because nobody but Johnny knew the Cadillac was in Johnny's name. There would be no A.P.B. out on that car, at least for a few days.

Karen was leaving the security of her life for the adventure of living on the dodge. She had had a son and had been involved in a custody battle over him with the husband that she had just left. She would not be able to see her parents again for a long time. Whether going with him was love, excitement or ignorance on her part, Eddie wasn't sure.

He had no real plan and he thought about it on the way to Chicago. He had plenty of cash, but now the law would be looking for him. There was no turning back to the straight life. He thought about a plan as he drove to Chicago. The only reason he had headed that way was because it had been the quickest and best exit out of Cleveland.

He knew he would need a new identity. Plastic surgery might not be a good idea, because it would arouse the surgeon's curiosity. He thought about growing a beard, but beards were uncommon and would attract attention.

But not if he went where beards were common. That was it—he would go to San Francisco and mingle with the arty dropouts, weirdos and beatniks. When he told Karen about San Francisco she was excited about the adventure.

"Gee, Eddie," she said, "this is just like a Humphrey Bogart movie."

At her suggestion they stopped at a motel to change their appearances with hair dye. Eddie's hair was dark brown and she had to bleach it four times to make it white. On the third bleaching it hurt so bad he had bent over in pain and banged the wall. She had burned his scalp something terrible. Eddie just knew the skin would peel off.

"My God," Eddie cried. "You've burned my fuckin' head off."

"I'm sorry, honey." And then she started coming at him with that bottle again.

"Oh no you don't."

"I've got to do it just once more, hon."

"Get away from me, wife of Dracula."

His head was on fire and he fled to the bathroom and soaked it in cold water. When he rose back up, feeling some relief, he looked in the mirror and there she was again with that bottle.

She told him she was an expert at this. Maybe she was an expert at something, but this was not her calling. After the next dye job not only did he feel as if the top of his head was burned completely off, he had a crop of what he considered the fruitiest looking red hair he had ever seen.

"Well, hon, I can go get another bottle and change it to something else."

"Oh, no you don't," Eddie warned her. "Not now, not ever."

They left the motel under cover of darkness, headed for Chicago and a new life.

They checked into a motel near O'Hare Field and that night Eddie counted his money. He had $74,000 plus all of the money that he had in markers in Vegas. Some of the cash would need to be laundered, so they would stop in Vegas on their way to San Francisco. If he played his cards right, he would be able to get into a business and just disappear into oblivion, get out of the jungle for good.

But he couldn't sleep that night for worrying about the law busting in and hauling him off to jail. Karen slept as if she didn't have a worry in the world—and she didn't. He knew that if he were to wake her up and tell her the truth, she would probably simply yawn and say, "Let's talk about it in the morning."

Eddie thought about sending her home, but he knew that she was set on going along. He could use the companionship, and nobody would be looking for a couple right away. But he knew that the federal authorities would be after him this time. They would be after Karen soon, too.

Eddie had always planted the idea in Al's mind that he would go to Florida if things got hot, and he knew Al would tell the police that when he talked. He also knew that Al would talk eventually, if he hadn't already.

But it would be safe to let Karen do the legwork of finding a place to live, getting IDs and doing the shopping; then they would settle down like regular folks. Perhaps he could create the impression that he was a traveling salesman.

At O'Hare field, Eddie was nervous. Airports are always full of police looking for people for various things, or just looking for anyone suspicious.

As they boarded the plane and settled in their seats, Eddie began to think about life on the run. He remembered back to what inmates had told him about their lives on the run, and what had tripped them up, how they got caught. He remembered what he had been told by Russ Clark, the last of the Dillinger mob.

Russ had said, "When the heat's on, don't stop. Move faster. Give them so much to follow that they stay confused. The more leads they have to check on, the more you can keep moving."

But Russ had failed to realize the flaw in his "M.O." of hitting banks. Russ never changed his style, and the banks and the feds finally were able to prepare for him; eventually they caught him.

Eddie looked at Karen, contented in her airplane seat reading a gossip magazine. She was an asset, but she could also be his downfall. She wasn't particularly bright or clever and she often acted without thinking. She would have to be watched and told what to do. She had a fantastic memory—God granted her that, at least—but she only remembered what she wanted to remember. She could and often did forget everything that didn't directly relate to her. He was sure that in a week she wouldn't remember the old apartment numbers in Cleveland. All she lived for was to dance and screw. She could live in a cardboard box if Eddie were to take her dancing regularly and pay attention to her in bed.

Karen questioned nothing, would pack and leave in the middle of the night without regrets. She didn't seem to miss Cleveland nor any of her friends or family. She just sat there in the seat reading her magazine and popping her gum, content to be on the run even though she wasn't sure why. They had decided that their new names would be Mike and Pat O'Shea, so Eddie became Mike O'Shea.

When they reached Vegas, Karen said, "Oh, by the way, my ex-sister-in-law was on the plane."

"On what? Your ex-who?"

"I didn't say anything because you told me not to do anything suspicious, and I didn't want to whisper."

"God almighty. Did she recognize you?"

"She looked right at me. But we never talk. She's my first husband's sister."

Eddie wondered how many of those she had and how many sisters-in-law they might be running into in the future.

He didn't spend a lot of time in Vegas. He didn't want anyone to recognize him from his earlier trips. Karen stayed in the room while Eddie took care of "some business."

He was Mike O'Shea to all those he would meet from then on, but at present he was still looking a lot like Eddie Watkins and he was hot as hell. He laundered his money and cashed in several of the markers as quickly as possible. Then he got Karen, and Mr. and Mrs. O'Shea were quickly on a plane bound for their new home, San Francisco—a place where he knew nobody and nobody knew him, a place that he figured would be absolutely perfect.

SIXTEEN

The O'Sheas spent their first night in San Francisco at the St. Francis Hotel. It was Eddie's first peaceful sleep since Johnny called him with news of Al's capture.

As he looked out over the sunny, peaceful San Francisco skyline, he wondered about Johnny. He thought for an instant that maybe Al wouldn't talk. But then he came to his senses. Of course Al would talk; he would talk like a magpie at a convention. If Johnny did what Eddie had told him, he might beat the rap.

But he found out later that Johnny had panicked and run for Canada. He also found out that Johnny sent money to his wife and, even though she needed it, she marched right down to police headquarters and turned it in as stolen.

Eddie informed Karen when she woke that they were going on a shopping spree. She would buy $2,000 worth of clothes and so would he. She was excited, and they went to the stores and kept coming back to the hotel with armloads of packages.

They found an apartment in the Mission District—not the greatest neighborhood in the world, but a place to sojourn while he grew a beard and all of the essentials were in order.

Eddie had begun to call Karen "Pat" and she had begun to call him "Mike." He found an apartment and she went and rented it. He had over $100,000 in an attaché case and his pistol in his belt to ward off anyone who might try to take it. The apartment was purposely on the second floor, to discourage burglars.

They would stay in the apartment for a month, then move to another, better one, using the previous apartment as their address for the past year. With a few months' rent in advance, no one would check closely.

Eddie needed a car. He found a Grand Prix that by bargaining he got for $4,000. He told the salesman he was going to put down $500, then go to his bank and bring back the rest in a cashier's check. When he decided it was senseless to leave a deposit, the salesman thought he was losing a deal and offered to drive him to the bank.

"Which bank, Mr. O'Shea?"

Eddie had that covered, too. He told him the downtown branch of the Wells Fargo Bank. He knew there was no place to park there and the salesman wouldn't go inside with him.

He had told the salesman that the car was for his daughter, Pat. He knew it would be easier to pass off Karen—at barely twenty years old—as his

161

daughter rather than his wife. At that age she could get a Social Security card and a driver's license without drawing suspicion. And by registering the car in her name they could establish a credible identity for her, even get bank statements. Then eventually this could be used to provide identification for Eddie.

After about fifteen minutes in the bank, Eddie came out with forty hundred-dollar bills to pay for the car. He didn't get a cashier's check because he didn't want to arouse suspicion of any kind at the bank. He told the salesman he had gotten the money from his savings, and no more questions were asked. After he had signed the papers in Karen's new name, he stopped by the driver's license exam station and picked up a manual for her.

For three weeks he stayed in the apartment and Karen handled all of the outside chores, and she drove, just in case they were to get stopped and ticketed. At the end of a month they moved into a better apartment.

Eddie had had no communication with Cleveland and he decided it was time to find out what happened. There was a friend he trusted in Cleveland, a woman he had known for twenty years.

When she answered and heard who it was, she said, "Don't even tell me where you're calling from. I don't want to know."

Eddie told her he had a new name and she said, "I don't want to know what it is."

By her answers, he knew that the worst had happened.

"They raided that apartment where you were living with the girl," she said.

"They did? When?"

"It must have been right after you went out the door, because the papers said there was a still warm cup of coffee on the table."

Eddie felt his stomach tumbling. The police must have come just as he and Karen were pulling out of the parking lot. Al must have talked that night or early the next morning.

"The newspapers are writing stuff about the Eddie Watkins gang," she said. "You're as hot as a firecracker and they'll probably come see me soon. They've checked out everybody else who knew you."

"If they grill you," Eddie said, "tell them about this call. You don't know where it's from anyway, and you won't be able to tell them anything they can use. I'd better get off the phone. Anything I can do for you?"

"Not a thing," she said. "Take care of yourself—and stay out of Cleveland."

For the next two weeks he had Karen buy daily papers from Cleveland and Detroit. The Detroit papers were just a precaution so some newsstand seller wouldn't start asking Karen about Cleveland. On Eddie's request, she changed newsstands often. He was taking care of even the smallest detail that might trip him up.

There was no mention of Karen in the papers, which was a relief to Eddie. For several days there

163

was news about Johnny, who had surely fled to Canada, although the papers didn't know where he was—only that he wasn't around and hadn't been caught. The papers claimed that Al wasn't spilling his guts, as Eddie had believed. It was possible that the police simply found out Al was working at the same company as Eddie and went to talk to Eddie routinely. Luckily for him, he had beaten them by a hairsbreadth.

Eddie shaved the top of his head to eliminate the bleaching, then dyed the sides of his hair dark red. He clipped a few hairs from his dye job and had Karen go to a toupee shop. They gave her a plastic hood and told her how to measure the bald areas for a fitting.

A month later they had a toupee ready for her. Eddie had not gone to the shop because he hadn't wanted them to know that he had shaved his head on top, or to see the dye job and get suspicious. In less than six weeks he had completely changed his appearance and he and Karen were beginning to establish a background. They were getting bills sent to their address and everything looked normal.

When Eddie got his driver's license, he took care of the thumbprint by smoothing down the ridges of his thumb with sandpaper and coating it with greasy hair oil. When the print was taken the ridges were not as high as those on his real thumb. He was sure that the grease, mixed with the ink, had caused a smudge. He shaved his head completely and removed his false teeth. When the picture had been taken he grinned. He had created a horrible-looking driver's license photo, but he had ID, and if the information were sent routinely to the FBI, there would be no resemblance in photo or print. If he got stopped for a violation, he could explain that he had gotten a toupee since the picture was taken. The policeman probably would feel sorry for him because he looked so ugly and wouldn't give him a ticket.

He began going out at night with Karen. They went every place where they could dance.

The next step was to buy into a legitimate business. He had scanned the classifieds every day looking for business opportunities, some kind of enterprise that Karen could run and he could use for ID and a front. He had never worked and knew little about business. He thought, and laughed to himself, that he should probably open a bank.

Then one day he saw an opportunity to buy a pet shop. Animals were nice. They weren't like people—they didn't cross you up, they didn't dump on you. They were innocents. Karen liked animals, too. For sure, she could handle this—or so he thought. How much schmaltz did it take to clean out a birdcage, anyway?

Eddie bought the pet shop. He was now Michael O'Shea, born July 1, 1925; Eddie Watkins existed only on the FBI's Ten Most Wanted List, making him one of crime's elite big timers. But Michael O'Shea was a pet-shop owner and liking it.

Michael O'Shea got a credit card at Kay Jewelers. He bought a $200 ring and filled out a credit application. Although his background was weak in credit standing, he counted on the greed of the salesman.

The salesman looked at the applicaiton and said, "Mr. O'Shea, how much do you intend to put down?"

"I'd planned to pay for the ring in cash, but I chose one that cost more than I have on me right now. I'll put down a hundred and fifty dollars."

He knew that he had more than paid for the cost of the ring, plus profit. The salesman got his credit approved and Eddie agreed to pay $10 a week on the remaining $50. He did the same with other companies and soon he had several credit cards. Karen got him a Social Security card, listing his age as twenty-three since age wouldn't appear on the card.

The pet shop was a lot more complicated to run than Eddie had figured it would be. No matter how much outside training he got for Karen, she continued to butcher the poddles when she clipped them. Then she told the owners that it was the new look, and most of them, not wanting to seem uninformed, accepted that explanation and paid their bill.

Tropical fish were a big problem. Every morning they would find many of them floating dead on top of the water. Eddie finally found out that Karen was filling the tanks with hot water. She didn't know any better. Then she started filling the tanks with cold water and the fish died in droves. She finally got some of the neighborhood kids to teach her how to care for the fish.

For weeks the cash register came up short. Eddie knew Karen was honest as the day was long, and she didn't need to steal. Finally, after wondering how they could be losing so much money, Eddie found out the problem. Karen did not know how to count. He was flabbergasted. You could give the poor thing a five-dollar bill and she'd give you your item and maybe hand you back eight. He managed to cut the losses somewhat by giving her a crash course in counting.

Eddie bought a white XKE Jaguar and gave it to Karen. They took a trip to Tahoe and stayed at Harrah's. It was more of a real atmosphere than the concrete and neon of Las Vegas. There were real mountains and things that grew and real trees and real water.

The tables were tough on Eddie that first night, and after heavy losses he and Karen went out to dinner. After the second drink a waiter came over, and looked at Eddie and said, "Excuse me, sir, but a gentleman over there said he thinks he knows you. His name is—"

Eddie was startled and couldn't hear the name. He told the waiter that he didn't know the man, that the fellow had obviously made some mistake. He had figured the disguise to be foolproof. Could it be somebody from his old prison days could see through the disguise? Or a federal agent?

When the show was nearly over the waiter came back and said, "Sir, the gentleman insists that he knows you from somewhere. He said he is the captain of the Nevada Highway Patrol; you might remember him by that."

"Look, I'm from New York," Eddie said. "I don't know any Nevada Highway Patrol officials. You're disturbing the show. Please don't bother us further."

Eddie was shook. They eased out of there and over to the crowded tables. He told Karen to bet some money on the tables and he'd be back in a minute. He went to the restroom and looked around. It was empty. He went inside a stall and stood up on the toilet seat so anybody coming in wouldn't see him. He took out his .38 and cocked it. Then he realized how ridiculous he looked standing on a toilet seat with a cocked pistol. What an awful way to get brought down, he thought. He could see the headlines: "EDDIE WATKINS DIES ON TOILET SEAT." That was no way to end a career.

SEVENTEEN

He and Karen eased out of the casino and drove back to San Francisco that night. Karen didn't think there was anything odd about that, because Karen didn't *think*. Karen just *was*.

With the pet shop sputtering and the money going out here and there, Eddie's savings were dwindling fast. He could envision poverty ahead, and poverty was not a luxury he could afford while being on the run. He knew that it took big money to stay obscure, so he decided he would have to hit another bank. He wouldn't do it in the city where he lived, though. He and Karen now knew enough about the pet-shop business to start making it work; eventually it might become a real income producer. He wanted to preserve what he had built up so carefully in San Francisco. But in the meantime, money still needed to be pumped into the business; besides, he and Karen had both been blowing cash as if it would never run out. So he decided that he would go back and pay a visit to the city where his talents had first surfaced: Los Angeles.

Then he decided that he might go to Vegas instead, maybe win money on the tables and not have to rob any more banks.

He flew to Las Vegas alone and checked into the Sahara. He had been there many times, but Vegas forgets you five minutes after you stop losing or tipping. He bought two thousand dollars' worth of chips and by four in the morning he had lost that and a thousand more. He had also met a lovely lady named Rosie. He wasn't sure what Rosie's angle was. Any time a lady took the dice and bet a dollar or two, he bet with her. Thus his meeting with Rosie.

She was a lovely lady, twenty-three or four years old, dark eyed and dark complexioned. She had a great figure and a nice sweet face. She was betting dollars and winning, and Eddie was betting hundreds and she was winning for him. Every time she made a number or a point he would toss her a five-dollar chip and she would place it on a longshot bet.

Eddie's first guess was that she was a hooker.

It was nearly daybreak when he suggested they have breakfast together. She agreed. They had a nice talk over breakfast and he said, "Would you like to go to my room with me?"

"I would," she said. "I think I'd like that."

When they got to the room Eddie said, "What's this going to cost?"

She glared at him, first with anger and then with hurt. "If you think I'm a whore I'm leaving right now," she said.

Eddie apologized awkwardly. He said he was sorry, but he had just assumed that with the age difference and all—

She sat down on the corner of the bed. "When you asked me to go to your room, I liked what I saw in you," she said.

"Look, I'm sorry," Eddie said. "I've always just had to grab love where I could get it. Everywhere I've ever been in my life somebody always had an angle. Somebody always disappointed me, all the way from my childhood, I've tried to live through it—and I'm sorry. I didn't mean to insult you."

"Do you still want to go to bed with me?" she said.

"Sure, of course I do."

Once her body was out of her dress, it was much more incredible than it had appeared all wrapped up in clothes. Eddie could not believe that she would want to go to bed with a man pushing fifty who had all of the miles on him that he did—at least for free. But she did.

After they made love, they talked. She was from South America and the man who married her had left her in Las Vegas with a kid to raise. She did have an angle—she was what she called a "good-time girl." She would hang around the tables placing small bets, and men would often make bets for her. Sometimes she won a bundle off what they bet for her, or they'd tip her heavily if she were winning for them. She would accept dinner invitations and sometimes go to bed with men, but she never charged them. That way she could get through the jungle without doing anything illegal. She had actually made a bundle from Eddie's bets and had it securely in her purse.

Later that night she left, but they arranged to meet again during the next two days of Eddie's stay. She was deep and intellectual and claimed to genuinely care about him, whether or not she actually did. Eddie wanted to believe that she did, and he didn't mind her angle. Everybody had to survive in the world. He liked women a little tainted; he understood them better if they were.

However, Eddie left Las Vegas $9,000 poorer than he came, and decided he would have to make that trip to Los Angeles after all.

EIGHTEEN

Eddie drove to Los Angeles and cased banks for two days, found one on Western Avenue and bought a used Ford for a getaway car. It was dependable and started quickly every time.

He wore an old pair of pants and decided not to change his face this time, since he was already living under an assumed name and this face wasn't the subject of any wanted posters. He shaved his goatee, however, and put black spray dye on his hair. He took off the toupee and parked the car in a supermarket parking lot, where the getaway Ford was stashed. Driving up near the bank's back door, he left the key in the ignition.

He was armed and ready. He walked up to the bank door . . . and it was locked. "Oh, hell," he said. "Have I hit some strange California holiday?"

Maybe he was early, he figured. He went to the car, drove closer to the front of the bank.

The next time he tried the door it was still locked. He thought to himself, *Maybe this is some kind of omen.*

He tried the door a third time and now it was open. He walked in, went to the manager's desk and said quietly, "In my left-hand pocket is a gun. My finger is on the trigger. The gun is pointing at your heart. Would you like to die?"

"Are you kidding?" the manager said.

"Shall I pull the trigger to prove that I'm not?"

"Of course not," the manager said, sweat already beading up on his forehead.

In seconds the manager was filling the bag with money and the employees were on the floor. Eddie said to the manager, "I'll hold you responsible for any alarms that are set off."

As he was easing out of the door he said, "Anybody gets up, I'll blow their ass off."

The rest was a routine getaway.

He switched cars before he even heard the sirens and was soon on his way to Vegas.

Back in Vegas, he counted the take: more than $32,000, mostly in twenties, some in hundreds, the rest in ten, fives and ones. He had laundered all of the money and was on his way to his room. In Las Vegas it is impossible to get from any one place to another without passing a gambling table. Casinos are designed that way purposely. The gambling urge hit Eddie and he started chasing the nine thousand that he'd lost three days earlier.

But the money ran too fast and he'd dropped more than $6,000 before he regained his senses. He realized he'd been at the tables drinking and playing for twelve hours. He'd lost three thousand dollars

174

on the last pass of the dice and decided he'd better get out of Vegas.

Instead of heading back to San Francisco, he drove southward to San Diego. He'd been there in the early thirties and it was time to return and see how the old town had changed.

He called Karen and said he was visiting some old friends and would be back within a week. He scouted out and hit another bank, and except for a woman screaming in the parking lot when he drove away, everything went smoothly. He got $22,000 from that bank and drove back to Vegas, laundered the money, and this time stayed away from the tables.

He drove back to San Francisco with nearly $50,000. He wanted to get back. He didn't want to leave Karen alone long enough to botch things up beyond repair. He kept pushing the thought out of his mind that one day she would do something really stupid and get him caught.

Eddie negotiated for a second pet shop, in Daly City, in the suburbs of San Francisco. It was a bigger shop than his first one and he figured he could hire a couple of girls to run it. Karen had a couple of kids helping her in the first shop, and she loved it and didn't want to leave. Eddie wasn't sure whether she loved the kids or the pets more, but whatever it was, it wasn't the money. Although they weren't losing money any more, they weren't turning much of a profit.

The second shop cost him $25,000, but it was well

stocked with supplies, had a second room for animals, a grooming room, an office and a large kennel for boarding dogs and cats.

Eddie's banker—he had his own now, and it was a unique sensation—told him that the pet shop in Daly City was a little rundown now, because the girl who had owned it last had inherited it from her mother and hadn't taken much interest in it. But when the mother ran it, it was a veritable gold mine. Eddie finally talked Karen into leaving the shop in Noriega and going out to Daly City. She eventually got to like the Daly City shop better than the first one, and with Karen out of the Noriega place it soon began to turn a profit.

Eddie bought a house on Skyline Drive in Daly City. By now he and Karen both had substantial bank accounts at the Bank of America. They had insurance policies and oil company and major department store credit cards. A Dun & Bradstreet representative had visited the shops for information about the growing business, and Eddie, as Michael O'Shea, was soon listed in Dun & Bradstreet's register of up-and-coming business executives. That put him not only on the exclusive FBI's Ten Most Wanted list but the also on the equally exclusive Dun & Bradstreet up-and-coming-executives list.

He had found out about the Ten Most Wanted list one day from a newspaper article. The report said that Eddie Watkins had robbed several banks in Ohio and other states, and was known to carry two guns; the report went on to give his old physical description. It also mentioned that his favorite meal was pork chops and buttered rice. When he read that he gave a sigh of disappointment; he knew Johnny had been caught. Whenever he went to Johnny's for lunch or supper, he would ask if they were having his favorite, roast pork chops and buttered rice. Whenever Johnny came to his place it was what Eddie cooked. Johnny was the only one who knew that, so Eddie realized that poor Johnny had talked and was now probably somewhere in the slammer.

He felt bad about that, and he wished to hell that Johnny had done what he told him. If Al hadn't talked it would have been hard to convict Johnny. Eddie felt bad because now Johnny's kids would be fatherless. And they would have to live with the stigma of their father's being an ex-con, a convicted bank robber. But if it weren't for Johnny, Eddie would never have gotten out of jail. He didn't blame Johnny for his own return to bank robbing, he took full responsibility for that.

Well, one thing, Johnny's worries about getting by would be over for a few years. He would have three squares and rent paid by the federal government.

Eddie was also a little shook up about making the Ten Most Wanted list. But after all they were after Eddie Watkins, and he was now Mike O'Shea.

Eddie had a close call not long after that, when he was dining out one night. Before the end of the show, three people sat down at the table next to Eddie's group. Eddie glanced over and, without thinking, said hello to an old acquaintance from the Ohio pen, a fellow named Don Eagle. As soon as he'd said it, he knew he shouldn't have. He'd spent many a night playing gin rummy with Don in the pen. Don glanced Eddie's way a couple of times and nodded but didn't speak. Perhaps he, too, had changed identities. They left about the same time and neither of them spoke to the other again. As they went out the door and turned right on Broadway they passed each other and Don spun around to walk back. He seemed disturbed. Eddie didn't think Don had recognized him; he thought Don must have figured he might be a lawman on the tail. When they passed, Eddie didn't look Don in the eyes. He was sure that Don didn't recognize him. If he thought he had, he would've changed identities again.

Eddie's life had improved immensely from the old days at the Ohio pen. He had the house on the ocean, the business, money in the bank, and the companionship of Karen. Karen had never asked him whether he loved her and he had never told her that he did.

But she was jealous, in a possesssive sort of way. If she caught Eddie flirting or fooling around, dancing too close with someone or making advances to one of her girlfriends, the woman soon disappeared. Karen ran her off. But several times Eddie caught Karen making advances to other men. Once when he walked into the pet shop he found her in the back grooming a poodle, with four healthy-looking young men watching her rear end as she groomed the dog's rear end. Eddie made a wise-crack and the men left. He found out that they were car salesmen from across the street who came in often, always on the make. Eddie and Karen finally had a confrontation about their jealousies. Once they aired the problems their relationship loosened up and improved .

A very lovely nineteen-year-old blonde named Sharon had gone to work for them at the pet store and had moved into one of the bedrooms in their house. Eddie was tempted by Sharon; he made some covert advances that didn't work. Karen was suspicious and watched them both very closely, hesitant to leave the two of them alone for any long period of time. She knew that Eddie's appetite for variety was insatiable.

On one occasion, when Karen went to bed early, Eddie slipped out of bed and went to Sharon's room. He had been hinting to her that night and she had seeemed receptive. But when he tried Sharon's door, it wouldn't open. He tried it again—no luck. Then he knew that she had been teasing him and had put something in front of the door to keep him out, and she was inside giggling about it.

Then one day Eddie was very sick; he had been vomiting most of the previous night with the flu. Karen recommended he stay home in bed while she went to the pet shop. Eddie stayed home. It was Sharon's day off, and the thought of her being down the hall in the next room was too much for

Eddie. He started feeling better quickly. Sharon had caused trouble between Eddie and Karen by hinting to Karen that Eddie was making advances. But Eddie had covered it by denial, saying that Sharon knew he had money and wanted to cause a rift between him and Karen so she could move in on Eddie's money. He was sure Karen didn't believe that, at least not completely—but she didn't completely disbelieve it either.

That day Sharon was in her pajamas in the living room, playing the organ. Eddie came up behind her and started humming along with the tune she was playing. She smiled at him, and that was all the encouragement he needed. He put his hands on her shoulders, then moved them down to her breasts and onto her nipples. She didn't budge. He slipped his hands down her waist and inside her pants. Soon they were in the bedroom.

A few days later Karen and Sharon got in an argument over cleaning out the kennels and Sharon quit. Eddie told her she didn't have to move right away, but Sharon was a little afraid of Karen and moved out. Eddie felt no particular love for her, just desire. He had simply wanted to satisfy his curiosity, more or less.

One day Karen confronted him and said, "You don't love me, do you?"

"I never said I did, Karen. I've never been dishonest about it. I never wanted to make you feel that I did when I didn't. I like you, I love to make love to you, you're great company and you've got many lovable qualities. But no, I don't love you. I've never loved any woman, really."

She sat there pouting.

"I made no promises," Eddie said. "It was you who insisted on coming out here with me."

When he got home that night Karen and three hundred dollars were gone. He waited until 9:30 and decided that if she didn't call by ten he would get in the car, leave everything but his money and vanish. He knew that if she left she would go back to Cleveland and she might tell her family about Eddie's identity. But she still didn't know that he was wanted for bank robbery.

She called at 9:35 from the airport, said she was about to leave, and asked if he'd take care of her Doberman and her pet monkey.

Eddie thought fast. "I'll sell them as soon as you leave town."

"You can't do that," she said, almost in tears. "That little monkey will die if you sell her. She needs special care."

"I'll just have to do it," Eddie said.

He knew that Karen felt rejected and that what she wanted was for him to ask her to come home. He held his ground. "Are you going to Cleveland?" he said.

"The plane leaves in a half hour. You can't sell my pets, Eddie."

"If you leave, the pet shop will be mine and I'll sell all the animals at cut rates just to unload them."

There was a long pause and then she said, "Can I

come home?"

"If you want to. It's up to you."

She came home. When she got back Eddie decided it was time to tell her the truth about himself. He dug out a clipping from a paper saying he was on the Ten Most Wanted list and read her the part about how bad he was, carrying two guns and bragging that he'd never be taken alive.

"Oh, you're not bad," she said, "You're a softie. You're good to everybody. You give half of everything away. People like you."

He went on to read the part about how he might be accompanied by a former strip-tease girl from a Cleveland nightclub. He had wanted to impress upon her the danger they could be in. Her only response was typical.

"I'll sue them," she said. "I am *not* a strip-tease girl. I'm a dancer."

She didn't seem to be shaken by the fact that he was on the FBI's Ten Most Wanted list, that he had robbed banks, that the police were looking for them, or that there might be danger involved. She just didn't want to be called a "strip-tease girl."

He told her that they could never convict her as an accomplice, and that if he were caught he would clear her name.

Eddie spent many hours thinking about his life with Karen, and it was true that he had never loved her.

Not long after he told her about himself, he took another trip to Vegas. He had been there about two hours when he ran into Rosie, the South American "good-time girl," again. She was happy to see him and she gambled with him at the tables for a few hours; then they went to see a show. Later they had breakfast and talked.

When they were through eating he said, "I'm going to my room, Rosie. I'd like you to come with me, but you aren't obligated."

"I am never obligated," she said.

He fiddled with a pat of butter. "I mean—I just wanted you to know that I have enough respect for you that you're not obligated. I know you're not, and that you don't feel you owe me anything; I just wanted you to know how I feel. But I would very much like you to come with me."

"I would like that too."

"Why?" he said.

She seemed startled, and at first she thought the question indicated rejection. Then she smiled and said, "Because you are a good lover, for one."

"What makes me a good lover?"

"Because you are very interested," she said. "Very passionate and very interested. Maybe there is more."

"Like what?"

"There is tenderness in your passion. It is as if something is trying to get out of you, something that you conceal."

Eddie looked down.

"That is not a judgment," Rosie said. "It is simply a comment. Many men are the same way. But with you—with you there seems to be something missing in your life, something you are reaching for, searching for."

"What do you think that something is?" Eddie said, putting down the butter and looking into her eyes.

"I don't know. Do you know?"

"I'm not sure. Let's talk about it upstairs."

He had never talked about these things to Karen. Karen would have slipped off in the middle of the subject to something she had read in one of her movie magazines, or complained about her chewing gum, or asked him something completely out of left field. Not that Karen was uncaring—it was just the way Karen's train of thought was: she had the attention span of a kitten.

The last time he had made love to Rosie, it was fiercely passionate and he had scratches all over his back. But this time it was very tender, and when it was over, they talked.

She asked him about other women in his life and Eddie told her, "I've never loved any woman and none has ever loved me."

Rosie looked at him. "I think that's tragic, if it's true."

"Well, it's true. My own mother abandoned me after she'd divorced my no-good father. She found another man and he wanted her, but not me. They bounced me around to relatives like a damn cue-ball. Every time I got settled with one I got bounced to another."

184

Then he stopped talking and said, "Look, I don't want to sing the blues. I don't want to sound like a damn soap opera."

"It's okay," she said. "I like to listen. It's important."

They talked intimately for a long time that night and made love again and then talked some more. It was good for Eddie, and Rosie seemed to get something from it too.

"The most important thing about making love," she said, "is the intimacy of it all—being close with another person, seeing inside that person's soul. That is what is best about it."

Eddie told her that he didn't feel any bitterness toward women; he never had. He just never knew anyone who loved him, anyone who really cared whether he lived or died. He told her about Karen, and confessed that he liked Karen, liked the lifestyle and the companionship and liked her in bed, but that he had never really loved her.

"You know," he said, "I've tried to think about love, tried to define it, to understand it, many, many times. But not really knowing what it is makes thinking about the subject kind of fragmented, you know? When I make love to women I sometimes give the thought of real love a few moments to roll around my brain, but it always comes up a question mark. It's like looking at modern art. It does something to your imagination, but you can't figure it out, so there's no use thinking about it."

"It's the one thing you can't get without giving

away," she said.

Eddie said, "A lot of times I'd like to know women deeper, but I never could really commit myself to crawling right inside their heads and souls so I could see what they thought. My attachment to any woman has never been so strong or lasted so long that I really care what they deeply think. My mother never gave me approval after she found her second man. I've visited her from time to time, even tried to impress her with my successes, or phony successes. I never really got any satisfaction from it. I must have been seeking that satisfaction, or I don't suppose I would have gone to the trouble of making up stories about my successes, would I?"

"I don't suppose so," Rosie said.

He reached over and lit a cigarette then lay back on the pillow. "I always went away from my mother feeling as if she were some distant relative that I didn't really know. Sometimes I've seen women who look so clean and pure and desirable that I just have to have them, but I find that I can buy most of them, or get to bed with them some other way, and then after I did, it wasn't love at all. It was just another experience. I've wondered often how you get someone to love you, to care for you, to touch you, to hold you when you're miserable, and I've wondered how you give that in return. Maybe I was born with a brain, an animal cunning, and lust, but no heart and soul."

Eddie would go back to Las Vegas many more times and he would always search for Rosie, hoping to run into her, but he never did. Rosie, like so many others in Eddie's life, simply vanished from it.

NINETEEN

Eddie's home on the ocean almost made him forget his past, and for several months he laid off banks. He and Karen had spent a lot of money having the house decorated and they were living well. Staring out of his picture window could make him forget that he had ever seen the inside of a penitentiary. The pet shops were making money and Eddie had almost gotten to the point where seeing a policeman didn't make him nervous. He was trying very hard to drift mentally, physically and legally into the identity of Michael O'Shea. He had once read something that said, "Change your name and you change your life."

Eddie liked children and Karen did, too. Like animals, Eddie felt that children were innocents, real and honest with their emotions. He had hired two brothers, ages ten and twelve, to help out in the pet shop. They cleaned the cages and swept up, and he overpaid them. He would always ask them if they had enough spending money, and even when they said yes he'd give them an extra dollar or two.

One day Eddie was tending the store while the boys were working late, and their father came in to pick them up. Eddie had a nice conversation with the father, and a few days later he asked the boys what business he was in. They told Eddie that their father was a police inspector. A few weeks later his picture was in the paper because he had caught some dangerous criminal. Eddie read the story and looked closely at the picture. Behind the man, on the wall behind his desk, he could see a wanted poster. It was from the FBI and was for one Edward O. Watkins. Eddie knew that his disguise was a good one, but he stayed away from the store from then on when the boys were working.

The policeman raised guppies and sometimes brought some in to trade. One day when Eddie was there the policeman asked him to help carry two delicate bags full of guppies. Eddie followed the policeman around a corner and right into the police station. Before he left he walked over and looked at the wanted poster. There, on the wall, was a picture of Edward O. Watkins, one of the FBI's Ten Most Wanted. Next to his photo was one of Karen, wanted for aiding and abetting a bank holdup. Eddie knew that she had aided and abetted nothing or no one. The pictures were very poor in quality and he could see why neither of them had been recognized.

Eddie said to the policeman, "These look like some bad characters."

"Believe me, Mr. O'Shea, they are."

From that day on, Eddie would drop in at the station from time to time, checking to see whether there was any new information on him, but there never was.

One night a couple of Karen's friends came by to watch TV. They were watching *The FBI Story,* and at the end of the show the star, Efram Zimbalist, Jr., did a spot telling people about the Ten Most Wanted list. And there was Eddie, front and side view, with Zimbalist talking about how dangerous Eddie was. Eddie looked to see whether Karen's friends, Tom and Diane, had noticed any resemblance. Diane said, "Doesn't that one look mean."

Everybody, including Eddie, agreed. But Eddie was still not certain that they wouldn't make some kind of connection later. So that night he took Karen to a motel, came back home and spent the night on the beach, a hundred yards or so from his house, checking with binoculars for police activity. Before going back he checked traffic in his block for anything suspicious. Finally reassured, he picked up Karen and they went home.

The pet shops were doing well. Karen had purchased an ocelot, and when it arrived it was eight months old, weighed about forty pounds and was still growing. Karen had no fear of animals and the ocelot immediately sensed it. But Eddie had an instant fear of the creature and the ocelot figured that out right away, too. Karen named it Diablo, and from the moment she had let it out of the cage, it took to her while more or less ignoring Eddie. They brought it to the house and it was better than a watch dog. It might let a burglar come in, but when the burglar felt safe the animal could rip him to pieces. The animal even kept looking at Eddie as if to say, "I haven't decided whether I'll actually let you stay here."

Once Eddie was watching TV and moved his elbow just slightly as the cat was reaching out its paw. It clawed Eddie across the arm, leaving bloody tracks, and Eddie grabbed it and threw it off the sofa. From that point they were bitter enemies. When the cat was loose in the house Eddie wore a leather jacket. Sometimes he dozed in a chair with his arm dangling down, and the cat would attack it as if it were a live chicken. Or it would play stalking games with Eddie. Eddie would pretend he was asleep on the floor and would watch the cat slither on its belly, climb to a high place on the sofa and get in a postion to pounce. Eddie would open his eyes and stare at the cat and the cat would nonchalantly swish its tail, blink its eyes and walk back to where it had been.

Sometimes Eddie would walk by when the cat was eating and kick the bowl. The cat would hiss and take a swipe at him with its claws.

Often the cat would look at Eddie and lick its lips as if Eddie were dessert. One night when Eddie was dozing off in his easy chair he felt a light mist, like falling rain. The cat was urinating on him. He called Karen, Karen spanked the cat, and that ended that bit of misbehavior.

But eventually Eddie and the cat got used to each other, even attached to each other. In fact the cat grew to like Eddie better than Karen, and Karen, always wanting to be number one, began to ignore the animal.

As life became easy, Eddie filled his need for excitement with heavy gambling, especially in Las Vegas. And with heavy gambling often came heavy losses. Eddie went to Sacramento and robbed another bank, meanwhile vowing to lay off the urge to gamble. He robbed the Sacramento bank and was in and out with a pillowcase full of money in a minute and forty-five seconds.

The FBI was frustrated by Eddie Watkins; they had no idea where he was. For many years there had been FBI suspicions about Eddie's robbing banks, but he had never been caught at it, and there was no charge until Al and Johnny were nabbed in Cleveland. It was no secret that J. Edgar Hoover was a proud, egotistical man, and the thought of Eddie Watkins eluding the FBI for all those years did not set well with J. Edgar's temperament. Memos had gone out and pressure had been put on to find Eddie Watkins. He was put on the Ten Most Wanted list even though he had never hurt anyone. Eddie thought about that and decided that money was more important to "the system" than human life. After all, there had to be hundreds of murderers, rapists and deranged violent characters running around loose, and they weren't on the Most Wanted list.

To Eddie, human life was more important than money; it was the most important thing in the world. It was really all there was that was real. Money to Eddie was just a stake, a way to buy freedom from the jungle. He knew he was in over his head, and many times he wished he had made it some other way. At first the bank robberies were more of a game to him than anything; they provided excitement as well as money. And they were his rebellion against his childhood poverty and rejections.

At the Ohio penitentiary his IQ had been tested at 135, which was borderline genius. The psychiatrist had made the comment, "Eddie, with smarts like yours, why on earth do you rob banks?"

Eddie asked him, "Doctor, are you a good psyciatrist?"

"Yes, I believe I am."

"Are you the best in the world?"

"No."

Eddie said, "Well, I'm the best bank robber in the world, the best one-man bandit in the world. At one point in my life I had a burning desire to be the best in the world at something. The avenues are limited, so I ended up being the best bank robber in the world. I've stolen millions of dollars and spent most of it. In my own twisted way that was my recognition, my success."

When Eddie decided to rob the bank in Sacramento, he arranged a code with Karen. When he got to the outskirts of San Francisco he would phone her. If she called him "Michael" in the conversation, he would know that the police were there. If she called him "Mike," the coast was clear and he could come home.

The Sacramento job had bolstered the cash flow again and Eddie was back into free and easy living. He spent a lot of money taking Karen out on the town, and at Christmas that year he gave her $3,000 to buy him presents and told her he'd spend the same amount on her.

They both started shopping a month before Christmas. Eddie went over the $3,000 limit for Karen. He bought her several presents and surprised her with a new Corvette, which he paid the saleman extra to deliver just before midnight on Christmas Eve. She was elated, but Eddie knew she probably would have been just as satisfied with a new pair of jeans.

But Eddie wanted her to have a nice Christmas. She deserved it. She had spent a long time away from home, away from her family and friends and everyone she knew, and she had not once complained about it. He felt that she was loyal and appreciative, and sometimes he wished to hell he could love her.

There were hundreds of presents in the house that Christmas. He even bought her a mink coat and put it in an old beat up sack so she wouldn't know what it was. He looked at the Christmas lights blinking on the tree and thought of all of the non-Christmases he had had as a child, alone and unwanted. Christmas had always been an unbearably lonely time for him. And there were all those wretched Christmases in prison. This was his best Christmas ever, but as he looked out at the serenity of the ocean on Christmas morning he knew it could all end at any time.

After Christmas Karen seemed a little lonesome for home, so Eddie gave her money and told her to go to Hawaii. Her friend Diane had relatives there and Diane could go with her. She was to come home when the money ran out.

A few weeks later Karen called and asked for more money.

"We made a deal," Eddie said. "You would come home when the money ran out."

"Eddie, I'm not coming home."

"What?"

"Not ever."

He talked to her but she wouldn't budge. After he hung up he thought about it. He figured she had met some fellow over there, and he didn't blame her for wanting another kind of life. But there would be a problem with his identity. There were a lot of things he couldn't cover now, and he was afraid at some point she might talk. He would bring her back and let her get a separate apartment if she wished. And if she wanted get out of their arrangement she could do it in an orderly manner, when Eddie had had time to establish a new identity.

He went to Hawaii to get her. He could not find her, but found Diane, and Diane was at a house with

195

Sharon—good old Sharon who had worked for him. They were reluctant to tell him where Karen was, so Eddie offered them both money, and that bought out their loyalties. They weren't sure of the address but they could help him. Finally he located her by tracing the address she had given to the rental car company when she renewed the lease on the car.

He went to the address and a little girl answered the door. Eddie asked about Karen but the little girl played dumb. Eddie pulled a bluff and said he was sure it was her father or brother who was with his wife. The little girl said that she would call the police if he didn't leave, and Eddie said, "If you do that, your brother is going to have a kidnaping charge against him."

He told her he would wait on the porch.

A few minutes later the girl came out and told him that his wife was on the phone and wanted to talk to him.

"What the hell are you doing here?" Karen asked. "I told you I wasn't coming back. We're through. You never loved me anyway."

"I don't care if you come back or not. But we're going to have to straighten this out face to face. I want to sit down and talk with you."

There was long silence. Finally she said, "I'm not going to meet you."

"If you stay here you're going to get me in a lot of trouble, and it won't be easy on you or him if that happens."

"I'm not afraid to meet you," she said.

"Don't be. I'm sure as hell not going to hurt you. You've put me in a terrible position."

She agreed to meet him at a club that evening. She was alone and she looked frightened, but was adamant about not coming back with him.

"If you don't go back with me," Eddie said, "I'm sure I'll get caught. And if I get caught because of you, you'll go to jail too. I'll see to that. If you do it my way I'll make sure the police never touch you."

"This guy has two children to take care of, and they love me, Eddie."

"We're leaving now; it's got to be that way. I know you're not too happy with me, and if you want to be on your own I'll rent you an apartment, and give you money after I sell the businesses and the house, But I have to keep my name clear while I do it. I'll establish a new identity that you won't know about, and then you'll be free to date anybody, get married, do whatever you want."

She looked at him like a lost puppy. "Eddie, I still love you."

And that was it. They were back on a plane to San Francisco.

Eddie knew she would forget the fellow soon; he was a passing fancy. Once she had heard a song while they were riding in the car and she told him it was her favorite. She said that it would be "our song." But a few days later when they heard it on the radio she didn't recognize the words, the music or the name of the song. She had an "erasable mind" which could barely remember what had hap-

197

pened the previous day. If he told her he was going to take her dancing a month from now, however, she would remember the date, even the hour, they were supposed to go, and would remind him every day until it was time.

So he knew that in a few weeks she would forget the guy in Hawaii. In three weeks she would forget his address, and in a month she probably wouldn't be able to remember his name.

When they got back, Eddie got the gambling urge worse than ever. He went back to Vegas and blew thirty thousand dollars at the tables, but kept on gambling until he hit a hot streak. He got nearly $50,000 ahead before a "friend" told him about a private game where the IRS didn't snoop around. Eddie got cleaned out in that game and barely had enough for gas money home.

The gambling urge was his biggest vice, and he used another vice to compensate for it—robbing banks. He got a pocket police radio with an earplug so he could actually monitor police calls while he was "working." He robbed several banks in LA and then was away like a wisp. The rash of bank robberies all had much the same M.O.

He decided that he needed to hit a few more banks to get back to where he had been before the gambling bug bit him.

This time Karen surprised him—she wanted to go along. "I love to travel, Eddie. You know that."

So they headed for Denver, Omaha, Detroit, Pittsburgh and then she pleaded to go back to

Cleveland, just to see it again. Eddie didn't want to, but his soft heart made him give in. She said she wanted to see the old town again and wouldn't call her parents or any old friends. Eddie said okay. They got a motel on the outskirts of town. Cleveland brought back mostly bad memories for Eddie, all the way from his childhood. He knew that he never should've gone there after his release from the Ohio pen.

But now he was back for a visit, and as he sat watching TV in his motel, he began to think about how hot he was there, how badly they wanted him. His resentment about Cleveland and his childhood reared its ugly head and Eddie decided that to shove it in their faces he would hit a bank while he was there. The more he thought about it the funnier it seemed. He decided to do one without disguise, just hit and run, Western style.

It was an easy job, and he ran out the door with his .45 in his hand, shouting obscenities and generally making an ass out of himself. It was a sheer ego robbery, just to let them know that Eddie Watkins was still around. It would also concentrate their search in the Cleveland area and keep them away from Michael O'Shea's trail in the West. It would also raise a boil on the head of old J. Edgar Hoover. The Cleveland office of the FBI would catch hell.

They drove back out West and went the southern route, through Albuquerque, where they stayed in a motel just outside the city. Karen loved horses and wanted to take a ride. So they went out to a riding stable on Route 66. It was a beatup place, with more wood missing from the barn than on it.

There was an old trailer by the barn, and a corral with about ten horses roaming around in it. Next to the corral was a Buick Wildcat, with a man and a young girl sitting in it.

Eddie asked whom he could see about renting a horse and the man said, "I'm the one." He introduced himself as Mike Naccaroto. His girlfriend, a very beautiful young woman with dark skin and silvery blonde hair, was named Darlene. She was part Apache. Mike Naccaroto was a very friendly man and they went in for coffee with him. He suggested that, since it was so late, Eddie and Karen should stay and ride tomorrow. They agreed. They would spend a day riding in the desert.

Mike was a widower with three boys ranging from age twelve to twenty. Darlene was in the midst of getting a divorce from her first husband. She lived in the trailer and Mike lived in a house in town.

The next day Eddie and Karen rode out into the desert and fell in love with it. It was peaceful riding out there and looking at the incredibly blue sky, pale blue like Darlene's eyes, and the dusky brown Sandia Mountains. After the ride they had breakfast with Mike and Darlene. Eddie liked the couple and, when Mike mentioned that times were tough and he might have to give up the place, Eddie suddenly made an offer to become half owner. He would duplicate what Mike had, buy ten more horses and gear, and Karen and Eddie—Mike and Pat O'Shea to them—would live in a trailer.

"Gee, Eddie," Karen said. "It'll be just like Roy Rogers and Dale Evans."

"Well, not quite," Eddie said, but he was as excited as Karen.

It was an impulsive thing to do, but Eddie did it because he liked the countryside and he felt the life would be good for him and Karen. It was time for a change, and it would help out Mike Naccaroto, whom he liked. Mike was very real and down to earth, and the age difference between him and Darlene was similar to the age difference between Eddie and Karen.

Karen and Darlene would run the stables, and it would be a nice life.

It would be fairly easy to sell what they had in California. By now Eddie had good credentials as Mike O'Shea: credit cards, bank accounts and a Dun & Bradstreet rating. Eddie had finally found what he wanted in New Mexico. He felt at peace there, different somehow.

Three days after he got back to San Francisco, Mike Naccaroto called him and said he wanted to sell the whole business. Darlene had gone off, back to her husband, and he didn't want to run the place by himself. Eddie thought at first that he was being scammed, but the price that Mike asked was very low. All Mike wanted was out. He offered to sell the horses at cost, let Eddie take over the trailer payments and rent land at a dollar a year. Eddie agreed. He then paid all his bills in California, sold the pet shops and his furniture and house, and put his "legal" money in a Crocker Bank account.

Before he left he got a call from Darlene. She'd tried to track down her ex-husband but couldn't find him and now she was in San Diego, dead broke. She wanted to know if she could stay with Eddie and Karen until they left for New Mexico. Eddie said yes and wired her a plane ticket for San Francisco.

They rented a U-Haul for their personal things. Darlene would ride with Karen and Eddie would follow in his car.

Eddie had some shaky feelings about leaving San Francisco, and some very ominous thoughts, but he dismissed them as fear of the unknown.

As it turned out he was dead right. The move would eventually cost him his freedom—and he would be brought down, ultimately, by an old, worthless leather jacket.

TWENTY

An acquaintance of Karen's helped them load up the U-Haul truck. It was warm and he had taken off his old leather jacket and put it in the trailer. A few things were piled on top of the jacket and they ended up taking it with them.

Before Eddie left he wanted to make a call to his old cellmate, Dr. Sam Sheppard, to see how he was doing. And he figured he could trust Sam to give him some information on what his status was in Cleveland.

Sam answered the phone. "It's me, Sam, how are you. It's Ed."

"Ed, I never expected—"

"Just traveling around. Calling from a pay phone, Sam. How's everything with you?"

"Not worth a damn, Ed. Things are tough. If they don't start improving, I may have to join you to make a living. I got married again, Ed, and I'm not doing well in the medical profession. The patients don't trust me. But maybe after a little time things will get better. I read in the papers, Ed, that you are a sought-after item."

"I'm doing fine, Sam. Spending money like there's no tomorrow."

"Better save some for a good lawyer."

"There's no such thing," Eddie said.

"I was thinking about you the other day, Ed, wondering where you were living. But for God's sake don't tell me. They caught some guy who was supposed to have robbed banks with you, and there was a story in the papers recently about a guy they thought was you, pulling off a hit-and-run job. I figured it couldn't have been you."

"It was me all right. Just wanted to show them that I'm not worried about being one of the ten most popular."

"You'd better watch it, Ed. They'd love to kill you."

"The way I feel about it, that's the only way they'll ever take me again, Sam. I'm too old to go back in the joint. They still on your back, Sam?"

"Damn right. They never let up. Watch yourself, Ed, and for God's sake don't come back to Cleveland. They want you bad here."

Eddie said his goodbys to Sam and wished him the best.

Eddie, Karen, Darlene and the ocelot were off to New Mexico. Karen told Darlene that she had a brother in Las Vegas and wanted to stop there to see him. It was an excuse to go launder the rest of Eddie's bank-robbery money. She laundered twenty grand in Vegas, and Eddie wondered whether she would come back. If she wanted to run, this was her time. But she came back, they all stayed at the Dunes, and the next day they were off to New Mexico.

Mike Naccaroto was surprised and pleased to see Darlene with them. He sold Eddie the rest of the stables. Eddie got a twenty-year lease on the land at a dollar a year. He and Karen began to shape up the place. They cleaned up the trailer, had a new corral built and bought thirty more horses, and a ten-thousand-gallon tank for water storage for the horses. Then they had several billboards erected along Route 66 near the stable.

Karen was as good at running the stable as she had been at running the pet shop. She hired an Indian to help her with the chores. She was making good money, sometimes several hundred dollars a day, and Eddie let her keep it all; he made her put most of it in a savings account. Knowing that he could get captured any time, he wanted her to have something with which to guy her way out of the rat race.

They built a cage for the ocelot, Diablo, and a few of the dogs that had come with the place decided to test the cat from time to time. They always came out on the worse end.

Eddie enjoyed Albuquerque and the horse stables. He rode nearly every day and bought Karen a fine horse of her own. Karen could never think of a good name for the horse, so she ended up calling it "No Name."

Eddie had dug holes and stashed money all over the desert. Finally they went house hunting because the trailer was getting to them. They found a beautiful house with three and a half acres of land around it, at the edge of town on Del Sur Avenue. They bought new furniture and kept four horses in a pasture so they would have horses for pleasure riding when friends dropped by.

Eddie had finally found his heaven. He had finally escaped from the dreary slums of his childhood, and the cold prison bars, to the wide-open peaceful spaces. He hoped dearly that this life would last.

Darlene stayed for a while to help run the stables. Mike Naccaroto was constantly bothering her about getting married. He was deeply in love with her, and Eddie couldn't blame him. Mike's pressure on her to get married caused bickering. One day as they sat in the trailer going at one another verbally, Eddie interceded.

"Hey," he said. "Why the hell don't the two of you get married? You argue like a married couple so you might as well be one."

Mike said, "I want to, but she keeps stalling."

Eddie continued, "Come on, Darlene, marry the guy. Hell, then the new Buick will belong to you."

"I'd have to be drunk or out of mind to marry him," Darlene said.

"Well," Eddie said, "if that's the problem, bring in some more drinks, Pat, and we'll get Darlene drunk."

Eddie began breaking down Darlene's resistance, and before long he was offering to pay for the wedding and give the couple a night in Las Vegas, at his expense—a night he guaranteed they wouldn't forget.

That did it. Darlene agreed.

Karen stayed back at the ranch while Eddie accompanied them to Vegas. They got their license and headed for the marriage mill for the ceremony. It was one of those quickie-marriage chapels that supplies the rings for an extra twenty bucks. Eddie checked in the newlyweds at the Riviera and gave them money to play with after they got tired of playing with each other. He then went to the tables himself and won $3,000.

It was a wonderful weekend and Eddie had made it all happen. He felt very good inside. He felt good about everything now—perhaps for the first time in his life.

It was May of 1966.

Not long after, the ocelot was stolen and then escaped from the thieves, only to be cornered by the police, shot and killed.

Eddie felt very bad about that. He lost something he had come to love, and it made him feel vulnerable.

Karen got the blues again, and took off once more. Eddie couldn't find her. He began to worry and he felt as if he could smell trouble. He gathered up all the money that was stashed in the house so he could be ready to make a run for it if he had to.

When he couldn't find her, he reported her disappearance to the police. Then he called a broker and listed the stables for sale, while nightly he cruised the streets and bars looking for her. He would like to take her with him, have her with him if she wanted to go, but if she didn't it would be okay too. He felt again that she might get him caught, and if she had decided to split he wanted her to do it the right way. Finally he tracked her down where she was staying with a man she had recently met. Eddie sat her down for a talk.

"Eddie, I don't love you any more," she said. "I want to be free of this arrangement. I just want my clothes, that's all."

"You can have your clothes and I'll set you up in an apartment," Eddie said. "But you've got to give me time. Stay here till this place is sold and you can have the cash."

"I don't believe you'll let me go," she said.

He explained to her again about the danger of the law, the FBI and prison. He told her she could go if she wanted, but that running away had to stop. Everything had to be ended in an orderly manner. She could keep the stable, her clothes, everything.

She finally agreed.

She was surprised to see that Eddie had already sold all of the furniture. They got her clothes and went to a Ramada Inn for the night, where they rented separate rooms. Then they went to a place called The Hitching Post for hamburgers and some country music.

It was July 19, 1966.

As they sat in The Hitching Post the manager came over and told Eddie, "Two police officers would like to talk with you in my office."

Eddie's stomach turned over. His brain began to spin. And then he realized that if the police knew who he was, they wouldn't send the manager—they'd come over with guns drawn. Remaining calm, he walked to the manager's office and introduced himself to the policemen.

"I'm Mike O'Shea. What can I do for you?"

One of them answered, "We're investigating the disappearance of your wife, Mr. O'Shea. We were just at your house and it's empty of all the furniture. What's up?"

Before he could answer, the other one said, "We noticed mounds of freshly dug earth on your place. Does that mean anything?"

Eddie laughed. "Look, I don't know what you're thinking, but my wife is with me now at the table. I called an hour ago and told the police that I found her. You can check with your desk."

One of the officers called the station. The story was true. He had called and told them he had found her.

But the officer kept asking questions. "What do you do to make so much money? I notice you drive a Cadillac."

"I own the Buffalo Stables," Eddie said. "On West Central. Actually, my wife owns them. I'm technically unemployed."

The officer said, "Hell, I work every day and I can't afford a Cadillac."

Eddie couldn't hold his cool. "The difference is, smartass, I'm probably more intelligent than you."

"Okay, wise guy. Where did you live before you moved to Albuquerque?"

"Eight-forty Skyline Drive, Daly City, California," Eddie said. "I owned Daly City Pet Shop and Noriega Pet Shop. If there's nothing else you want to know, I'll be on my way. I'm busy and my wife is waiting for me."

"You're a wise-ass, " the officer said. "We still want to talk to your wife."

"Well, I'll ask her. I don't know whether she wants to talk to you."

When he got back to the table, he filled Karen in. "Be careful what you tell them."

Karen handled it well, and they drove back to their house and found that the yard had been dug up. The police had apparently been looking for a body. They went back to the motel and the police were following them. In the motel room, Eddie had a dismantled .30-06 with a half-moon clip that held fifty rounds, a Colt .45, a .38 and a two-shot Derringer. He also had nearly a hundred thousand dollars cash in the room. Marked and unmarked police cars were outside. The police were watching the front door, so they slipped out the back window and Karen got everything in the car without being seen. Eddie covered her with the .45 and then ran to the car.

Eddie pulled away and when they saw him leave with the lights out they followed. But Eddie turned a corner and pulled into a driveway with his lights out, and they roared by. Then he drove out to the stables and ditched the money and most of the guns, all except the .38, which he could explain, and which would be legal to carry in his car if it wasn't concealed.

He drove back to the motel and the police came from all directions when he pulled into the parking lot. He wasn't worried about their questioning him. He was sure they had been doing background on him from San Francisco and he knew he would check out. He had not, in his wildest imagination, realized what they were about to hit him with.

It was the jacket—the one that the fellow left in the trailer when they moved from San Francisco. He had written and asked for the jacket back, and Karen was slow in sending it. She had mailed it back only a few weeks before. But the jerk in San Francisco reported her as having stolen the jacket when he didn't get it. He had said the coat was worth $100, which made the charge grand larceny, technically. They took Karen away in handcuffs, mainly because they found the .38 in the car.

They took Eddie in with her, because he was speeding, they said. "You're a liar," Eddie told the officer. "I wasn't speeding."

The patrol officer said, "Don't call me a liar or I'll kick your teeth in."

Eddie reached for a longshot. "If you do that,

you will surely hear from my friend Sheriff Jones."

Actually he wasn't really friends with the sheriff, but he knew a Mexican who was very prominent in the sheriff's campaign effort, and Eddie had contributed $500 toward the re-election. That cooled the officers down, but when they got to the station they found the Derringer in Eddie's pocket. He had forgotten to take it out, and he was irked at himself.

That was a concealed-weapon charge, if they wanted to press it, and was a reason to keep him in jail and fingerprint him. They could hold him long enough for those prints to get to the FBI office, come sailing back like a bombshell and land right in his lap. He cursed himself for having been so harebrained.

He decided he had better change his tone of voice to the police now. No more Mister Smartass. They had him and they could keep him, if he didn't work fast.

He called his Mexican politico friend and told him the problem. His friend said he would do what he could. After all, he didn't know that Mike O'Shea was Eddie Watkins, the notorious bank robber.

They fingerprinted Eddie before his friend could do anything, and while they were fingerprinting him, Eddie was looking right at his own wanted poster on the wall.

The bail was $60 on the gun charge and Eddie paid it. As he was paying it, the cop who had brought him in asked him to empty his pockets.

Eddie had fifty $100 bills in one pocket and $12,000 in travelers' checks in the other pocket. That would really arouse suspicion.

But just then the desk sergeant said, "Hell, if he's making bail, I ain't going to inventory his pockets."

That kind of money would've made them so excited they would've booked him on suspicion. He paid his bail and the speeding ticket and left the jail. Then he found his Mexican friend, who made a few phone calls to get Karen out.

Eddie was worried about his fingerprints. He told his friend a lie, that he'd walked away from an army hitch twenty years before and was afraid he still might be prosecuted for it. He asked if the prints would be mailed to Washington, to the FBI. His friend said that there was no computer hookup between the local police and the FBI office in Washington, and it would take several days for the prints to get there.

The same suspicious police officer was waiting for Eddie later when he went to meet Karen, after his Mexican friend had secured her release. Her story had checked out; she had mailed the jacket back.

"Mr. O'Shea," the policeman said, "why do you carry two guns?"

"Because every day I read in the papers where citizens get blown away just for looking prosperous. I drive a Cadillac and carry cash on me. I don't plan to give it up without a struggle."

"Mr. O'Shea, I'm a cop and by nature very suspicious. So if you don't mind, we'll hold the guns and send them to Washington for a check at the FBI lab. If everything checks out they'll be returned to you. Could you tell me where you purchased them?"

Eddie told him that he didn't remember the exact name of the gun shop in California, but that he had the receipts at home and would drop them by. They called the police precinct next to Eddie's old pet shop in San Francisco. The police inspector who had bought all the guppies told them about how his two sons had worked for the O'Sheas, and gave them glowing reports about the couple. Karen was quickly released, and the moment she got to the car she and Eddie made plans to hightail it.

Karen held back the tears until they got to the car; then she told Eddie about how horrible the jail had been. Her cellmate was a big dike-looking woman, and Karen had remembered Eddie's telling her there were lesbians in jail who would rape her. She had slept with her clothes on and was terrified the whole time she was in jail.

"It's your own fault for not mailing that goddam coat back," Eddie lamented. "Maybe now you realize what will happen if the FBI gets you in one of those places for life. Our cover is blown. We'll lose your car, my car, the stables, the horses, everything we have. We're going to get out of town right now and never come back."

They headed out toward Route 66, having stopped just long enough to pick up a few things they needed. They left a note for friends to keep some of the things that were left, as they knew their friends would be stopping by. Then they got the cash and headed out to Albuquerque. Eddie wanted as much lead time as he could get. He would have to ditch the car and get another one the first chance he had. Karen now had the necessary fears about jail, which she had just had a small taste of.

Eddie didn't have the slightest idea where he was heading. But wherever it was, it was so long to Albuquerque, and so long to dreams of the good life, to peace and tranquility, the very things he had finally realized he had been searching for and had, for a few months, found. He had lost everything because of a rotten, twenty-dollar leather coat.

He was back on the run again, back in the jungle.

TWENTY ONE

They drove to Flagstaff, Arizona and checked into a motel. Eddie shaved off his goatee and Karen bought an old Ford junker. Eddie was upset about losing a life that he had wanted to hang onto—a normal existence. For once he had been "real folks" with fewer cares and worries than he'd had in a long time. Now it was gone and the fear quickly turned into bitterness and anger. He felt naked, helpless, an easy target for the police.

His first thought was money—the more the better to run and hide with. They drove to LA and Eddie robbed two banks in one day. At the first bank he went in and announced to the manager, "I'm Eddie Watkins. You've no doubt heard of me." The manager had. "Well, then," Eddie said, "you must know why I'm here." The manager did. Eddie was in and out in less than two minutes.

Karen had bought an old Rambler station wagon and Eddie drove the Ford. He robbed the first bank and gave her the money, and she drove to the second bank and waited for him there while he robbed it.

He also used no disguise. He wanted the police to find out that he was in Los Angeles, to confuse them.

As he was leaving the second bank he told the manager, "When the cops and the FBI get here, tell them Eddie Watkins was here and I have a few more places to visit before I retire. Can you remember the name?"

"Yes sir, Eddie Watson."

"Watkins," Eddie said. "W-a-t-k-i-n-s."

That night they drove to Vegas and registered at a small motel as Mr. and Mrs. Henry Small. Eddie stayed in the motel while Karen laundered the money. She tried to get a driver's license, but for that she needed a birth certificate, and she did not have one.

They left for El Paso, Texas, but on the way they checked out New Mexico to test the heat on them. Eddie called his Mexican politico friend and his friend told him he didn't think the guns or the fingerprints had been sent to Washington after all. Eddie and Karen drove to the friend's ranch. The man had connections at the central police station and called to check whether or not the police had mailed the prints.

Eddie hoped for the best but feared the worst. He listened as his friend was calling the station.

"My friend Mike O'Shea—did his prints check out or aren't you going to check them? You heard some mention about it this morning? Well, could you check it out for me now?"

He smiled at Eddie and Eddie managed a smile back. Then Eddie saw the smile disappear from his friend's face. "The Ten Most Wanted list? There must be some mistake."

His friend hung up and Eddie ran a bluff. He acted very indignant and said that he was going right over there to clear it all up.

"Do you want me to go with you?" his friend said.

"No," Eddie said. "Wait until your friend calls back. We're heading down there to clear our names."

He knew he shouldn't have come back. He headed out of town quickly, out Coors Road and hellbent for Texas. He had left the Cadillac in Flagstaff and had made sure that his friend had not seen the Rambler when he drove up. They had parked it out of view.

He stole some New Mexico license plates just in case, and they drove all night, Eddie with two loaded guns in his lap, until they reached El Paso. At their motel he saw his picture in an El Paso paper and decided to push on. Karen bought a used Cadillac. They had left the Rambler parked near the dealership, but took the risk of coming back to move it so the police wouldn't check the dealership to see who had bought cars.

They drove straight for Kansas City. They had eight wigs with them and it would be fairly easy to disguise themselves. Karen dyed the fringes of her hair and Eddie bleached out one of his toupees to make it white. They found a furnished apartment, and while Karen was going through one of the drawers she found a birth certificate for one "Dee Johnston." Now she would be able to get a driver's license and could buy cars and rent apartments. Eddie would go by the name of Robert Johnston, but he had no ID and no time to get any. Karen bought a Pontiac in the name of Dee Johnston, and Eddie robbed a bank, using the El Paso Cadillac for the robbery.

They drove the Pontiac to Council Bluffs, Iowa. Eddie was going to rob a bank there, but he picked up a paper and found out that the FBI was on the right trail. They were looking for him in the El Paso area and the story described the Cadillac with Texas plates. He decided to pass on the Council Bluffs bank and they traded the Pontiac for a Ford LTD station wagon and pushed on to Seattle. There they checked into some cottages as father and daughter. Eddie was going to hit a few banks and then find a place to lay low. He had decided on Montana.

At one of the Seattle banks, he more or less got robbed while he was robbing a bank. He was cleaning out the Greenwood Savings and Loan and one of the female tellers was filling his bag with cash. Occasionally he saw her reach up to her breast, and at first he hardly noticed it. Then he saw it happen again. And a third time. Watching more carefully, he saw her stuffing money into her bra. He smiled at her and winked. It was okay with him. He figured they probably underpaid her anyway.

Out of curiosity, he wanted to look inside her bra to see how much she had gotten, but he didn't want to pick up the paper and read about himself as the sex-maniac bank robber.

He heard the TV report that night. The report showed his picture and, although he had grown the goatee again, and hadn't said his name, they identified him as the notorious Eddie Watkins. He was shocked that they had pegged him so quickly. But when the commentator said how much money had been taken, Eddie laughed. Their count was short of his by $2,000. The little lady had stuffed twenty $100 bills into her bra and they would never know. Eddie certainly was never going to tell them.

But now they had to get out of Seattle. Eddie sent Karen to the store and she came back with what he needed. He shaved his face very closely and put on pancake makeup. Then he slipped on a pair of women's slacks, padded up a size-44 bra and put on a blouse and sandals. Karen fitted him up with one of her wigs. He wore dark women's glasses and he and Karen left looking like mother and daughter. There were police cars stationed all along the route out of town, but no roadblocks. There were also police cars all along the road to Spokane, but none ever stopped them.

"You look weird," Karen said.

"Talk to your poor old mother with respect," Eddie said, and laughter pierced the extreme tension.

They drove on into Montana, to Missoula, where they registered in a motel as mother and daughter.

Through the local classifieds they found a place to rent twenty-five miles outside of Missoula, in the town of Florence. It was a farmhouse owned by Mr. and Mrs. Ray Stratton, a retired couple who lived farther up the road in a bigger house. For the first time Eddie could close his eyes without having nightmares about FBI guns and handcuffs and his own cemetery stone.

They bought two horses, both Tennessee Walkers. Eddie grew a mustache and died it gray to match his hair, which he had also dyed gray.

The heat was off and they spent their days riding in the mountains and enjoying their freedom. They became very good friends of the Strattons. Eddie liked them right away, and so did Karen. These were the type of people that Eddie had fantasized as his parents when he was young. They were good, solid stock, honest, real, open and friendly. He told them he was a retired engineer. Not wearing his dental plate, he look like a harmless old cuss. There were plenty of young women in the area and few eligible men, and Eddie almost wished he'd chosen a younger disguise.

But he enjoyed the bear and deer and other wildlife, and slept to the tune of horses feeding, snorting and grunting, far from the madness of the jungles of cities. The first thing he heard when he woke up was the tinkling sound of a nearby brook outside his cabin window. On nights when he couldn't sleep well he would walk out into the pasture in the moonlight, talk to the horses and rub their noses.

They became friends with Carol and Stacy Homme, two girls who lived on the next farm. Eddie knew that life must be frustrating to Karen here, because she was young and stuck out in the country with no young men for company. They had grown tired of one another romantically; they were together only because they had to be.

He told her that he needed to make one more trip to Vegas to launder his money, and that when he got back he would send her to a new city with a new identity and plenty of cash. She could find herself an apartment and he would send her a thousand dollars a month for the rest of her life—or until they put him out of business.

He had acquired a driver's license and credit cards as Robert Johnston, but he didn't take them with him to Vegas. If he were caught there he would be forced to run, and he didn't want to be caught as Robert Johnston. He took his Michael O'Shea identification with him, drove to Vegas and hit a bank on the way, carefully laundered his money and put sixty thousand dollars into markers. He took the long route home, robbing a bank in Omaha and another in St. Paul before heading westward to Florence.

One of the local stations started carrying the FBI show into Florence, and Eddie knew they would eventually show his picture on the "Most Wanted" segments. So he put up a large antenna that got the program from a Butte station an hour earlier than it would be telecast in Florence. When he saw his picture come on, he and Karen went to the Strattons' and the Hommes' and messed their antennas so they would not get that particular segment.

In October he went back to Vegas and drove on to Council Bluffs, Iowa, checked into a motel, got a plane, rented a car, made a big score and came back to Council Bluffs. The FBI would trace him from Vegas to Council Bluffs, but he would be gone before they had picked up his trail. The Council Bluffs motel clerk would identify the FBI photo as Eddie Watkins, and would verify that he had stayed there for two nights. They weren't sure why he was in Council Bluffs, and although they thought he had pulled off the other job, they weren't sure how, since he couldn't have been in two places at once.

In late November he headed for St. Paul to rob what was going to be his last bank job ever. He would retire. He had gotten back what he figured he'd lost by having to run from Albuquerque, and what he had had to leave buried, and this was going to be his last job ever. He would simply retire to Montana as Robert Johnston. He'd taken their money, but he'd never hurt anyone other than financially, and he figured he had been more moral than someone who swipes some little old lady's last fifty dollars. After all, the banks and the FDIC would get over it and survive.

He had done many things in his lifetime that he regretted, but what was done was done. Karen talked him into her going with him to St. Paul. They checked into a motel in Minneapolis and scouted out a St. Paul bank that was too big for a one-man job.

Karen had gone out to get something at a drugstore, and when she came back she told him, "I've found the perfect bank for you."

Eddie dismissed it at first. "I'm the one who picks the banks."

"Look," she said, "right across the street. On the second floor of that building on the corner."

She was right. It was the first savings and loan that he had ever seen on a second floor. No passersby could see him through a window. No policemen would come through a rear door. He checked out the bank and it was, indeed, perfect. Only one man and two girls worked there. He didn't need a getaway car, either. He could simply park his station wagon around the corner and Karen could sit there with the motor running.

It was an ideal bank. He was leery of it only because Karen had picked it out. He thought about the James Gang hitting Northfield that fateful day. It was suppose to be so easy, but most of them were surprised and wiped out.

At a nearby store he bought a floppy hat and went in looking like what he figured to be some kind of Russian immigrant. His eyebrows were thickened and darkened by mascara, and he had his hat pulled down over his ears.

The bank manager's name was Gorman. Eddie introduced himself and said, "Have you ever been robbed?"

Mr. Gorman said, "Are you kidding? This bank? Certainly not."

"You're sure?"

"Of course I'm sure. Why?"

"Because I'm breaking the maidenhead," Eddie said. "This is a stickup. I just got your cherry."

"What?" The manager's face fell into a frown. "Oh my God."

"Don't waste time. Let's get this over with so that I don't have to kill you."

That made the manager very nervous. He gave Eddie all of the money in the tellers' cages, and Eddie told him to get the money from the safe, too. The manager didn't want to upset Eddie, so he started being a little too helpful. He started putting in the heavy rolls of coins and Eddie's sack broke. The money went all over the floor.

"It was an accident," the manager said. "I swear."

"Find another bag," Eddie shouted. "Quick."

"Okay, okay. Just don't do anything rash."

He found another sack and was hurriedly filling it when it broke again. Again the money spilled out all over the floor.

"Jesus Christ, mister. What the hell is the matter with you?"

"Nothing, I swear. Please, please. Let me use my briefcase."

He got his briefcase and filled it. Eddie was so perturbed that when the manager had finished putting in the paper money he said, "The coins, too."

"But you told me you didn't want the coins."

"Goddamit," Eddie barked. "Put the damn things in there."

The manager put the coins in there and from the moment Eddie picked up the briefcase he regretted it. The bag had to weigh nearly 100 pounds and Eddie weighed only 160.

He staggered down the steps like a one-legged rooster through the barnyard. He was hopping and struggling with the briefcase. He bumped it down the stairs and out to the street. He had to literally drag it around the corner, then heaved it into the car and was sweating like a tired horse when he got in. Karen started laughing and Eddie said, "Drive, dammit, drive." She was laughing so hard that she could barely steer the car.

"If that isn't comical," she said. "You looked like that poor wolf in those Roadrunner cartoons."

She kept laughing and Eddie started laughing, too. They laughed all the way out of town and back to the motel.

In Fargo, North Dakota, he opened the briefcase and found out that the nervous manager, eager to please, had stuffed in envelopes containing a lot of nonnegotiable things like records of people's payments, as well as the money.

That was to be the last bank robbery, and Eddie had left them laughing—or at least he had left laughing.

"Always leave them laughing," he told Karen, but she didn't know what he meant.

Eddie took the wheel in Fargo and drove back toward Montana. On the way back, Karen started talking about horses and told him about having broken a saddle cinch. She had taken the saddle back to the store where she bought it and talked them into giving her a new one even better than the one she bought. When they returned she wanted to take the saddle back. Eddie didn't think it was a good idea. The FBI had put their pictures a lot of places and might even have them in a western store.

Karen began to pout. Here she had done something smart, something right, and Eddie wasn't going to let her enjoy her little victory.

"I thought you'd be proud of me."

"Oh, all right," Eddie said. "Take the thing back."

His mind was on the future, and peace and tranquility and freedom in the Big Sky Country.

Eddie didn't know it then, but when Karen went back into that western store it was a big mistake. A twenty-dollar leather jacket had put them on the run and caused them to leave their paradise in Albuquerque. Now a cinch on a saddle was about to send Eddie on his way to federal prison.

TWENTY TWO

The FBI had converged on Eddie's Albuquerque home and stables. In the house they discovered many empty bottles of Clairol hair coloring. They sent fliers, with mug shots of Eddie and Karen, to every distributor of Clairol products in the country. In Albuquerque they had discovered Eddie's and Karen's interest in and love for horses, and they papered every western wear and saddlery store in the country with mug shots.

Eddie and Karen had fairly good disguises with the wigs and hair coloring and they felt relatively safe and well hidden. Eddie believed that he could now do in Montana what he had wanted to do in Albuquerque—just blend into the world and be gone as "Eddie Watkins" forever.

It was nearing the Christmas season and Eddie knew that it would be his last one with Karen. He was going to set her up in an apartment in Vegas and take good care of her financially, as he had promised. Then he was going to stay in Montana and live in the peaceful way he had never been able to before. He wanted to make it a good Christmas for Karen.

On the morning of December 2, 1966, they were both up early for a shopping trip to town. There wasn't any snow on the ground, but it was bitterly cold. Eddie thought about staying home by the fire, and later wished to hell he had. Many times when he traveled he tuned in on the police radio to listen to calls. On this morning he did not.

They left the house at 8:30 and Karen drove. About two miles from the house was the Florence post office, where Karen pulled in to check the mail and see whether her newspapers and magazines had come. Eddie stayed in the car with the motor running. As he bent over to coax a little more heat out of the stubborn heater, he thought he heard voices over the noise of the radio music and the humming of the heater.

Suddenly he saw the flash of a shadow across the side window, and then he heard, "Come out of there with your hands up."

He raised his head and there were at least a dozen guns pointed at him. An obese policeman was grinning and pointing a shotgun at Eddie's head. His car was hemmed in and more police cars were coming as backups. Eddie had a gun in his hip pocket and another in the glove compartment, but he didn't make a move. He had no choice but to open the car door—very carefully—and get out.

An FBI agent moved in, spun Eddie around and said, "Put your hands on the car, Watkins." Eddie's heart sank when the FBI man said his name, but he thought maybe, just maybe, he could bluff out of it again. He tried.

"My name's Johnston . . . Robert Johnston. You're making a mistake."

The FBI man said, "Bullshit, Watkins, we know it's you."

Eddie tried threats of lawsuits, but it was no use. His heart sank even further when he saw Karen being led out of the post office handcuffed.

They had forgotten to get his Beretta, which was in his back pocket when they frisked him. He heard one of the police officers say, "That looks like her, all right, but we could be wrong about him." The rotund policeman got in the back of the car with Eddie. Karen was in a different squad car. He knew he could have reached for the gun any time on the way to the jail.

When they got to the jail a police sergeant asked, "Have they been searched?"

The FBI agent, whose name was Moe, said, "He's clean, but we didn't have a matron for her."

The sheriff's assistant spoke up. "Search them again. Both of them." When he said that, Eddie felt depression sneak up his shoes, through his head and down into his back pocket where the gun was.

The FBI agent said, "I'm an FBI agent. Don't worry about the search. He's clean."

Eddie breathed a sigh of short-lived relief.

"Search him," the sergeant said.

The deputy searched him and spotted the bulge in

his back pocket, reached in and pulled out the gun. He held it up in the agent's face, which was a crimson blush.

"Don't they teach you G-men that pants have back pockets?" the deputy said.

The obese policeman, who'd been riding in the back with Eddie, said, "Jesus, I can't believe it. He's on the Ten Most Wanted list and a damn FBI agent searches him and misses a gun. Hell, he could've shot me dead." Then he turned to Eddie and said, "How come you didn't do it when you had your chance? You probably could've got away."

Eddie looked at him and said, "It's a little complicated to explain, so I just think I'll let you wonder about it for the rest of your life."

Eddie's freedom ended with the click of a cell-door lock. The good life, the freedom, the moonlight walks were over. The Strattons would probably never speak to him or Karen again when they found out who they were. Eddie wanted to be dead at that moment rather than go back to the misery of prison.

Karen had been spotted when she took the saddle back to trade it for the new one. Her poster was in the store and the owner notified the FBI that he thought she was the same person. The FBI and the local police had a dragnet out for them.

Eddie felt especially depressed about Karen's going to jail. If there were a way to get her out of it he would. He had told her that he would, and he planned to hold true to his word. She had been loyal and he knew she wouldn't tell the police anything about him.

He had one more mission before they shipped him off. He had to save Karen.

TWENTY THREE

Karen was put in a separate cell and they were both booked on bank-robbery charges. They set Eddie's bail at $100,000 and the FBI man told him that if he could make bail they would just charge him with another robbery "and slap another hundred grand on your ass, and I'll bet you run out of goddam money before we run out of goddam charges." Eddie knew he was goddamn right.

With the four thousand dollars he had on him when the FBI made the arrest, Eddie hired an attorney. He had several hundred thousand stashed, but there was no way to get at it, at least not now. He was housed in a wing of the new jail with several other inmates. It would be a simple jail to get out of, he thought. Karen was in a single cell across the hall from him, as they had no women's facilites.

The attorney advised Eddie to cop a plea while in Montana.

"Hell," the attorney said. "The judges here never handle anything bigger than drunk Indians and never give them more than two to three years, no matter what they did. They'd think a fifteen-year sentence was a lifetime."

Eddie told him to try it.

Eddie had Karen sign over the station wagon to the Hommes for one dollar, as they could use the car. The Strattons and Hommes came to visit him and Karen in jail. The Strattons, to whom they had become very close, told them they would take care of the house, the horses and the rest of their things until they got out. They seemed to think Eddie would be back in a few months, but he knew better.

Eddie wanted to get out of jail; he could do no good while he was in there. He set to work on a plan. After about a week he noticed that one deputy would always open the control-box door and look down the aisle before telling the inmates to go from the day room back to their cells. He could have looked through the glass door and used the speaker to order them to move out, but he never did.

Eddie was sitting with another inmate, an Indian named Stan Many White Horses. "Do you want to escape?" Eddie said.

"Sure. Hell yes," Many White Horses said. He was nineteen and wild as hell and in on a car-theft charge. But Many White Horses had a friend, Ronald Ingrahama, who had been caught with him, and he wanted to take Ronald along. Eddie said okay. He told them to flatten out a tobacco tin and make a knife. The next night he would be at the other side of the door and would grab the deputy, lock him up and take off.

Once he was out, he could get Karen out by admitting everything. And he had enough money to buy her freedom. The police didn't have anything substantial on her at all. She'd never gone in a bank with him and no one had ever seen her. And, after all, she hadn't known his true occupation until long after she'd run off with him. He could clear her and be free himself.

The next evening Eddie was there when the deputy opened the door. He grabbed him fast and put the makeshift knife to his throat. "One move and you're dead," Eddie warned.

"Easy, Watkins," the deputy said. "I won't give you any trouble."

Eddie yelled at Stan and Ronald, but by the time the other deputy got to the door they were doing a war dance of some kind. As he came through the door they froze.

"Grab the deputy," Eddie yelled. Many White Horses jumped up on the deputy's back as if to mount a wild stallion. He was yelling and whooping, but his friend just stood there.

"Goddamit," Eddie yelled, "help your friend."

The second Indian hesitated, then finally jumped the deputy. Then the other Indian let him go and headed for the door. Eddie could not let his deputy go, because he knew he would reach for a gun. The second deputy had managed to get his hand on the microphone and yell something into it. Eddie took the first deputy hostage to the door. In the scuffle he lost his slippers in the corridor. At the door, he let the deputy go and the man bolted. There was fresh snow on the ground and Eddie ran through it toward an alley. The police station was across the street from the jail and the lawmen swarmed. They beat Eddie to the mouth of the alley and he was faced with a half-dozen guns.

"Stop or we'll shoot you down," a policeman yelled.

Eddie yelled back, "Go ahead, you bastards. You'll have to shoot me to stop me."

He was so mad at his two companions for messing up a perfect escape that he didn't care. Out there in the snow it just didn't seem to matter. A deputy came up behind him, tossed a towel over his head and pulled it tight around his neck, and the other policemen were quickly upon him.

When he got back to the jail he heard Karen yelling his name. "What's happened? Eddie, are you all right?"

"Take it easy," Eddie said. "I just tried to escape, that's all."

"Oh," Karen said. "Are you okay? Did they hurt you?"

"No, I'm not hurt. How close are you to me?"

"I don't know, Eddie. Where are you? I can't tell."

"They put me in the cell naked," Eddie said.

"Naked!" Karen said. "They can't do that. You can sue them."

"That's right, honey. They're in a lot of trouble now, aren't they?"

When they brought the Indians back in, Eddie looked at them, shook his head and said, "Jesus, I don't see how Custer ever lost."

The FBI agent came in later and commented dryly, "Tried to leave us, Watkins?"

"Johnston to you," Eddie said, frustrated. *"Mr.* Johnston to you, asshole. And heavy on the 'mister' part."

Agent Moe said, "This gives us another charge against you."

"No shit," Eddie said. "I'm underwhelmed."

"The state might put an attempted murder charge on you, too."

"Great. Tell them to take their best shot."

"I guarantee you'll never get another chance to escape from here."

"Look," Eddie said, "this is a ridiculous conversation. You are perhaps one of the great assholes of our generation. I don't have time to talk to you right now, so hit it."

Later he hollered out the details to Karen and she hollered questions back. Tired of the constant yelling, the deputies moved them into adjoining cells.

Eddie could have no more visitors after the escape attempt except for his attorney. The latter seemed very interested in finding out where Eddie's money was hidden, and very anxious to handle Eddie's affairs. He badgered Eddie so much that Eddie gave him a power of attorney, phony leads to nonexistent bank accounts and a phony map showing where the money was hidden on the Stratton place. Eddie didn't hear from the attorney again, except by way of the Strattons, who told him that the man had started boarding horses at their place—which was a long way for him to go to board horses. And he was making many visits. Eddie had one comforting thought: the attorney would die from blistered hands before he found any money with the bogus map.

Eddie instructed Karen to keep her mouth closed and said the police would release her once they got to Cleveland. They would have to go back because the FBI had blocked his attempt to be tried in Montana.

Eddie continously told the police that Karen hadn't known he was wanted, but they didn't believe him. They had her on aiding and abetting in a bank robbery, aiding and abetting a fugitve, and harboring a fugitive.

On December 19th the hearing to move the trial to Cleveland was held. The newspapers and the TV station in Missoula had a great time with it all. It was one of the biggest events ever to happen around there. Later, when a book was written on the Bitter Root area, Eddie's capture was listed as one of the historical landmarks.

Eddie's identity was proved through fingerprints and he and Karen were moved to jail in Cleveland to await trial. Karen refused to talk unless Eddie was there, so they came and got him. She wouldn't answer any questions until Eddie told her what to say. Throughout the trial she answered all questions with "I don't remember," except those questions to which Eddie had specifically given her the answers. Knowing Karen as he did, he believed that she really didn't remember the answers to most of the questions. A perfect witness.

TWENTY FOUR

Instead of the wonderful Christmas Eddie had been planning for Karen, he spent the holiday season shackled in a crummy little jail in Rapid City, South Dakota, in a 4 x 7-foot cell with a mattress on the floor. The marshals made the jailers there so wary of Eddie that when they fed him (bread, gravy, beans, potatoes and watered-down coffee), they brought his meal tray to a spot ten feet from his cell, set it on the floor and then shoved it to him with a broom.

The Christmas presents were back in the house in Montana. There had been no gifts, no laughter, no music and no revelry for Eddie on Christmas Eve, 1966. He fantasized about Christmas back at the Strattons' house, and the previous wonderful Christmas in San Francisco. Karen, too, was jailed and would be flown from Missoula to Cleveland later.

Eddie wondered on Christmas Eve, as he looked for the first star in the East, how many public officials who ran prisons had ever spent a night on a cement floor with no linen on their mattresses.

On Christmas Day one of the jailers finally worked up enough nerve to talk to Eddie.

"What was that Christmas dinner?" Eddie asked.

"It was supposed to be chicken," the jailer said, picking his nose and examining the result as if it were evidence in an important case.

"I guess I missed the chicken part of it."

"Supposed to be two parts chicken," the jailer said.

"Well," Eddie said, "I guess the two parts I got must've been the feathers and the asshole."

"It ain't my fault you're in here," the jailer said. He did not sound mean.

"I know that," Eddie answered. "Certainly prison is not supposed to be a country club. And it's the criminal's fault that he's inside. But how he comes out after he's served his stretch is society's problem."

"Well," the jailer said, "I ain't one of 'em, but there's lotsa people would just as soon take every criminal and, instead of housing 'em and feeding 'em, just shoot 'em all, dig a hole and bury 'em."

He offered Eddie a cigarette and Eddie took it through the bars.

"Inmates usually come out of jail more violent people than when they went in," Eddie said. "If you want a society that shoots people for stealing, then you're saying that society puts a higher value on property than it does on human life. And then you're going to have to shoot car thieves and parole violators and speeders and jaywalkers. You want to live in a society like that?"

The jailer took a drag on his cigarette. "Tell you the truth, 'bout all I want is my paycheck every week, sorry as that sounds."

"That's why the prison system is never going to improve," Eddie said.

The jailer had to go back to his office. "Merry Christmas," he said.

"I'll do my best to have one," Eddie said. "Thanks for the smoke."

The next stop on the way to Cleveland was Minneapolis. There, Eddie was thrown into a police lineup for a Minneapolis bank job. He hadn't done it, but it was almost certain that he'd be identified as the bandit. He knew that the FBI man would take his mug shot into an office and call the robbery victims, then excuse himself from the room, after telling them that Eddie had all but admitted to the crime. He would leave the mug shot where the witnesses could get a look at it, and they would certainly identify Eddie. They did. He was innocent of that one but he was fingered for it nonetheless.

The next stop was a crummy jail in Rockford, Illinois. Then it was on to Cleveland. The marshals stopped at a toll booth and waited for several minutes so police cars could come and escort them into Cleveland, as if it were the circus come to town. The police wanted a little TV credit for the capture of the nation's most notorious bank robber.

242

That night, Channel 3 in Cleveland made it sound as if Eddie were suspected of every crime that had occurred in Cleveland since his release from the Ohio pen.

At the jails where he'd been housed on his trip back, he had become very depressed at the thought that he would never have anything better for the rest of his life. But once back to the Cuyahoga County Jail he started to think about getting out again, and about how if he had just had a file he could saw those bars and be gone.

On January 4, 1967, the FBI came to see him. Agent Pat Burke spent many hours talking to him, trying to get him to foul up his alibis on the thirteen bank robberies they had indicted him for and the eighteen others they suspected him of.

Eddie rather liked Agent Burke. He was good at what he did and not a wise-ass like Agent Moe, who had grilled him in Missoula.

They definitely had Eddie cold on thirteen counts. He had been positively identified in some, and had identified himself in a couple of the California jobs.

Eddie refused to admit to any of the robberies. A conviction on one count would get him twenty-five years; a second would probably get him fifty years. And fifty was more years than he could ever serve. Furthermore, he was a parole violator from the Ohio pen and could owe them twelve years for that.

There were many news stories about Eddie Watkins and the "Eddie Watkins Gang" in Cleveland papers, on the radio and on TV. Eddie was a local celebrity.

The sheriff allowed him to have a TV and a radio in his cell and let him order one meal a day from a restaurant. He also let Eddie out of his cell to exercise in the yard in front of it.

Just before they flew Karen back, Agent Burke called and said, "Look, Eddie, you might as well discuss these cases with me. Karen will be here tomorrow and we'll get everything out of her."

"No you won't," Eddie said. "First, she doesn't know anything. And besides, she has a terrible memory. Even if she wanted to tell you anything she couldn't remember."

"I was on the L.A. vice squad for six years," Burke said. "I know how to talk to women!"

"With all respect," Eddie said, "you'd be just as well off to go fuck yourself. Even if she knew anything, if her brains were gunpowder she wouldn't have enough to blow her nose."

The next morning Eddie saw a deputy pass by with Agent Burke. They had Karen with them. Eddie called out, "Hold tight, Karen, they don't have a thing on you."

They interrogated Karen. She couldn't remember what city they'd been in three days after they left it, let alone now. She confused Reno with Vegas, and couldn't remember which year they were in San Francisco.

The next day Agent Burke called Eddie out to the interrogation area. Eddie looked at Burke, who had a pleading look on his face.

"Eddie, either she's the best liar I've ever seen or she's utterly stupid. In all my years of interviewing people I've never met one like her. How did you ever put up with her for two years?"

"She has her good qualities," Eddie said, "Brilliance may not be one of them. But tell her you're going to take her dancing, Burke; give her a specific date and hour when you'll pick her up. She'll remember that promise exactly but she won't remember anything else. I told you she wouldn't."

Burke shook his head. "Jesus, what did you two ever talk about for two years?"

"Mostly about dancing, clothes, cars and fooling around."

"Eddie, why don't you confess so we can clear these charges against you? You won't have a chance in court." He gave Eddie a cigarette.

"When will you let Karen go?"

"That's up to the D.A."

"You're not talking to some rookie, Pat. If you tell the D.A. what she's like he'll listen. She was never in on a single job. It's me you want, not her."

"What about St. Paul, Eddie? She was with you. How about the car for that job?"

"I told her it was for a daughter from a previous marriage, Pat. She believed whatever I told her."

"The bank employees identified her."

"They lied. I was never in a bank with her on a job. She never knew what I was doing."

"Didn't she know where the money came from?"

"I could've told her a genie brought it, Pat. Realize here that you are dealing with someone who has the inertia quotient of a sack of rocks."

"She didn't know you were a fugitive?"

"Thought I was running from alimony. I swear it. Hell, she doesn't read papers or magazines; she doesn't even watch TV, except soaps."

"Between you and me, Ed, she's guilty as hell."

"You can't prove a thing and you know it. So if you want cooperation from me, you get her out of the case."

Burke went on to tell Eddie how they had caught up with him. Burke had been assigned to Eddie's case exclusively. When Eddie became too tough to find, he had sent out thousands of circulars on Karen to drugstores, western stores, nightclubs. Agents in other cities hadn't been too anxious to link Eddie Watkins with any robberies in their area, and if they showed his mug shots to victims they did not press them to identify Eddie Watkins as the robber. If they did, J. Edgar Hoover would send the special agent in charge of the city's bureau a scathing letter telling him how incompetent he was. J. Edgar had become obsessed with catching Eddie Watkins.

"I went through Washington," Eddie said. "Why didn't old J. Edgar catch me himself if he was so smart?"

His offer to make it easy for the courts and the FBI worked. All the charges against Karen were soon dropped and she went free. Eddie felt good about that part, but now he had to take care of himself.

He had a nineteen-year-old cellmate named Ronald Watson, also a bank robber. Watson wanted out in the worst way. The city hired a new deputy, Eugene Fetcho, who had resigned from the Cleveland Police Department under pressure. He was assigned to guard Eddie, and he told Eddie that he was deeply in debt and needed cash badly. Eddie told Fetcho he'd pay a good price for some sawblades, and Fetcho agreed to get him four of them for $750. In the meantime, Ronald Watson's mother, who had been making Sunday visits, had managed to get her son four sawblades. Since Eddie could not tell Deputy Fetcho that Watson's mother had already brought them, he went through with the deal.

Eddie also asked Deputy Fetcho for two dark-colored sweatsuits, and Fetcho made Eddie pay him for those with two checks Eddie had received, one for $84, the other for $89. Fetcho made the mistake of cashing those checks in the presence of another deputy, who would later testify against him.

Eddie and Watson went to work on the window bars. They had been saving bedsheets for the escape attempt; the plan was to tie the bedsheets together and drop to the third-floor roof, then to the ground and away.

Fetcho was to act as lookout, and to intercept the other deputy when he came by on his rounds. They sawed at the bars and were nearly through; freedom was a quarter inch of steel away.

But the other deputy didn't come past Fetcho that night—he came the other way, directly to Eddie and Ronald Watson's cell, and nailed them cold. As the deputy rushed to the phone for help, Fetcho came by demanding the sawblades and Eddie gave them to him. This escape attempt had failed, but Eddie still had two blades taped to his feet.

The bars would be replaced and Eddie kept quiet about Fetcho's part in the attempt. However, the other deputy had seen the checks Fetcho had cashed, which had belonged to Eddie, and that would lead to Fetcho's downfall. Eddie would refuse to testify against him, but Ronald Watson did. In fact Watson even testified against his own mother.

Meanwhile Eddie had found out too late the meaning of real friendship and kindness, the type that wasn't for sale. The Strattons had stuck by Eddie and Karen in spite of finding out who and what Eddie really was. They saw him as a kind-hearted, generous and giving person, even though the law and society saw him as a taker.

The Strattons had sold all of Eddie's horses and belongings and put the money into his bank account. They sent Karen's clothes home to Cleveland, and Mrs. Stratton sent a letter to Eddie warning him that Karen's parents were on the make.

Eddie knew that although Karen had never gotten along with her father she was easily swayed by her parents. They came to see him and tried to find out the location of the money that he had buried. They knew about the markers in Vegas, too. Mrs. Stratton had told Eddie that she had sent his color TV and his electric watch to Karen's parents, and that she later felt it was a mistake. She was right. Karen's father came to the jail wearing Eddie's watch.

Karen's mother tried to give Eddie a sermon saying that stolen money wouldn't buy happiness, but he knew it was a ploy to find out where his money was. What she really meant, Eddie figured, was that the stolen money wouldn't buy *her* happiness— unless she could find it. Eddie pointed at the watch.

"That watch doesn't seem to be making your husband unhappy. And I know you sold my color TV. Those items were bought with stolen money, so I assume that money is making you terribly depressed."

They left then, but they sent Karen back and she tried the same approach. That depressed and bothered him, but he didn't really blame Karen for it. He knew she was easily led.

Eddie had bargained his way to a guarantee of concurrent sentencing, which would still leave him with forty-five years to serve. That meant he could be paroled in ten years, but he was still aware he would be an old man when he got out.

Karen showed up at the trial with a tattoo of a cross on her forehead. Eddie was shocked, and so was Judge William Thomas. When the judge asked her about it she said, "I'm planning to turn Catholic."

"I know a lot of Catholics," the judge said, "and I've never heard of tattooing as a prerequisite." But then the judge didn't know Karen.

Eddie had given her another $500 and she had given it to her parents to pay off what they owed on their trailer.

Eddie would see her once more, just before he was to be sentenced. She was still on a religious kick and asked him, "Eddie, did you ever wonder whether God wants you in prison to spread His word?"

Eddie told her he believed that her parents were trying to take advantage of her, and she'd be better off away from them.

They were talking through a screen in a holding room. She said, "Eddie, I love you and I'm going to wait for you."

"You aren't going to wait for me—we both know that. Let's part friends. You find some nice guy and settle down, but drop me a line once in a while. It's lonely in jail and I won't get many letters."

"I'll write to you every day," she said.

"Come on Karen. You didn't write to me twice all this time I've been in the county jail. Be realistic—just drop me a line sometime. Let me know what's happening to you."

They touched fingers through the screen, and that was the last time Eddie would see her until thirteen years later in Lodi, Ohio, across a police barricade. He knew he would miss her and he hoped that the world wouldn't chew her up.

Eddie still had two sawblades, and in April, before his sentencing, he tried another escape. He worked carefully on the bars in his seventh-floor window, which had four small windowpanes surrounded by metal. The windows opened on a slant, just enough so Eddie could stick his arm out. He was working on the pins that allowed the window to slant, and the work couldn't be detected as long as the window was shut. "D Day" was planned as April 29th. But that afternoon he was summoned to the office of the chief deputy, who started riding him about trying to saw his jail down.

Eddie wondered how he could know about the escape attempt, because he hadn't told anyone. But then he realized that the chief deputy was still irked about the attempt Eddie and Ronald Watson had made before. He started on Eddie about how he wasn't going to give him any more visiting privileges, riding him, trying to belittle him to make himself seem tough in front of his deputies. Eddie lost his temper and shot a couple of insults back. The chief deputy ordered Eddie stripped and searched and they found the blades.

Eddie knew that the FBI liked to have all of their cases solved; so, for admitting to some of the robberies, many other charges weren't pursued and Eddie was allowed to serve his sentences concurrently. This meant that neither he nor Karen would be tried later on state charges—the Feds had seen to that, at Eddie's insistence.

251

He would, at least, be sent to a federal penitentiary, where the facilities would be better than at a state pen. Temporarily he would be sent to Atlanta Federal Penitentiary, but Agent Burke told him that he'd do his best to get Eddie transferred closer to Montana, which he had hoped for.

Eddie was sentenced May 29, 1967, to five consecutive nine-year sentences to total forty-five years, and eight consecutive nine-year sentences to run along with the forty-five, for a total of one hundred seventeen years. He thought back about it and remembered Al Marks, the drunken bum who was his downfall. Al was serving twenty-to-life at the Ohio pen. Poor old Johnny was in a federal prison in Terre Haute, Indiana, and would end up doing eight years.

Eddie had thought a lot about the Strattons. They had written to him often during his ordeal, and had given him the spiritual support that he had never received before during his life. He began to wonder—much too late in his career, sadly enough—whether there might not be a lot of people like the Strattons out there in the free world. He had never managed to stay out in it long enough to find many like that. He would later discover that Judge John Thomas, who had tried him in federal court on the charges, was also a true friend. So was Agent Pat Burke. They were people who seemed to care about him, and he wondered why he hadn't met more individuals of their quality in his forty-eight years.

Before he left for Atlanta, Eddie talked with Burke.

"There's no telling how far you would have gotten in this world if you'd stayed away from crime," Burke said. "You are one clever man. You kept the FBI offices in a state of confusion for two years. All of these agents want to come by just to look at you, to see the man who was the subject of all those Hoover memos." After a long silence Burke added, "But, Eddie, you have ruined yourself."

Eddie could feel the tears trying to well up in his eyes but he fought them back. "I know, Pat. I know."

Eddie had resigned himself, once again, to prison life.

He left Cleveland shackled and handcuffed. The marshals didn't even know their way out of Cleveland to Route 71, so Eddie directed them. He took them purposely by the apartment where he had met Karen, and past Johnny's now-empty office. He wanted to breathe in everything, to lock all of the pleasant thoughts in his mind so that he could recall them during the many long lonesome nights he was about to spend in prison.

TWENTY FIVE

After years of suspecting him and trying to get him, the FBI had finally nailed Fast Eddie Watkins for robbing banks. The Atlanta Federal Penitentiary was a huge, bleak old fortress with cellblocks that looked to Eddie like something out of a traditional prison movie. The cellblocks were stacked on top of one another, with guards in little cement offices in the corners, their ever-watchful eyes on the five tiers of cells.

Inside, inmates got twenty cents an hour to make mattresses and mailbags in the textile mill, or wooden park signs in the wood factory.

In Atlanta, Eddie heard from Karen only a few times—and that was at the very first. However, he did hear from Judge Thomas quite often. He was suprised the judge was so concerned. Eddie also heard from Agent Pat Burke, and the concern of these two eased the pain of doing time.

Eddie decided to get some oil paints and canvas and try to learn to paint. He developed remarkable talent at painting scenes of old barns and broken-down wagons, and after about a year his paintings were good enough to sell for as much as $100 in the prison art show. Judge Thomas bought some of them and got his friends to buy others. Eddie was saving the money from the sale of the paintings and from working as a clerk. He was a model prisoner, kept all the rules, and didn't cause any trouble, hoping to make parole.

In the outside world, things were changing. The free-spirited thinking he had sampled in San Francisco had caught on and become a cultural revolution. The hippie lifestyle was spreading and the antiwar movement was too. Robert Kennedy and Martin Luther King had both been assassinated, and Nixon had become President. And while the youth culture was warning its adherents not to trust anyone over thiry, Eddie Watkins had turned fifty. Eddie had robbed at least one bank for every year he was alive. Considering that he hadn't robbed any until he was nearly an adult, and he had spent lots of time in prison, he was rivaling Jesse James as the busiest bank robber in American history during his active years.

For all of his notoriety—the Cleveland press, especially, began to make a folk anti-hero of him—he was nonetheless faced with the humdrum reality of being fed, housed and clothed by the government behind the stone walls of a federal pen.

Eddie concentrated on his artwork while in Atlanta Federal, with all the hurts and frustrations of his past life providing fuel for his creativity.

It was a dull and lonely existence, but for some it seemed to provide a macabre sort of security. He would indelibly carry the memory of inmates, on two separate occasions, who had made parole and were to be released—but who, rather than face the outside world, hanged themselves in their cells.

What Eddie dreamed about mostly was being out in the wide open spaces, on a ranch, with horses and cattle and some kind of inner peace he wasn't sure he knew how to achieve.

He had had an evidentiary hearing for a new trial, and Karen—who incidentally had stopped writing to him altogether—was more harmful than helpful to him in court. He did not get a new trial, but on his third review in front of the parole board he was released. On June 7, 1975, after eight years, he was again a free man.

He was by now the nation's best-known bank robber. But he was fifty-six years old and the parole board reasoned that he was a harmless old coot who was ready to go straight.

Eddie had been paroled to work on the ranch of Dr. Peter Briesch, in Idaho. Dr. Briesch was an old acquaintance whom Eddie had met in Montana.

He left the prison that morning and, although it was a hot humid Georgia day outside, it couldn't be as uncomfortable as the sweltering cells of the Atlanta Federal Penitentiary.

On the way to the airport he stopped at the Trust Company Bank's downtown branch—not to rob it, but to withdraw money he had made honestly by his painting. He withdrew $300 in cash and the remainder in travelers' checks. As he signed the checks he told the girl who was working behind the desk, "You sure are lucky."

She was startled. "Why is that?"

"Because this is the first time in years that I've withdrawn money from a bank without a gun." Eddie laughed, but the girl did not.

He went to a clothing store and bought a pair of slacks, a jacket and a shirt and tie. The salesman said he would put his other clothing in a bag.

"Don't bother," Eddie said. "Just throw it in the trash."

Eddie wasn't sure whether Dr. Briesch would recognize him after all these years, but he did. He was waiting at the airport with his wife and two daughters. The girls were aged nine and six respectively, and Eddie had never seen them.

The smell of the pines and the clean air seemed to cleanse his soul. The blue sky, the cold mountain streams and the peace he felt warmed his heart.

There was one trip Eddie wanted to take, and that was to Las Vegas to collect the $60,000 in markers that his friend, the pit boss, had been holding for him. The latest letter Eddie had received from his friend indicated that he had purchased a couple of points for Eddie in a casino. He explained that points were the same as stock, and interest could be collected and the stocks cashed in at any time.

Eddie felt fortunate to have had at least one person on the outside whom he could trust, who did not take advantage of him as so many people had during his lifetime, all the way back to his childhood.

He decided that he would give his friend $10,000 for holding the money for him. That would still leave Eddie with $50,000, enough of a stake to start building a retirement account, even if he never recovered the buried money that the police were keeping a watch for.

On the phone, Eddie found that his points were now worth close to a hundred thousand dollars, and he decided he would give his friend $20,000. He planned a trip to Las Vegas to pick up the money, and his friend said that it would be waiting at a casino desk at 11:30 p.m., June 15, 1975. Eddie was excited. That money, plus some he had hidden away in Montana, would be enough to buy him a ranch. Certainly it was stolen money, but he felt as if he had paid dearly for it so it was now his. Maybe, he thought, he could even go into partnership with Dr, Briesch. He had told the doctor he planned to buy $20,000 worth of cattle for the ranch.

He took a Hughes Air West flight to Vegas and walked around like a tourist, looking at the sights and resisting the old urge to hit the crap tables.

At 10:45 he went to the casino to pick up his money. At 11:15 two men came up to him and said, "Are you Eddie Watkins?"

Eddie admitted that he was. He was sure that they weren't policemen, but he let them escort him to a small office near the slot machines. If they were police, he could be in violation of parole and go back to prison.

Policemen they were not. The bigger one said, "Watkins, you're a parolee. You're not welcome in this casino. Get your ass out of here now and don't come back. Ever." He stuck his finger in Eddie's chest. "If you ever come back here again you'll go to jail." The other one slammed Eddie against the wall and started roughing him up.

Right then and there Eddie knew the score. His old "friend" was no friend after all. He intended to take Eddie for $100,000, and these two goons were in on it. Eddie didn't want to draw attention to the matter, so he left for the airport and a plane to Idaho.

Back at the ranch, he thought about it. What a fool he had been! He had been going to give his pal $20,000 and, just like everybody else in his life, the friend had turned out to be just another uncaring, two-bit taker. Eddie had offered the man friendship and the man had tried to use him. The more he thought about it the more he burned.

The thought stayed in his mind day and night; it got up with him and went to bed with him. He couldn't digest food. He began to dwell on memories of his childhood, and being tossed out and rejected. The fifty-cent piece his mother had put in his hand when she sent him out into the freezing-cold night, and the $100,000 his friend was trying to cheat him out of, were like one and the same thing.

It was the principle of being cheated that bothered him—not the amount of money nor even the need for it.

Then one day he threw down his shovel and went to the gun store, bought a pistol and flew to Las Vegas. He was wearing a red goatee and he had dyed his mustache red. His hair had thinned out and what was left was also dyed red.

Eddie bribed a busboy at the casino where his friend worked to find out his friend's address. That night he took a cab to within three blocks of the man's house, and walked the rest of the way. There were lights on inside and Eddie knew the man must be there. He tried to pry open a window next to the garage, but it was locked. He tried to raise the garage door but could not. Then he was able to break a small pane of glass in the garage window and unlatch the lock. Inside the garage were a Cadillac and a Lincoln Continental. Eddie thought about how well his old friend must be doing on his trust money. There was a stack of old tires in the garage, and Eddie climbed inside the pile, and hid himself and waited. He slept there all night.

Early the next morning he was awakened by noise outside. He heard footsteps and then saw the door swing open. He could see his friend in the doorway light, the morning sun at his back. Eddie rose slowly and pointed the gun.

"Hello, asshole," Eddie said. His friend took a step and squinted, saw it was Eddie and froze.

"Eddie," his friend said, "I've been waiting for

you. Where the hell have you been?"

"Your two goons scared me out of town."

"I don't know what you're talking about. I went there but you didn't show."

"Don't bullshit me."

"Really, I thought something had happened."

Eddie wasn't buying it. "Something is about to happen, buddy boy. You are about to die unless you get all of my money, now."

"I don't keep that kind of money in the house, Ed. I can go get it for you."

"What do you take me for, shithead? You better have a big chunk of it in your house, or else you won't live to see another day."

His "friend" had thirty thousand in cash in the house. Eddie gave him an address and told him to send the rest in cash or he would come back and finish him off.

Then he went directly to the airport in one of his friend's cars while the man was tied up back at the house. He flew to Los Angeles.

Eddie was disgusted and depressed about what his friend had done. He sulked and cursed, and the more he thought about it, the more all of the old hurts came bubbling back to the top. He had checked into a motel on Sunset Boulevard, close to La Brea Avenue. On the morning of July 5, 1975, he set out looking for a bank to rob, and that day he robbed a bank. He nearly cleaned out the Family Savings and Loan on La Cienega Boulevard. He took it like a big dog chewing up a small bone; he was down on the world.

The next day he rented an apartment at 1736 North Sycamore, in Hollywood. The landlord was so anxious to rent that she didn't even ask him to fill out a lease.

Later Eddie would get back most of the money that his friend had tried to keep—but he'd already crossed the line. He'd broken parole and had assumed an alias, and he wasn't even clear on why he had done it. He'd blown all his plans for the future and there seemed no way to turn back now.

Soon he hit another Family Savings and Loan, in Pasadena. During the robbery one of the tellers dropped a bundle of twenties in the safe room. As Eddie reached down to pick up the bundle, his finger nervously tightened on the trigger and the .357 magnum discharged against the floor. The bullet ricocheted around the room, hitting a bank customer in the arm. It was only a scratch, but Eddie was emotionally torn up by the incident. It was the first time he had ever fired a weapon in a bank and the first time anyone had ever been hurt in any of his robberies. The noise ruptured his eardrum and, as he drove away from the bank, he could hear nothing. It was difficult for him to determine whether or not he was making the tires screech. Eddie went to the doctor about the ear problem and got medication to relieve the pain although he would continue to have a ringing in his ear and occasional balance difficulties.

He was dejected about having gone back to the

old life, and he wasn't really sure why he had done so. But once he started living it up again he began to forget about it. He kept his apartment stocked with liquor and young women. To finance his lifestyle he was knocking off banks regularly.

But he was beginning to get the jitters when he was on a job. He could actually see his heart thumping in his chest. Again he had baffled police with will-o'-the-wisp bank jobs, disappearing without a trace, in and out faster than an alarm could be answered. But he decided he was getting too old to live like that. His heart couldn't take much more.

But Eddie was, in his own twisted way, like any other champion. There was always one more big one, one more challenge to meet. He hated the thought of fading away into ancient history.

He drove to Vegas and laundered money; then, for some odd reason, he headed back toward the Midwest, in the general direction of Cleveland. He would find the perfect bank—one with two doors, front and back, and no smoked-glass windows or offices that he couldn't see into, just open lobbies and tellers' cages. The bank had to be ripe and right.

He did not find the perfect bank in Denver or Kansas City, so he headed for St. Louis. On the way, his fingers suddenly began to go numb, so he changed routes and headed for Cleveland. He knew a heart attack was coming on, but when he got there he was afraid to expose himself to medical help. He rested in a motel in Cleveland, then drove back to

L.A., taking his time and resting often.

He got back to L.A., thankful to be alive. In that town he took it relatively easy, more concerned about his heart than about his vendetta against Cleveland.

On September 29th he had such a bad heart attack that it felt as if a pair of hands were inside his chest, squeezing his insides and wringing them out. He made it home in spite of incredible pain, stumbled into his apartment, and called a couple next door, Wayne and Jori. Telling them to look after his Doberman, Dutch, he gave them his apartment keys and called an ambulance. Jori went with him. The pain got worse and the ambulance took him to an emergency clinic, where the doctor told him he was having a myocardial infarction—a heart attack. He sent Eddie away in the ambulance, with attendants working on him until they arrived at the hospital—L.A. County. The doctor there told him it was "the big one." "Mr. Baxter," he told Eddie— that was Eddie's new alias—"we are admitting you immediately. This is serious."

But Eddie stubbornly talked his way out of the hospital and somehow, with Jori's help, made it home, weak and exhausted. She stayed with him for the next week until he started feeling better. He had another attack on October 9th, but he was prepared for this one. He packed a bag, took his dog to a kennel and drove to Hollywood Presbyterian Hospital. He knew that it was a private hospital and he could pay in cash, with no questions asked. He checked in, feeling secure with his dog in a kennel, his apartment door locked and double bolted, and a gun inside his car, which was parked just outside the hospital. The hospital visit was an orderly process with no loose ends. He only spent three days in intensive care.

Eddie had brought cash with him to pay the bill, which was $375 a day. The hospital accounting department figured him to be just an eccentric, and they didn't ask questions. The doctor recommended that Eddie stay and rest two more weeks but he refused, got a prescription for peritrate nitro and codeine tablets, and went home with orders to take it easy for a while.

When he felt better he decided to disappear. He had plenty of money and it was time to vanish into thin air, leave the old life behind, and never be heard from again. He gave his stereo and many other possessions to Wayne and Jori, and asked them to take good care of Dutch, his dog. Then he got in the car and began to drive.

He drove toward the southwest, then decided it would be better not to stay in that part of the country, so he headed eastward. As so many times before in his life, the road seemed to lead him to Cleveland. It was as if the car had its own brain, and Eddie found himself back to take one last nostalgic look at the city. Then it would be goodby forever.

The day he arrived there he picked up a copy of the Cleveland *Sunday Plain Dealer.* And there was an article about the famous crooks of Cleveland's history. There was a photo of Bill Rooney, one of the most famous safecrackers of all time; and there was Louie "The Dip," a notorious and talented pickpocket. Also there was a photo of Fast Eddie Watkins being taken to court in 1967.

Eddie had cut out cigarettes, liquor, and even his fondest desire, women, and he was feeling good again. He saw the blurry door to the future that was in front of him, and the door to the past about to close behind him. Taking a drive over to his old neighborhood in South Euclid, he parked near his old house at 1326 Sheffield. He walked over to where the ballfield had been located during his youth. There were houses there now. He looked at the corner lot where his father had dreamed of building a house—a busted dream, a broken promise.

He smiled as he saw the old oak tree where he'd had his treehouse, the smile becoming a grin as he noticed that the old house was still there. Then he looked at his old home and it was as if he were in a time warp. He could see the bedroom in his mind's eye, the bathroom that his dad had added on, the pantry with the ladder leading up to a ceiling doorway, to an attic where he had played and dreamed on rainy days. He thought of his electric train, his Hoot Gibson cowboy suit, his mother. Where had it all gone?

He drove to a house where his friend Bill Manzo had lived, and he could almost hear Bill's voice calling to him as they played in the basement. He sat in the car, his eyes misty, remembering.

Then Eddie drove toward Green Road and Mayfield, past Victory Park School where he had met his first love, a freckle-faced redhead named Isabel. He wondered what had happened to Isabel. Had she married, had she had children, had she had a happy life or a miserable one?

As he drove toward his aunt's old house he began to feel the old resentment that his brother had been raised in a loving home and he himself had been turned away like a stray dog. Why, he wondered, didn't anybody want to love him? Was it something about him? How could they hate a child? He felt no happy memories when he drove past his aunt's old house, and none when he drove down Crawford Road where his mother and grandmother had lived.

A deep melancholy set in. He glanced absently at the newspaper on the car seat beside him, while his mind was busy thinking of all the wasted years, the prison cells, the robbing of banks and the going wrong. He had never been able to buy happiness and the few moments he had had of glory had cost a terrible price.

A paragraph in the paper caught his eye. Police Inspector Stanley J. Deka was reported as having made the comment that old bank-robbery gangs, and bank robbers of the past like Eddie Watkins, couldn't operate in the world of modern electronics and law enforcement. That brought a gleam to Eddie's eye.

He read further and on the next page he saw a full-page ad with an old wanted poster picture of himself that read: "EVEN FAST EDDIE WATKINS WOULDN'T TRY OUR BANK. YOUR MONEY IS SECURE AT SOCIETY NATIONAL."

"You son of a bitch," Eddie said to himself. "We'll see about that bullshit." He folded the paper, his mind made up; he had decided to take the Society National Bank.

He stayed in Cleveland and the next day cased the bank. He counted the employees; everything looked good. With a makeshift bomb, complete with a dynamite plunger, in his briefcase, he took his loaded .357 magnum and headed for the bank.

Eddie arrived at the front doors of the bank at 2:22 in the afternoon, set to clean it out completely. He fingered the bomb-device, a square box wrapped in masking tape. The tip of its aerial stuck out of his briefcase. When he entered the bank he stopped; there were five customers inside. It would be the fifty-fifth bank robbery of his career and, he hoped, the very last.

As Eddie stood there, an attractive young lady approached and greeted him. "May I help you?"

Eddie looked at her. "Yes; I would like to speak with Mr. Hahn."

She nodded and walked away. Mr. Hahn, the bank manager, was with customers, and Eddie had to wait. He looked out the window and noticed a police cruiser slowly moving down the street.

Finally, Hahn shook hands with the couple at his desk and they smiled. Good, Eddie thought, they're getting their loan. He watched them leave, and then Hahn motioned toward Eddie and asked him to have a seat.

Eddie put the box on the manager's desk and the briefcase on the floor. Slowly he pulled out a letter and handed it to the man. "I have a money problem that I think the bank can solve for me," Eddie said. "The letter will explain it."

He slowly removed the plunger from his pocket and placed it in view on the desk. Hahn looked up, first startled, then with fear in his eyes.

"Don't look at me," Eddie growled. "Read the letter."

The letter read, "This is a holdup. Sitting on your desk is a box of dynamite and in my hand is an electrically controlled plunger. One wrong move and you are dead. Smile if you intend to cooperate."

It was a smile inhibited by pure terror. Hahn stared first at the box, then at the plunger in Eddie's hand, and finally up at Eddie. "What do you want me to do?"

Eddie knew he had the manager where he wanted him. "Go behind the counter," Eddie said. "Call everyone together and tell them exactly what is happening. Tell them to stand in the center of the room. You are to completely clean out that vault—" Eddie pointed—"and then put the money in this briefcase. Do you understand all that?"

"But the safe is on a time lock and won't open

until two forty-five," Hahn pleaded.

Eddie looked at him. "I'll wait."

He told the bank manager that he wanted everyone away from the alarm buttons, and he threatened to blow the building to hell if they did not comply. He also warned Hahn that if the cops got there before he left, he would blow the bank apart, killing himself, Hahn and everyone else inside. Hahn did not want to die; Eddie had already sensed that. Hahn did not know that the "bomb" was harmless; it was not a bomb at all, just a box made to look like one.

Eddie had the .357 out as they filled the briefcase with money from the tellers' cages. At exactly 2:45 the safe opened; they added the money from that. There was nearly $100,000 in large bills, all told. Eddie was ready to make it back to his old Buick and be gone from the bank, from Cleveland and from the practice of crime forever.

Then it happened. He felt the numbness in his hands, and arms, the tightness in his chest, the sharp pain. He couldn't move, he was having another heart attack. His head was spinning; the pain grew worse. He reached for his medicine, then remembered it was in the car's glove compartment. Finally the pain let up a little and he began moving toward the door. He didn't know how long he had been standing there; when he looked up at clock it was blurred. He began backing toward the door, the eyes of all his victims on him. Suddenly he heard a voice say, "Drop it."

Eddie froze for a second and then turned slowly around to see a policeman pointing a shotgun at his head. He had been all but out the door when the heart attack gripped him, and now he was cornered. His mind raced. Slowly he raised his hand, showing the plunger. Looking at the officer, he shouted, "Get the fuck out of here or I'll blow all of us to hell."

He stood silent, his eyes on the officer, praying the policeman would think of his wife, his children, his dog—anybody he loved. The officer's face became white; he looked at the plunger, at Eddie, and around the bank. Finally he began to back up slowly. He was shaking. "Take it easy, buddy. Just take it easy." Finally Eddie was out of the bank, but it was too late. He looked at the door. He should have been long gone; now there were other police cars screeching up to the bank. Eddie jumped over the counter. Everybody in the bank was on the floor, expecting shooting. Eddie clutched his chest and looked at the door again. The great bank siege of Cleveland had begun.

There were two hundred policemen and FBI agents against Fast Eddie Watkins, a heart attack victim with his fake bomb and nine hostages. It was a situation that Eddie would never forget.

TWENTY-SIX

Before this momentous bank siege ended the hostages would feel as if they, too, were under assault by the law, especially the FBI.

Eddie Watkins had robbed fifty-four and a half banks and had pulled off some seventy-five other robberies in his life of crime and rebellion. But he knew now, as he saw police cars pulling into view of the window like an endless line of hotdogs coming out of a clown's pocket, that he should never have tried this bank.

He was cornered and his face looked pale and drained of blood. He knew the hostages could see it, too; he could tell by the looks of fear on their faces. He did not want them to know that he was having a heart attack, nor did he want them to realize that his bomb was a fake.

He looked at the faces of the hostages again and knew that they must be thinking they were going to die a violent death, crushed under concrete and steel, at the hands of this maniac bomber. Eddie felt a little sorry for them as he looked at each one individually. Meanwhile he held his chest, not wanting to show that the pain was coming back. He knew, though, that he would soon need the isodil, peritrate, digoxen, valium, nitros, and codeine that were in his car. He had to think fast and get everything set for what might now take place.

Knowing he was a clay pigeon for sharpshooters as long as he stayed in that lobby, he herded the eight employees and one customer into a back room of the bank. There were six women and three men.

The place was a makeshift lunchroom that had a stove and a refrigerator. Eddie found out from Hahn that there were two secure walls and one weak spot, the wall next to the bathroom. He looked at it closely. It could be broken through by police teams.

The L-shaped area was very small for ten people, but they crowded in and Eddie shut the door behind them. There was no lock, so he put two chairs against the door and told two of the girls, Maureen Masterson and Jane Veydt, to sit on them.

Suddenly Eddie turned and faced the group. "Somebody set off the alarm," he accused. No one answered. Eddie wanted them to be scared, but as he looked at them he knew he did not have to worry about that. "Whoever did it is going to pay." He kept searching their eyes. "You've risked your lives for federally insured money, bank money, not even your own. This would not be happening if one of you had not pushed the alarm."

He wanted to explain to them that their chances of being taken hostage in future situations would be minimized if they forgot to use the alarm button. Then he wondered to himself why he should be worrying about their futures when he was in this position. It was fruitless to think about the future with hundreds of policemen, sharpshooters and FBI agents surrounding the place.

His chest pains were increasing and his mind was running wild. He checked the air vent overhead and reminded himself to listen for sounds in the ceiling. He was sure that the police would never try the door. They would come in through the ceiling or come crashing through that south wall. He walked over to the wall and looked at it closely again, trying to blot out the pain and concentrate on it. It was now 2:55, and very quiet inside the room. Eddie wiped the sweat from his hands and looked at the nine faces staring at his.

"I'm in big trouble and so are you." Nobody said a word. "If I don't get out alive, none of us will. If anyone makes a move on me, they are dead." Again there was total silence.

Daniel Niestadt, assistant manager of the bank, took a step away from the wall and said, "Sir, no one is going to do anything foolish like that."

"You're damned right they aren't," Eddie snapped back. "You're all going to play this game with the cops my way. All your lives mean nothing to me at this point. Mine comes first. Do you understand?" They all nodded.

Eddie looked them over; Jan, the secretary, maybe twenty-five years old; Maureen, whom they called "Mo," no more than twenty, very small and cute; Mrs. Brazine, about fifty, the motherly type and the calmest of the group.

There were two more older women and another young one, who weren't wearing teller's name tags and who were all very nervous. The manager, Hahn, was a tall, slim man who had played basketball at the University of Tennnessee. Timothy Russ, a customer, had a bad case of the shakes. Niestadt was very calm and helpful and suggested he make a pot of coffee. Eddie told him to go ahead, but not to try anything, like tossing the hot water at him, or it would be his last, fatal move. There were nine in all, mothers, grandmothers, sons, fathers, daughters and one beat-up old bank robber who could die from a heart attack at any moment.

Eddie asked the people their names and they told him. He tried to smoke a cigarette but that made the pain worse. The cigarette shook in his mouth, and when he took it out he noticed that his hands were shaking, too. He hoped the group were not very perceptive.

One of the older women looked as if she were in the same shape he was. All he needed was for her to have a heart attack and they would put a murder charge on him. He decided that he would have to let her go; he would also release the shaker, and maybe a third person. He thought about it for a moment and figured he could trade the three of them for something, perhaps his medicine.

Looking at the vent, he could imagine the police

trying to get through it with a high-powered rifle or pistol. He made one of the girls cover the vent with newspaper and tape. If he heard even one sound through that vent he would unload the magnum into it.

He was still worried about that vulnerable south wall, knowing the Cleveland police might be stupid enough to storm the room and risk killing the hostages. He hoped the FBI would be more clever. They would try to negotiate, divert his attention, or wait him out; then, if all else failed, they would attempt to take him by surprise.

The atmosphere was as quiet and tense as a razor fight. Eddie was sweating, the hostages were sweating, and, outside, he knew the police were sweating.

Finally a ringing phone cut throught the silence. Eddie reached over and picked up the receiver. "What's going on back there?" the caller inquired.

Eddie looked at the receiver, "What the fuck do you think?" he replied.

The caller asked Eddie to give himself up, and he wanted to know Eddie's name.

"You figure it out," Eddie replied.

"What do you want?"

"Out of here."

"If you let those people go, and they walk out of there, I guarantee you won't get hurt."

Eddie laughed. "Damn straight I won't get hurt, asshole, because I'm not coming out. And, if anybody comes in, it's these innocent people who will get hurt, and the blood will be on police hands and the FBI's hands."

Eddie told the unidentified caller about the bomb and the gun and the caller responded, "What kind of bomb is it? How do you set it off?"

Eddie laughed. "You piss on it and wait five seconds."

The caller, who was FBI Agent Bernie Thompson, did not answer Eddie; instead, he asked if he had done any time. Eddie paused and then told him he had, in several places. But he still would not let Thompson know who he was.

The phone conversation was interrupted by a pleading Hahn. "Look, mister, do you realize how many innocent people's lives are involved? We have families, wives and children. Would you like to see us dead and our children orphans?"

Eddie had put the phone down and was sure the FBI agent was still listening.

Eddie held up his hand. "Please, Hahn, no sermons at this point."

Niestadt spoke up. "But we haven't done anything to you. It's not fair."

"One of you pushed an alarm button, and that's why we're all here," Eddie blurted. "One of you worried about this goddam bank's money more than his own life. Now I don't want to hear any more of your bullshit."

"No one pushed the button," Hahn pleaded. "I instructed them not to. That safe is so sensitive a woman's dress brushing against it could have set it off. We've set off the alarm several times by accident."

Eddie turned and hung up. Quickly the phone rang again. It was the same caller, the same line of conversation.

By this time Mrs. Hood was shaking violently. Eddie looked at her and said to Thompson, "Look, I'm letting one of these hostages go. She's an old lady."

"Why don't you let them all go?"

Eddie was angry. "Now listen, asshole; they can all stay here and blow up if they want to. Do you want her or not?"

"Hold on," the agent said. Eddie could hear the scurrying in the hallway outside. He knew by what the agent had said that there must be sharpshooters aiming at the door, waiting for Eddie to make that one mistake, just to poke his head out the door for an instant. Thompson came back on the line, "Don't open the door till I say so." Silence again. "Okay, let her come out." Thompson waited.

Eddie didn't like it. "No tricks. I have my gun on the back of the old gal's head. If I see anything wrong, she dies."

"No tricks," Thompson shot back.

Eddie had Mo and Jane ease one of the chairs away from the door and Mrs. Hood squeezed out through a narrow opening. Everything became quiet again.

Niestadt made another pot of coffee and Eddie continued to check the wall. He was sure sharpshooters were going to crash in. He didn't want to die that way—or any way.

Jane was the next to speak. Eddie had told them his first name but nothing else. "Eddie," she said, pointing at Lillie Bender, "can't you let this girl go too? She has a bad heart."

Eddie looked at her. "You seem healthy to me."

"I'm on medication for a bad murmur."

Eddie picked up the phone and asked for Bernie Thompson. "Thompson, I've got a girl with a bad ticker. I'm going to let her out."

"Eddie, why don't you just let them all go?"

Eddie's anger took over again, "Dammit, Bernie, I don't want a fucking lecture every time I get soft-hearted." He slammed the phone down. Following the same procedure as with Mrs. Hood, he let Lillie Bender squeeze out the door. And now there were seven.

The minutes passed slowly. By now they had been holed up in the tiny room for two full hours. Soon it would be dark outside.

Eddie was watching the vent, trying to think and wishing that he had his heart medicine, when the phone rang again. He answered and heard a woman's voice.

"Are you the bank robber?"

Eddie looked at the phone. Another police trick? "No, I'm Huckleberry Finn." He waited. By now the whole city must know about this situation, he thought to himself.

"I'm serious," she said. "Are you the bank robber?"

Eddie played along, "Yes, I am."

"Well," the caller continued, "be careful. They have the whole place surrounded."

"I appreciate your concern." Eddie was a little bewildered. She went on, "I understand your problem. The little guy doesn't have a chance in this world any more. The rich get it all. I don't blame you for what you're doing. Please don't hurt the hostages, though. They're little people like us." Then she flabbergasted Eddie by adding, "If you get away, here's my address." She gave him her address and said he could come to her place and she would not turn him in.

Eddie thanked her for her concern and her offer and hung up. As the minutes squeezed by Eddie got more calls from women including one who said she would lend him her car to take him out of the state; she even offered to drive. Eddie could not believe what was happening. He had created a fan club.

Finally Thompson got through again. He asked Eddie if that Buick out front belonged to him, and Eddie told him it did.

"Then your name is not Eddie," Thompson said. "We checked out that car. You're an old convicted bank robber who served time in Joliet." At first Eddie thought he was making up the story, but then he realized he had purchased a car that had, by astounding coincidence, belonged to another bank robber.

"We can't let you leave," Thompson said.

"You can and you will," Eddie fired back. "I

have ten sticks of dynamite in this box and I know how to set them off. I'll blow everyone and everything to hell."

"You aren't the type to kill," Thompson replied. "We know your background."

Eddie smiled. Thompson would not believe that Eddie wasn't actually the bank robber who had owned the car before—which would have been great if he'd just had a secret tunnel by which to crawl out and disappear.

He assessed the situation again. He had to let Thompson believe that he was dangerous enough to kill. If they looked up the Ten Most Wanted background on Eddie, they might just go for the bluff. When Thompson called back, he asked again that Eddie let the hostages go; then maybe they could make a deal.

"Monte Hall couldn't even make a deal with me without these hostages for bargaining power," Eddie snapped. "I am Eddie Watkins, not that other asshole, and with these hostages I am truly desperate. So you do what I say."

Bernie kept talking, but Eddie was sure he was in there scribbling notes asking for information on Eddie Watkins. Eddie decided to let another hostage go at this point. He figured that with the time she had spent in the room with him she could advise the FBI on his bomb and gun, and possibly convince them he was not kidding.

He turned and looked at them. "I'm going to let another one of you go. This will be the last one until

281

I get out of here. It'll either be Mrs. Neely or Mrs. Brezine."

Mrs. Brezine looked up. "I'm the mother hen of this group, Eddie. I'm staying until the last one leaves. Let Mrs. Neely go." Eddie admired Mrs. Brezine's spunk. She was actually turning down freedom!

Mrs. Neely didn't offer any objections and they followed the same procedure as before in letting her out the door.

Again the Mexican standoff continued. Eddie had a little time to get to know the hostages better and they all sweated it out. He discovered that Jane was married and had one child; Mo was single but had a boyfriend.

"He's probably outside now," she said. "We're supposed to have a date tonight."

Eddie leaned back. "Afraid you won't make it."

She dropped her head and after a long pause said, "Me too."

TWENTY-SEVEN

Through the long wait, Eddie could hear his heart ticking like a clock. He had a time bomb of his own, a real one, inside him—one that nobody knew about. Niestadt kept making fresh coffee. There was plenty of coffee and canned goods in the cupboard.

Again the phone rang. Thompson said he had checked out Eddie Watkins. He asked Eddie questions about when Watkins had been paroled, how many banks he had hit, who the judge was on his 1967 conviction. He went into the Ten Most Wanted list, his partners who were caught with him—Johnny and Al—and where he had served time.

Eddie told Thompson about Karen, and even about trying to saw his way out of the Cuyahoga County jail. When he was finally convinced that Thompson believed he was Eddie Watkins, he said, "I want out of this place really bad, Thompson. You know now that I have nothing to lose. If you guys get me again you'll put me away forever. So you listen. I want you to get me a van and load in one hundred thousand dollars in twenties. I want a light plane with a pilot waiting at the airport. I will take nothing less. Now do we understand each other?" Eddie stopped.

"That's a big order, Eddie." A pause. "It'll take a while."

"You have two hours." Eddie hung up the phone. He had made the biggest bluff of his life. Would it work? Again there was quiet. The time rolled by. The hostages had to use the bathroom, and the resourceful Mrs. Brezine solved the problem by suggesting they use one of the cooking pots in the corner—the girls first, with the guys turning their backs.

Eddie wiped his forehead. All of a sudden he jumped up and grabbed the phone. They had turned the heat up full blast in the room to make him uncomfortable.

"Bernie, you got the heat turned up in the room, you miserable bastard. You trying to make me and my friends here a little bit uncomfortable? Well, asshole, either the heat goes off or we stop negotiating."

"Eddie, I wasn't under the impression that we *were* negotiating. I'm just trying to fill your demands."

"Bullshit." Eddie was dizzy. "You must think I have the IQ of a piss ant. Have the fucking heat turned off now."

When Eddie slammed down the phone, Dan told him that the power to the stove was off. Eddie knew the FBI was playing its little game. Now they had completely cut the power in the room.

"That miserable son-of-a-bitch," Eddie swore. "Play your silly games, assholes!" he yelled.

Then he looked over at the young man who had been so nervous before. "No more shakes, Tim. What happened?"

"Well, Eddie, as soon as I heard you tell the FBI you were on the Ten Most Wanted list, and all the banks you robbed, I felt a hell of a lot better. I know now that you're a professional, and professionals don't go around killing people just for the fun of it. See, at first I figured you were just some crazy nut. Now that I know you aren't, it makes me feel better."

Everybody in the room laughed and it loosened things up quite a bit. They began to tell Eddie about their lives and he was able to tell about his. All the while he kept listening for noises on the roof and sounds in the vent and around the area of the south wall of the room.

Pains in his chest came and went and came again. He did not reveal to the hostages that he had had a heart attack, and he certainly didn't tell them about the bomb.

Eddie heard a noise on the roof. He listened quietly; maybe he was imagining it. Then he clutched his chest. A sharp pain had come. He looked around the room. Nobody had noticed it.

He motioned toward Dan. "Is there any more coffee?"

"There is, Eddie, but it's cold." The assistant manager shook the pot.

"You people have any sterno in the cupboard?"

Jane jumped to her feet. "I'll look." She searched the cupboard. "Nothing."

"I guess they're going to try and starve us out now." Eddie looked at the door. "That's not going to work." He lit a cigarette. Again the pain.

Once again Eddie heard a noise on the roof—footsteps. They were up to something there. He raised the gun slightly toward the roof and Jane said, "Eddie, please don't point that gun at me. Even if you're good at this, something might happen. You could make a mistake and pull the trigger."

Eddie said, "Don't worry. I don't plan to hurt anyone, but I do expect to get out of this place—and soon."

The FBI was waiting for Eddie to make the first move, and Eddie knew it. It was a war of nerves and wits. Certainly Eddie didn't want to kill any of these hostages. He was thankful for Dan Niestadt's casual talk, which kept everyone's spirits buoyed. If Eddie had to shoot anyone, it would be the Cleveland policemen, whom he didn't like. He didn't like the sheriff or his deputies, considering them to be leeches. But he had respect for the FBI and saw them as a challenge to be beaten. He was, in a strange way, like an athlete in the big game.

Eddie called Bernie Thompson and threatened to blow the place up if Bernie didn't turn the heat down. It was unbearable in the room for everyone.

Finally Bernie turned down the heat, but he wanted something in return—to take a look at the dynamite. Eddie told him that if he stuck his head through the door he would see the dynamite and then, for an instant, a bullet coming at his head, right between the eyes.

Bernie had done his homework thoroughly. He asked Eddie if he'd seen Karen since he came back. Eddie said that he hadn't, and what's more he didn't care to.

"Sure you do," Bernie tried. "You loved her, you know you did. Want to talk to her?"

"What I really want right now is some cigarettes. Pall Malls."

"Sure, Eddie. What about everybody else's brand?"

"We'll share," Eddie said.

"If I get them can I get just a peek at that dynamite?"

"Just the cigarettes. No peek."

Eddie had finished his last cigarette, sharing it with the hostages who passed it around as if it were a marijuana joint.

Eddie didn't want to talk to Karen, except out of curiosity about whether she'd gotten married and was living a normal life.

William Hahn had maintained his employee-employer relationship with the rest of the group and had been very aloof. Eddie tried to loosen him up. He asked Hahn how much money he'd had when the cop came in.

"I don't know," Hahn answered coolly.

Dan Niestadt, who had gotten the group over several rough spots in the past few hours, told Eddie that there had to have been about ninety thousand dollars in the bag. Eddie had made his big score; he could have been out of there and on his way to the sugar-white beaches and warm sunshine of Florida if it weren't for the heart attack.

Tim, the customer, said, "I wish I'd gotten the hell out of here when I could."

Eddie said, "That's what you get for standing around flirting with Jane."

"I wasn't flirting," Tim said. "I was talking when I should've been walking."

Everyone laughed.

"Well, we're all in big trouble now," Eddie said.

Dan said, "No we aren't. You'll get out and we'll help you, because when you get your freedom, we'll get ours. Anyway, the bank's money isn't worth any of us dying for—not even you, Ed."

Hahn scowled at Dan.

Tim said, "That's right, Ed; now we're on your side, I guess."

Eddie said, "Look, if we leave in a van, the minute I'm sure I will not be tricked I'll let all of you go. I really, honestly don't want to harm any of you, and I don't want to see any of you get hurt."

By now, Bernie Thompson had the cigarettes and wanted to slide them through a crack in the door. Eddie wasn't buying that one; he made Bernie take them out of the packages and send them in one at time under the door to Jane.

Jane said, "Darn you, Ed, I had quit smoking and now I'm smoking again like a chimney."

Eddie stretched to tap part of the upper wall with his gun butt and a sharp pain bent him over double. He nearly blacked out. Sweat began to bead his forehead.

Jane said, "What's the matter, Ed?"

He slid down the wall and looked at all of them. He could barely maintain consciousness.

Eddie said weakly, "It's my heart. I would have been out of this bank, and none of you would be here, except that I had a heart attack at the door."

Mo spoke up. "What can we do?"

"Nothing," Eddie said. "I'll be all right."

"You don't look all right," Dan said. "You're turning gray."

"I just need a little rest."

It was then that the phone rang. Eddie motioned for someone to hand him the phone. It was Bernie.

"Eddie, we have your van and the money. How are we going to work this out?"

"I'll call back and let you know," Eddie said.

They had filled his request, but now he couldn't leave. He couldn't stand up, let alone walk out.

Very soon there was another call. Someone had gotten through from outside again. The caller said, "The van they are giving you has no oil. They drained the oil out of the crank case and painted a luminous sign on top so they can track you with a helicopter."

Eddie thanked the caller and then hung up. When Bernie called back, Eddie yelled at him for draining the oil and told him that the luminous sign wouldn't help either. There was silence. Bernie was amazed and dumbfounded. Eddie said he'd inspect the van and would have his gun cocked and pointed at the heart of one of the hostages while he did so. And if anybody so much as moved toward him he'd kill at least one person, maybe more, before the police got him.

Eddie knew there would be a beeper in the bag of money in the van, but he had his own plan. He would drive the van to his second car, which was stashed, leave the money in it, and leave the car and the money behind. He would take a female hostage with him, and he felt sure that under the cover of darkness he could escape. But the pain in his chest was intense, and he knew he wouldn't make it under any circumstances if he didn't have the strength to walk.

Bernie called back again and told Eddie that he had sent trained dogs past the door to sniff for explosives and the dogs hadn't smelled a thing.

Eddie answered back, "Well, come on in, then, Bernie. You can blow up with the rest of us."

Eddie knew that the FBI was stalling for time now. He also knew that the noses of the dogs weren't infallible and that the FBI wouldn't bet all of their chips on those dogs.

The heat in the room was still intense, and Eddie began hallucinating—drifting in and out, on an iceberg one moment and in hell the next. Mrs. Brezine brought him a cold towel and wiped off his forehead.

The phone rang again and this time Bernie had Judge Thomas on the line. "The old Welshman's in trouble again, eh, Ed?" the judge said.

"Fraid so, Judge."

"Well, Ed, its not all that bad—not if you let them go and come out."

"Judge, you and I have always gotten along fine, but I'm through with jails. I'm making my last stand here. All the FBI can do is kill me, and that's not as bad as prison."

"Eddie, you have a lot of innocent people in there with you. Do you want them killed?"

"Judge, you know me—I don't want to hurt anybody, but if I don't get out of here, all seven of us will die."

The judge said, "Ed, you wrote me from Atlanta about how happy you were and that you didn't think you'd be in trouble again. I believed you, Ed."

"I know, Judge, and I really believed it, too. But here I am in trouble again and looking for a way out. I have these hostages. They are very nice people, and I mean that. If I can walk out of here and get into my own car, one that I'm sure isn't rigged, I'll let them all go and then the FBI can declare open season on me, because they'll never find me again."

"Ed, I still have the paintings you sent me from Atlanta. You have become quite an artist. They're hanging in my office. You could've gone straight."

"I know . . . but for some reason I didn't. I'm in here and I'm planning to walk out. Now, tell the FBI that I'm serious, and they should get everything ready as fast as possible. And, Judge, thanks for everything. Whatever happens, I want you to know that I appreciate how you tried to help me."

The pain in his chest had subsided but he was still weak. The heat was back on in the room. Eddie called again and asked for Judge Thomas.

"Judge," he said, "I'm an old timer and I've been beaten and thrown in the hole with nothing to eat—you know that. But Bernie has the heat in this room turned up to boiling. You know and I know the heat isn't going to kill me, but it's making these other people very uncomfortable, and I don't want them to suffer, Judge. Tell that slimepit to cut off the goddamned heat."

The judge called back several times and Eddie finally told him about his heart attack. "I've served all the time I'm going to serve in prison. I don't have much time left on this earth anyway, so these final years are going to count. I'm near the end of the line, Judge, and I don't have a damn thing to lose."

The judge said he would get Eddie's medicine from the second car. Eddie had exposed part of his getaway plan by telling the judge about the other car, but he needed that medicine. The judge told Eddie that Mrs. Brezine's husband was outside and had told him she had a serious illness. She would be needing her medicine too.

When Eddie put the phone down he said to Mrs. Brezine, "You didn't tell me you were ill."

She said, "I didn't think it would matter to you."

"Well, you were wrong. You'll be leaving us through the door just as soon as the judge get back with my medicine."

Mrs. Brezine said she would refuse to leave until everybody, including Eddie, was safe. He argued with her, but when the judge came back with the medicine she still didn't want to go.

When she finally agreed, she hugged everyone individually and gave Eddie's hand a squeeze. As she inched out the door she had tears in her eyes, as if she believed she would never see any of them again.

Bernie had called and said there was a loose wire hanging from the trunk of Eddie's car and he wondered if the car was booby-trapped.

"Bernie, tell the judge that if it was a certain FBI agent named Bernie, or a fat Cleveland cop, I had sent to that car, I would wish it *was* booby-trapped. But since it's the judge, you can tell him that not only *isn't* it booby-trapped, but I'm glad it isn't."

"Are you sure, Ed?"

"Why don't you have your dogs check my car? I'm sure you trust them. Of course they blew it back here, didn't they?"

Bernie said, almost to himself, "Oh yeah, the dogs." Some FBI agent, Eddie thought. He had to suggest the dogs to him. Eddie felt as if he were doing Bernie's job for him, and he had enough problems without that burden.

The judge had brought the medicine back and they had slid it through the door. Eddie took eight nitros one after another. He worried that the police had poisoned the medicine, but he trusted Judge Thomas, the most upright and honest judge he had ever known. Eddie remembered other judges he had met, crooked ones around Cleveland. Once Eddie had carried a payoff from a hood named Smiley Lanero to a certain judge who was to sentence Eddie to the Ohio state pen. The judge had sat there downgrading Eddie, telling him what a lowlife he was, but that judge was as crooked as Eddie. Judge Thomas wasn't like that, though. He didn't hand out sentences quickly, and though he lectured about the evils of crime, Eddie had always felt that the judge was above doing anything wrong. He trusted Judge Thomas more than any other man he had ever met. Nonetheless, he wasn't taking any chances with the medicine.

As Eddie was checking the walls—knowing the FBI might speed up their work now that they knew he was in a weakened condition—the plunger slipped through his fingers and dropped to the floor. Everyone in the room jumped to his or her feet.

Dan screamed, "My God."

Tim said, "Please put that thing in your pocket, so there won't be an accident if you black out or something."

Eddie did as he asked.

Dan said, "Ed, we're on your side now. We honestly hope you get away, and we believe you when you say that once you're free you won't harm us."

"Be honest," Eddie said. "No one here is on my side."

Jane said, "I am." The others all said that they were too.

Mo handed him a glass of water for the pills. He told her he wasn't going to take them because he was afraid they were poisoned.

"Would the police do that?" she asked.

"They'll kill me quick if they ever get a clear shot," Eddie said.

The hours were stretching out into late night now. The next try by the FBI was to have Karen call.

"I wanted to talk with you, Ed," she said.

"Why the sudden interest?"

"Because I still love you."

"You love me, Karen? Well, if that's true, you are without a doubt the most stupid, half-baked nut I have ever known. Did you love me all those years I was in the Atlanta pen?"

"Yes."

"How come you didn't write?"

"Well, I wasn't sure what part of the prison you were in, Eddie."

Eddie shook his head. "You idiot, you wrote me several times during the first three months and I answered all your letters. Did you forget about that? Anyway, Karen, you're a pathological liar."

"I don't know what that is."

"Never mind."

"Eddie, please let those people go. Please do it for me."

"This is not 1965, fluffhead. The *please* won't get it. Tell the feds their chances are decreasing, with you on the phone pitching for them." He hung up in disgust. Karen had tried to con him out of his money and hadn't given a damn if he rotted in Atlanta Federal—after he had made sure she didn't serve a day. He remembered his evidentiary hearing when he had a chance for a new trial or at least an early parole, and her testimony had all but ruined that. She had blown him away at that hearing and now he hated her.

The pain, Karen, and the FBI agents had him angry now. He would have to stall all night and hope that by morning he would be mobile enough to get away. A daylight escape would be risky, but he knew he had to wait. He felt, at that moment, that he was surely going to die in that room.

As time ticked on, he thought about what would happen if he surrendered. He figured he'd never get out of jail again. Vividly he could see the bleak, dreary prison walls, the marches to the chow halls, the loss of any semblance of dignity, the verbal abuse that one didn't dare respond to, the hole they would shove you into if you did respond, with perhaps a nightstick on the head for good measure; the bread and water, no showers in the hole, sitting there sweating and smelling. If there were blowflies in the hole with you, you were a target, for they would certainly mistake your odor for something that was dead. Eddie would rather be dead than go through that again, and he tried to think of a way out.

As the tension held and the night wore on, he dozed and dreamed and hurt. And throughout the night Bernie Thompson kept digging up old friends—even an old cellmate, Bill Rooney, who, by the sound of his voice, was certainly not rooting for Eddie. They put the wife of a deceased cousin of Eddie's on the line, and even Johnny, his old compadre from the window-washing business. Eddie refused to talk to Johnny, because he had found out that it was Johnny who had talked to the FBI about Eddie after being caught for the bank robberies.

The FBI kept the heat on in the small room and it was roasting. The stove was off and the hostages couldn't have coffee. Eddie leveled with the hostages. "The only reason they don't rush this place and kill you, too, is public opinion," he told them. "They'd look bad if somebody messed up and one of you died. Otherwise they probably wouldn't be too concerned."

Tim said, "Eddie, I'm beginning to think you're right."

"As the night goes on," Eddie told him, "you'll see how right I am. We're almost out of cigarettes. They'll stall bringing us more. They'll make us wait for everything. I'll have to start acting nuts and begin again with the threats before they'll do anything to make you comfortable."

Bernie tried again; he was back on the phone now. "Eddie, don't let Judge Thomas down. He likes you and will push for rehabilitation programs for you."

"Come on, Bernie, enough. I'm a three-time loser, wanted for this job, for taking hostages and for half a dozen other charges here, plus five banks in California. If I go away it's forever. So forget it."

The FBI was stalling, but it was helping Eddie. The chest pains wouldn't have permitted him to walk out even if they all just went home and left him the key to the bank and a private helicopter in which to escape.

The pain kept coming in waves and his whole body ached. Mo told him his eyes looked hollow, suggested he take some medicine. Eddie was touched that she really seemed to care about his life.

The hostages were trying to sleep. Eddie guessed they would all catch a few winks stretched out on the hard floor. He looked at them, wondering if they knew that convicts did it all the time in prison. Sometimes they went for weeks without ever crawling onto the stingy mattresses on the iron bunks. He wished he were in the hostages' position instead of his own. He knew that they were going to get out of this alive and he doubted that he would. Even if by some miracle he did, he would be back behind those dirty walls. He put his head down. He could not bear to think of that.

Jane was curled up across the two chairs blocking the door. It looked as if she had been crying. Eddie was sorry for what he had done to her, to all of them. He knew they must have believed that he was going to kill them or make some mistake and push the plunger, and that would have been all for them.

Eddie tried to get up to go over and talk to her, but at first he could not. By struggling, though, he managed to pull himself to his feet and walk over. He bent down and whispered in Jane's ear, "Please, don't worry."

She looked up at him.

"I'm not going to kill you."

"Thank you," she said, and a look of relief flooded her face.

He wobbled back and slumped against the wall, then looked around again at the people he was holding hostage. They had been in the room now for over ten hours. They had been strangers then; now they were mostly friends for whom he felt extreme compassion. But he could not release them without bringing about his own capture or death.

There was no way he could ever kill any of them; he knew that. People who are companions facing together the possibility of death, forget their petty problems and see deeply inside one another. This bizarre intimacy made Eddie Watkins feel attached emotionally to each and every one of them—even William Hahn, who was so cold and aloof. Eddie had found out that he had recently been ill; in fact he had only been discharged from a hospital the previous day. He wasn't fully recovered and had come to the bank the previous day only to attend to a few urgent tasks.

Outside the door were nearly two hundred lawmen who believed that they were dealing with a deadly, crazed bank robber who might at any moment try to blow everybody to pieces. They did not know they were actually dealing with a tired, sickly old papier-mache tiger who would almost sell out right then for a guarantee that someone could make his pain go away.

It was very strange: the hostages were safe from Eddie. Their only chance of death would come from the police if they rushed in shooting, or tried to pick off Eddie and accidentally hit one of the others. Eddie knew that his chances were not very good, but at that moment death seemed better than prison, and he would hold out until they had to carry him out of there.

At about one in the morning the phone rang. It was Bernie asking Eddie if he were hungry. Eddie said he was not, but that he figured the others were.

"Anybody hungry? The FBI is treating—hamburgers and Cokes, anyone?"

"Why don't you just release them and we'll all have a big meal together?" Bernie said.

"I'm not that hungry, Bernie. Why don't you try me say in ten years?"

Bernie warned him, "You're not walking out of there with those hostages, Ed—not ever. You know it isn't done that way in the FBI training manual."

"If I don't come out alive, Bernie, I'll come out dead, and so will a lot of innocent people. It's not in the manual for you to let any of these people die."

While he waited for the hamburgers, Eddie took some .357 shells out of his pocket where he could get to them fast. He'd fire five shots through the door if they rushed him, then reload while he still had one bullet in the chamber. He thought that he could get off ten or eleven shots before they killed him.

When they came to bring the hamburgers, Eddie had to maintain a front. He held a cocked pistol to Mo's head—but his thumb was between the hammer and the firing pin, in case they were to shoot him—so that he wouldn't accidently shoot Mo. It hurt Eddie to have to hold the gun to her head, and he knew she was terrified.

Everybody took a hamburger but Eddie. Jane said, "Aren't you going to have one, Ed?"

"Nope. They might be doped with pills or something."

"How could they do that, Ed? They don't know which one you'd get."

"They might all be doped," Eddie said. "I'll just wait to see if all of you fall asleep." But they weren't doped, and after a while Eddie ate one of the hamburgers. It was one of the crummiest-tasting hamburgers he had ever eaten. The FBI had gone out of their way to get crummy food for them. The hamburger didn't help his physical condition, either. His left arm became numb all the way to the fingertips. By now he was getting short of breath, and just tapping the walls exhausted him.

He had a thought: If the pain didn't ease up soon, he might have to take himself out of this bind with a bullet.

TWENTY EIGHT

Eddie was deeply into self pity, but Dan Niestadt brought him out of it. Dan came over and talked to him. "Ed, did you serve a long sentence before?"

"Eight years," Eddie said. "Actually eight and a half."

"That's a long time."

"And that's not the half of it, Dan. In all, I've spent nearly thirty years of my life behind bars. That's why I can't go back. You wouldn't believe what it's like. One time I served twelve and a half years at the Ohio pen without one single visit. Nobody came to see me and I didn't get one single letter in all that time. I've served weeks at a time in the hole on bread and water. And in the old days it was common for guards to beat inmates."

Dan said, "What about your parents—they never came to see you?"

"I was like an orphan, because neither of them wanted me. I'm not trying to make you feel sorry for me, but I've been sitting here thinking about the old days, and maybe it means there aren't going to be any more days for me."

Bernie called again. He asked Eddie if he was getting tired and he wanted to know how the sandwiches were.

Eddie said, "Bernie, those were the cheapest sandwiches I ever ate. I know you FBI types are on a government expense account. You could have done a lot better."

Bernie said, "Are you ready to leave, Ed? We have a van ready."

"You stalled too long, Bernie. I'm waiting for daylight now so I can see your sharpshooters." Eddie was stalling to have time to rejuvenate his body.

Tim spoke up. "Let me talk with him, Ed."

Tim got the phone and started cussing Bernie out. He gave it to Bernie much harder than Eddie had done. He told Bernie that everyone was damn tired of sweating in there while he stalled. "We trust Ed," Tim said. "Now pull all your men back and we'll walk out of here surrounding him. We'll all get in the van, and when he gets clear of here he'll let us all go and you can chase him to hell and back. I'm betting on Ed—but dammit, get on with it."

Eddie grabbed the phone. "You heard him, Bernie. They all feel that way. They want to go with me."

Bernie said, "I don't believe that crap. You probably made him say that."

Eddie held out the phone and circled the room, asking each hostage if he or she wanted to go with him. When he got to Jane she asked to speak with Bernie.

"We want to leave here with Eddie," she said. "Once he's sure he's gotten away, we know he'll let us go. We trust him more than we trust you. We all want out. Now help us."

Eddie took the phone. "Bernie, they know you'll use them to get to me. You've shown that by being so unconcerned about their comfort. You've kept the heat on in here; you don't give a damn about them and they know it. You're the one who's holding things up. So how about it? The van, the money, and everybody clear out."

Bernie said he couldn't do that, and also he didn't believe that Eddie would kill anybody. Eddie said he was right about that—their blood would be on Bernie's hands.

"My hands are clean," Bernie said.

Eddie answered, "Your and Pontius Pilate's, Bernie."

Bernie didn't answer.

Eddie said, "Your concern is the motherfucking image of the big, tough, FBI. That's all you really care about."

Mo interrupted Eddie and told him that Bernie needed to send their purses in, because Jane was starting her period and needed tampons.

Eddie told Bernie, but Bernie didn't deliver. Eddie wondered if Bernie was getting some sadistic satisfaction out of all this.

Eddie explained to the group how they would walk out of there at eight in the morning. They would surround him. He looked at Mo and said, "Mo, my gun will be at your head, but dammit, my finger will be between the hammer and the firing pin. The gun can't go off. Even if one of their marksmen picks me off, I promise you—I swear—you will not get shot by me."

The plan was that Tim would drive the van and Mo would go along. Two hostages would be enough. On the way to the airport Eddie would commandeer another vehicle, in case the first had been tampered with. When he got to the private plane only one hostage would go along—Tim. And as soon as the plane landed Eddie would release him.

Eddie knew that the moment he left the room sharpshooters would be aiming at his head. He wanted to be certain that when and if they shot at him, he made no mistakes that would get Mo or any of the others killed. He decided that he would have the hammer of his gun pulled back on an empty chamber. If he had to use the gun against the police he could get the other five bullets out quickly.

The sun was coming up when Bernie made his next call. Eddie asked for some breakfast for everyone. When he hung up a wave of chest pains hit him again. He had been feeling good enough to try his getaway, and now the pain was back. He was desperate enough to go for one of the codeine pills.

Dan looked at Eddie, alarmed. "Ed, you look awful. Is there anything we can do?"

"Afraid not, Dan. The old ticker is acting up

306

again. I'm not sure I'll last till breakfast."

"Sure you will, Ed. You'll get out of here, too. We'll help. We won't let you down."

Eddie figured that Dan was just comforting a sick old man, but he was grateful for those words. At that point Eddie decided that the easiest thing to do was to turn the gun on himself and end it all. He aimed the gun at his head.

Dan was wide eyed in terror. "Don't do it."

Jane said, "Please don't, Eddie."

"I have nothing to lose," Eddie said.

"Yes you do," Jane said. "Life. Life is prescious. Don't do it. The life of a very sweet man would be taken. Please don't. You'll make it out of here."

Eddie was dumbfounded. One pull of the trigger would bring an end to this whole mess for them, and they were begging him not to do it.

Eddie could feel a stream of tears coming down his cheeks. He couldn't hold them back. He wished right then that he had met these people under different circumstances. He had not really known their world; he had always believed that it was a world of squares, people with big dreams who were too meek to take what they wanted. Now his world looked like the square one. God, how he wished he had lived in their world.

By now William Hahn was very sick and getting feverish. Mo and Jane put water-soaked towels on his head. There was medicine in Hahn's desk and Eddie called Bernie and asked for the medicine. Bernie refused. He said if Hahn were sent out they would take him to a hospital.

"They won't bring the medicine," Eddie said in disbelief. "They want you to go to the hospital."

"No, I'll stay," Hahn said.

At that instant Eddie saw what was going on, and what he had been missing all of his life: people caring for other people. The group had been forced into a situation where they felt a responsibility for each other's lives. Eddie knew right then that it was the way the world was supposed to be.

The anger of he hostages was not directed at Eddie at all, but at the FBI. The hostages were in a situation where they felt a responsibility to one another, and to Eddie, even though he had caused them all the trouble. There was something very noble and holy in all of that; it seemed to blot out the memories of prisons and rejections and frustrations, and come floating up to a place in the highest part of his brain, some secret place that was like a sanctuary in his mind. He thought that maybe he was experiencing God.

Whatever it was, Hahn was still there and he was getting worse. Eddie told him he would have to leave, and called Bernie to come get him.

And then, when the door opened just a crack, Eddie said, quietly and softly, "Open it all the way and walk out of here. All of you."

They looked at him in disbelief. "I mean it. All of you move out, now."

Mo turned and hugged him. "Eddie," she said, "please don't kill yourself. We'll walk out of here with you if you'll come."

Eddie was leaning weakly against the wall. "No. I'm not coming. Send Bernie in here alone."

"I'm going to stand by the door," Mo said, "and make sure he's alone."

The ordeal had lasted more than twenty hours, and now it was over.

When Bernie came back he was alone. Eddie had the hammer of his .357 cocked, but Bernie ignored the gun. "Ed, we have an ambulance waiting."

Eddie eased the gun down and Bernie helped him rise. A few minutes later Judge Thomas came in. The two of them walked Eddie outside into the sunshine.

The hostages were outside and they led the applause when Eddie came out. When the hostages cheered Eddie, the crowd began to cheer him too. Throngs of people began to cheer as if he were Julius Caesar come home to Rome.

Tears rolled down Eddie's face as they led him toward the ambulance.

Bernie said, "I almost forgot, Ed. The bomb—you're still wearing the bomb. Can we take it off without any danger?"

Eddie smiled. "If Domino Sugar explodes we'll all go to hell. It's nothing but sugar rolled up in newspaper."

"Are you sure, Ed?"

Eddie looked in the direction of the hostages and he looked at the crowd and he thought about everything that had happened inside the room. He said, "Bernie, I'm not sure of anything any more."

TWENTY NINE

Eddie's next weeks were spent in a hospital where he was treated for the heart attack suffered in the bank. He stayed in the intensive-care unit under twenty-four-hour guard. During this time he looked back on the few months of freedom he had enjoyed.

His hopes for a bright new future were smashed and a trial and many charges, from bank robbery up, were facing him. He didn't want to go back to the big house.

After being released from the medical facility Eddie's trial was brief and he was once again sentenced to the Federal Penitentiary in Atlanta. The drive through the gates was familiar. The big gray house was still sitting beckoning. Eddie glanced out the rear window of the marshals' car at the streets of Atlanta. They were going to be only a memory, a quick glimpse. He was ushered out of the car and into the waiting area. He looked around. Nothing had changed.

A con walked by and noticed the old bank robber. "Hey Eddie, welcome back."

Eddie looked at him. "Thanks." The old con waved.

Eddie was printed, mugged and given a bundle of clothing. He was ushered into the cell area and once again he could hear the heavy metal crunch as the doors slid closed.

For the next couple of years Eddie worked hard on his paintings. He was becoming quite an artist, with many of his works being used in prison art shows. Also he received letters from friends and aquaintances asking him to paint one for them. But he remained a loner, rarely getting involved in prison politics or anything that would cause any more time to be added to the 125-plus years he now had to serve.

His medication was seemingly helping his bad heart and he was scheduled for his every-three-months checkup soon. It was five years since the Society National Bank and the last big attack he had had. But his heart couldn't wait for the checkup. One night, just after mess, Eddie felt the pains hitting him. He notified authorities and was rushed immediately to the medical ward and then out the gates and into Baptist Hospital in Atlanta. Doctors saved his life again but this time it was decided that the only way to keep him alive was a triple-bypass operation.

An armed guard sat at the door of his room. They were not going to give him a chance to get away this time. "You think that will do the trick, doc?" he asked.

"Yes, Eddie. That old heart of yours has about had it and repair is the only way you can hope to survive."

"When are we going to do it?"

The physician headed for the door. "I've set you up for in the morning. Make sure you get some sleep tonight and stay calm."

"Well, I guess a trip to underground Atlanta is out, then," Eddie said to the guard. "You'll have to find yourself another date." They both laughed.

The doctor opened the door. "Hey doc," Eddie called after him, "make sure you cut straight. You know how women are—they don't like sloppy work."

The next morning Eddie underwent surgery at Baptist Hospital. After eight hours in the operating room the operation was announced as being successful.

Eddie lay in the intensive-care unit for a number of days, recovering quickly. Then, after another four weeks of convalescence, he was returned to the medical facility behind the bars at the Atlanta Federal Pen. Three weeks later he was back to work as a clerk in the records department of the prison. But Eddie was getting itchy and he would spend as much time outside the office as he could. He was never one who really enjoyed record keeping and the only counting he liked was assessing the loot from one of his jobs. He needed to get outside and the warden was his only way of making the move.

Eddie sat at his desk watching the clock, waiting for the warden to arrive at the office. He had told the lieutenant that he needed to see Warden Hanberry as soon as he came in. It felt like hours before the guard approached Eddie and told him the warden could see him.

As Eddie walked into the office Hanberry was reading reports on his desk. The walls were dreary and the office reminded one of a seedy operation that was about to go out of business. Eddie walked up to the desk. The warden, a graying man in his fifties, never raised his head. Eddie stood erect in front of his desk.

"Sit down, Watkins." The warden kept his head lowered. Eddie pulled up the chair and sat at attention, his hands in his lap. He wanted everything to be right. The warden finished up the paperwork and pushed the big pile aside.

The warden looked him straight in the eyes. "Okay, Eddie, what's so important?"

Eddie fumbled with his hat. "I have a special request to make, sir."

"Well, what is it?"

"I would like to be transferred from the records department to the landscaping crew."

The warden got up from his desk and walked over to the window. Eddie watched him closely.

The warden kept peering out of the window. "The landscaping crew?" He slowly turned and walked toward his desk. His face was serious. "What's the matter, Watkins, don't you like being one of my clerks?"

Eddie had to think fast. Hanberry didn't have the greatest sense of humor and was not known to be considerate of inmates who disagreed with his decisions.

"Yes sir, I do. But, well you know, Warden, I've been here almost six years this time and . . . well . . ." Eddie was noticeably lost for words and the warden turned and looked at him. Eddie looked down. "Well, I don't know how many years I have left. Hell, I'm past sixty, and with this heart . . . I thought that maybe if I got a little more fresh air and stuff it would help the old ticker and maybe keep me around a few more years."

The warden sat back behind his desk and turned away from Eddie in his swivel chair. The room was quiet. "You know, I'm very, very disappointed in you, Watkins." The warden kept facing the window. "I thought you had learned your lesson. You have a good head on your shoulders and a natural gift as an artist. Why you're back here just makes my blood boil."

Eddie lowered his head and looked at the floor, seemingly abashed.

"Why, man, why?" The warden got up from his desk again. "You've had more chances than most men, and yet you continue to live your life in a destructive manner. I read your mental evaluation and it shows that you have an I.Q. of 145. Why in God's name can't you use your intelligence for something more worthwhile than robbing banks? You've

315

thrown away three-quarters of your life, man. Don't throw away any more." The warden turned and looked out the window. Eddie knew he was waiting for an answer. The warden was a persuasive speaker and Eddie always felt he had been fair to him. He noticed the tenseness of the warden's back.

"Warden, I'll level with you." Hanberry glanced over his shoulder at Eddie and then looked back out the window. "When I was a young punk I figured the only way I'd get my hands on the good things in life was by taking them. So I started taking them and I got those good things. When folks used to ask me why I robbed banks I would always tell them because that's where the money is. But when I got older. . . ." Eddie stopped.

The warden turned. "Yes?"

"Well, it's hard to explain. Tell me, do you think you're the best warden in the prison system, in the world? Are you the best warden who ever lived?"

Hanberry turned and leaned on the desk. "No, Eddie, I don't think so. I think I'm fairminded, I'm dedicated, and I would say that I'm a good administrator. . . but I would not go so far as to say that I am the best warden in the prison systems of the world." The warden looked hard at Eddie. "What does that have to do with your situation, anyway?"

Eddie looked up. "Well, Warden, I'm the best bank robber in the world. It's the one trade I really know and it's made me some big money and a big reputation. Warden, I'm the best at what I do, and when you're the best, it's something you have to do.

You have to keep proving to yourself and to others that you cannot be topped." Eddie stopped. The warden turned and looked at him almost sorrowfully. "Does that make sense to you, Warden?"

"I suppose it does, in a way." The warden turned again and walked around the office. He stopped and tapped his pen in the palm of his hand. "You realize that you'll never get out of here. You're listed as an incorrigible . . . a career criminal. In this system that means you're not fit for the outside world."

Eddie said, "Yes, sir, I guess I am incorrigible."

"And your painting—you haven't asked for paints or canvas for quite a while now. You haven't signed up for the art classes. But your painting, Eddie, can definitely ease the years ahead."

Eddie looked around the office, "I see you took down all my paintings."

"Yes, that's right. When you started doing business again I sold off or gave away your pictures. You conned me, Eddie. I went to bat for you many times while you were here the last time, I even helped you with the parole board. And what did I get back? Tell me." He looked at Eddie and the expression on his face suggested that Eddie shouldn't try to answer.

Hanberry continued, "I thought we were friends, I thought you were playing it straight with me. And there's your health: I don't know any man who has survived the heart attacks you've had—even one while robbing a bank. Then you survived openheart surgery too. It's a miracle you're alive, and why, Eddie? It sure as hell isn't so you can go out and rob more banks. I don't know, Eddie . . . I don't believe you any more. My faith in you is gone."

Eddie murmured, "You're right, Warden, and I don't blame you for feeling the way you do."

The office became very quiet as Hanberry paced around the floor, occasionally looking out the window. Suddenly he stopped, walked back to his desk and looked straight at Eddie. "I might be stupid, and I probably am, but I'm going to give you one more chance, Eddie. You've been a model prisoner since you came back; I've no beefs about that. Because you have only a half-working ticker I made you one of my clerks. You helped me straighten out my files, and you're a good office manager. I really need you where you are, but I'll give you that transfer to landscaping if you'll do something for me." Hanberry paused. "You must start painting again." He looked at Eddie. "Is it a deal?"

Eddie smiled inwardly; he had pulled it off. He looked at the warden and nodded quickly.

"Okay, then we have an understanding. I'm not saying I'm going to start another Eddie's wall—" Hanberry looked around the office. "I'm not asking you to paint a picture for me. But dammit, I want you to use your talents, your gift, and paint. It can make you happy and in the long run bring happiness to many others as well as you."

Hanberry pulled a pad from his desk drawer and began to write. "I'll put through the transfer papers right away. Now I'm not going to let you do any of the heavy landscaping work, because of your heart. How about driving? Do you think you can handle a truck?" The warden looked up.

"Yes, sir."

"Okay then, you'll be a driver. You know, you'll deliver bushes for planting, and tools, sod and stuff like that. I'm planning to ring the walk area with some pretty gardens and flowering bushes. It's sort of a beautification program, and maybe you can bring some of your creativity in the form of flowers." Hanberry finished writing.

"I appreciate the transfer, sir." Eddie extended his hand and Hanberry took it.

"We'll shake on it, Eddie. You help me with the planting, get yourself back into painting, and time will go faster for you and you'll feel twice the man you were."

Eddie turned and walked out of the warden's office. He set his hat neatly on his head and grinned. You could see the twinkle in his old eyes as he walked briskly out the door.

THIRTY

There was almost a week of nervous anticipation for Eddie as he continued his duties as clerk in the warden's office, but finally the word came down. Eddie was standing at the filing cabinet when the lieutenant walked up.

"Eddie?"

Eddie turned and placed a folder on his desk. "Yes, sir."

The guard handed him a piece of paper. "Your transfer came down from the warden, so, in the morning, you report to Sergeant Green in the landscape office. He'll fill you in on the rest." The lieutenant turned and headed for the door.

"Hey, Lieutenant!" He turned. "Thanks," Eddie said. The guard waved and left.

"This is the life," Eddie said to himself as he drove the orange federal truck around the prison.

The end of the cold weather had begun and Atlanta temperatures were getting springlike. Eddie pulled up his truck beside a lonely young tree in the far north corner of the yard. Slowly he climbed out from behind the wheel, grabbed a shovel from the back of the truck and began digging the young tree out of the ground—gently, making sure he did not hurt the roots. Finally the tree leaned over and he pulled it free. Placing it on the ground, he brought a bush from the truck, placed it in the cavity and covered its roots. He took a watering can off the truck and gave it some water. Then he lifted the tree, placed it on the back of the truck, drove to another area of the yard and began the same procedure. He dug a deep hole, moistened it with water, removed the tree from the truck and planted it. As he turned to get back into the truck he waved to the guard, who returned the gesture.

For the next two months Eddie worked hard on the landscaping crew. The warden's dream of beautification was becoming a reality and the prison yard was taking on a parklike look. It was sad that such a work of art should be spoiled by the old gray-walled building in the background.

Spring had finally set in and the weather had began to warm up. By now Eddie was a veteran behind the wheel of the two-ton truck. On April 17, 1980, he began his chores in the routine way. He went over to the northern part of the yard and began working on his bush, then went over to the tree. Today, however, Eddie was taking a closer look at the activity going on around the front gate. Delivery trucks came and went, normal for the early part of the week as food, supplies and other necessary items were brought to the federal pen.

Eddie jumped into his truck and headed for the gate. A smile adorned his wrinkled face as the gate opened and a laundry truck headed in. Eddie just kept driving. He almost couldn't believe it; he was out of the yard and onto the streets of Atlanta. Looking carefully in his rear-view mirror he saw that nothing was happening. He listened for the sirens—again nothing.

"Fuck," he said to himself, "this went better than I expected. At least I didn't have to knock the gates out."

He wheeled the truck down Boulevard and, about a mile from the prison, quickly made a right turn and pulled the truck over a block from the main street. He pulled a hat from his pocket and carefully examined the painting on the peak. "The warden said I should paint and this is one of the best jobs I've done in a long time." He put on the hat and looked in the truck mirror.

He removed the prison shirt, revealing a colorful sweatshirt; the removal of his prison pants turned Fast Eddie into Atlanta's newest member of the jogging set. Throwing the clothes on the floor, he left the truck. Carefully looking around, he saw that everything was quiet. He walked to the corner and looked toward the prison; he could hardly see the old stacks. There were still no sirens, either.

About then a group of joggers came past and nodded to Eddie. He returned the gesture and fell in behind them. Finally reaching a service station about three miles from the prison, he walked toward the phone booth. He dialed information, got the number of a cab company and called a cab to his location. Then he walked over to the vending machine and got a cold drink.

The station manager walked over to chat. "Beautiful day today."

Eddie looked up at the sky. "Sure is. Hope the weather stays this way." He sipped his coke.

"You know something," the manager said, "I'm going to try that one day."

Eddie looked at him strangely. "Shit, what is this son-of-a-bitch, a mind reader?" Eddie was ready to crack him with the bottle. "What do you mean?" He waited tensely for the answer.

"That jogging."

A smile came to Eddie's face.

"Yeah, it sure is good for ya." Eddie put down the bottle.

"That's what I hear tell." The manager walked toward the office.

Eddie reached in his pocket for another coin. "Shit, I need a plane out of here." He dialed information and got hold of an airline. After a short conversation he hung up and sat down at the curb. He pulled out a pencil and wrote down the flight number on a piece of paper. "Los Angeles, here I come."

The wait for the cab was about ten minutes and during that time Eddie kept a close watch on the Boulevard. He was waiting for the police cars to come screaming around the corner, sirens wailing. Nothing. Eddie jumped into the cab and looked out

323

the back window as he pulled away.

"I need to go downtown for a minute." The driver nodded. "Anyplace in particular?"

"Yeah, I need to pick me up a new suit and a few other things." Eddie lit a cigarette as the cab wove its way through the early-afternoon traffic.

Eddie looked at his watch; it was one-thirty, his flight was scheduled for three-twelve. He reached into the inner lining of his jogging pants, pulled out a small roll of bills, flipped through it and then shoved the roll into his sock. Sitting back he happily breathed the spring air. He turned quickly when two young blondes crossed in front of the cab.

"You see that?"

The cabbie smiled. "All day long." He turned the corner.

"Man, they really look good." Eddie leaned back.

"Hell, girls like that are all over. Where have *you* been? Shit, these streets are loaded with them."

Eddie didn't speak for a minute; he had to collect his thoughts. He had almost blown it with the remark. He was glad the cabdriver wasn't quickwitted enough to put the pickup spot and the remark together.

The cab had pulled onto Peachtree. "Any store in particular?"

Eddie's eyes quickly scanned the street. "That one over there." He pointed to a men's outlet shop. He had intended to hold the cab, pick out some clothes and then head to the airport. But he wasn't sure what the cabbie might be thinking while waiting, and he couldn't take the chance. He paid the driver and looked around the street before entering the store. Picking out a shirt, pants and jacket, he dressed, then looked in the mirror. It was a big change from prison garb. He walked over to the counter and pulled the money from his pocket. "That's a nice-looking outfit." The clerk started to make out a sales slip. "Will that be cash or charge?" Eddie showed the money. "That will be one hundred and thirty-eight dollars." Eddie counted out seven twenty-dollar bills and laid them on the counter. He looked at his watch; it was already two-twenty. His plane was probably getting ready to take off. The clerk handed Eddie the change. "Now do you want that all boxed?"

"No, I think I'll wear these clothes." Eddie pulled off the labels.

"Fine, I'll put your other clothes in a box."

Eddie said, "No, just throw them out. I won't be needing them."

He walked out onto the busy street. Suddenly he looked down and realized he now had a fancy outfit but he was still wearing tennis shoes. There was a shoe store directly across the street. Eddie looked at his watch. It was late, but he noticed a line of cabs moving along the street, most of them empty. It took Eddie only ten minutes to get what he needed in the shoe store and then he was hailing a cab to the airport. He kept watching the clock. The cabbie was moving along too slowly.

Eddie tapped the cabbie. "Hey Mac, I'm late for a flight. There's another five in it for you if you can move faster." The cabbie forced his way through the traffic. A grin crossed Eddie's face. Money always talked; it was the only way to go.

Finally they were at the airport. He looked out the window at the jets sitting in line waiting for takeoff. Leaping out of the cab, he dropped the extra five to the driver. Luckily there was no line at the ticket counter and Eddie was able to pay and run. He made the plane with about two minutes to spare.

Relief showed on his face as the doors of the plane were shut and the big bird slowly moved away from the gate. He had been free for three hours. The first place they should have looked for him was the airport. He wondered what had happened back at the Federal Pen, and hoped they still thought he was planting trees and bushes. He laughed. The stewardess approached him with her rolling bar and Eddie was in the sky, Atlanta only another black memory.

THIRTY ONE

Warden Hanberry was working on a large pile of papers at his desk. Occasionally he would sit back and stretch. The paperwork in the Federal penal system was enormous and the warden's job was tiring. Suddenly the intercom buzzed and Hanberry picked up the phone.

The voice was tense. "Warden, ah, we sort of have a problem."

Hanberry rolled his eyes toward the ceiling. "Okay, what is it? I'm busy in here."

"Well, Warden, it's the landscaping truck. It's missing, Warden." Hanberry's face turned ashen. "We've checked everyplace, Warden, and it's just not around the prison area."

"That's ridiculous. How the hell can you lose a two-ton truck, painted orange, inside a prison?"

"Well, sir, it's not in the prison, sir. Eddie took it."

Hanberry jumped up from his desk screaming, "What?"

"Warden, Eddie Watkins drove the truck out the front gate."

Hanberry fell back in his chair. He was shaking, angry, confused. "Make sense, man. How could he? Who let him do that? What are we running here?"

"The guard at the gate thought you had okayed it."

Hanberry interrupted, "Okayed what? A prisoner escaping in a two-ton truck?"

"No, Warden, they thought you were sending him into town for something."

"In a prison truck? Call the F.B.I., call the Atlanta police, get me the chief on the phone and bring my car around front. And do it now."

Hanberry slammed the receiver on its cradle. "He did it again." He slammed his fist down on the desk. "He did it to me again."

The plane started to make its descent. Eddie looked at his watch; it was a little past seven. He reached over and set the timepiece back three hours, then leaned back and wondered about the goings on in Altanta. By now, he knew, they were looking for him. The airport in Cleveland was probably full of Feds and police departments across the country would once again be flooded with wanted posters on him. The plane started its bank and Eddie could see the smog-shrouded outline of the City of Los Angeles. He pulled the seat belt tightly around his waist.

The landing was smooth and Eddie headed out of the plane. He was back in Los Angeles, where he had a couple of things to do. One was to see a cameragirl named Joan Roth who had done an interview with him at the Atlanta Pen. Eddie had liked her from the start. She was young and smart, and above all she had a big pair of breasts. Eddie and Joan had written to each other after the interview and after she took a network position in Los Angeles. He had done some paintings for her, and the two of them seemed to get along well . . . at least by mail.

His other job was financial. Eddie needed a new stake and Los Angeles had the banks to provide this for him. But always in his mind was Cleveland. He was not going to go out a loser in that city. He had done so as a child, as a man and as a bank robber, but he was still going to show them a thing or two.

Eddie walked out into the warm California air. There were a number of things he had to do before checking into a hotel. He had no luggage, his only clothes were those on his back, and naturally he had to fatten his money roll quickly. His savings from prison were running out.

The cab ride into downtown L.A. was slow, Rush-hour traffic made the cab crawl. But finally they were downtown.

Eddie spotted a department store and left the cab. He shopped for about an hour, picking up a suitcase and other necessary articles. Then he again hailed a cab. His next stop was a Holiday Inn. He was no longer a suspicious-looking vagrant, but a traveling businessman with packages and a suitcase.

In his room, he threw the key on the dresser and

placed his bags on the chair. Slowly he lowered himself to the bed. It had been a long day. Again he looked at his watch. It was seven o'clock. He propped the pillow under his head and lit a cigarette; the smoke slowly circled around. He was wondering how everything was back in Atlanta. It was lights out by this time and he bet that plenty of high Fed brass were trying to figure how to find the elusive Fast Eddie.

He pulled some papers from his pocket and finally located his little telephone book, then reached for the phone and dialed. The line was busy so Joan was probably at home. Again he lay back. Just this morning he had been in prison; now, just ten hours from when he woke in his cell, he was twenty-five hundred miles away, a free man. He reached over and again tried Joan. The number was still busy. Eddie then dialed room service and ordered his supper. Occasionally he would stop eating and dial Joan again.

"She must be the most longwinded broad around," he thought. He could picture that young body and those good looks, and he felt fine knowing she was only thirty minutes away. Eddie was in his glory. He finished his food and began emptying his shopping bags and sorting everything carefully in the drawers. He knew the nosy housekeepers would be looking around, and he wanted no slipups at this point. He was a hot number all over the country by then and he had to make sure everything was handled in the right way. After arranging his clothes, he jumped into the shower, shaved and used a bit of the new cologne he had just purchased. Then he dried himself and went back to the phone. Again the busy signal.

Eddie put on his jacket and left the room. In the lobby he stopped at the rental-car desk and arranged for a lease. He put the car keys in his pocket and went out, hailed a cab and gave the driver the address Joan had always used on her letters. After about twenty minutes the cab pulled up to the house. Eddie told the driver to hold on until he checked to see if anybody was at home. He knocked on the door and a voice from inside answered, so he went back to the cab and paid his fare. Then he mounted the steps and again knocked on the door.

The voice questioned, "Who's there?"

"It's me, Eddie Watkins."

He stood back, straightening his jacket. This was going to be a hell of a night. Eddie just kept standing there and the door remained closed. He knocked again. Still no response. Eddie slammed his fist into his hand. He was pissed off that he had not taken the car he had just rented. Now the cab was gone and here he was stuck in the dark with a dizzy broad playing games.

Eddie knocked and waited for about five minutes, then he looked around. "The fuckin' broad is probably calling the law," Eddie said to himself. He bolted down the steps and quickly headed up the street. Finding an area of trees and bushes, he hid behind them, keeping Joan's house in clear view.

Suddenly a set of headlights turned the corner and slowly moved down the street. Eddie crouched. The car stopped in front of Joan's house.

"No time to lose my cool," he thought. Backing through the bushes, he made his way to another street and then onto a main drag, where he lucked out and found a cab. He jumped in and told the driver to take him back to the hotel.

In the room, he reached for the phone to call Joan, then placed the phone back in the cradle. He could not let his anger get him caught. What was she anyway—probably not even a good piece of ass. She had always written nice letters, he couldn't figure why. But he was not going to leave his room tonight. He had had enough shit for one day and rest was the best prescription.

The sound of horns blowing woke Eddie. He looked at his watch; it was nine A.M. He rolled over and reached for the phone, ordered breakfast and a newspaper. He needed to know if anything had been printed in the L.A. *Times*. Quickly he jumped into the shower and was drying off when a knock came on the door. For a second he became panicky and looked around for his gun. He didn't have one. "Shit," he muttered, "I knew I forgot to get something."

Then his common sense again took control. For a moment he had forgotten about ordering breakfast. He opened the door and picked up the tray. The newspaper was there too. He closed the door and set the food tray on the dresser. Sitting at the window, he went through the paper page by page, his anxiety building up as he could find nothing on the escape of a famous bank robber. He turned to page one again and examined the paper even more closely, again with the same results—Nothing.

"Guess they haven't had time to inform the West Coast." He needed to get a copy of the Cleveland *Plain Dealer*. But for now it was breakfast time and time for a look at the yellow pages under banks.

THIRTY TWO

The next two weeks in California were lively, as Eddie proceeded to knock off five banks. He was reckless but crafty. He now had the start of a new bankroll and it was time for him to go back to where his roots were, Cleveland.

The trip home was slow, as Eddie knew he was a hot item again and was being hunted across the United States. Thinking about the banks in Los Angeles, he smiled as he recalled how easy it had been. Now he was well heeled and had a suitcase full of new clothes and a new car. The only area where he had not done well was with Joan.

He arrived in Cleveland late in the evening, wanting to make sure no one would spot him coming into the city. He found a hotel, moved all his belongings in, and looked out the window at the sprawling city, thinking about the old days. Then he ate and hit the sack. Eddie knew he had his work cut out and he needed all the rest he could get.

For the next few days he moved cautiously around the city. Every time he passed the Society

National Bank his heart would begin to pound. That bank had caused him more trouble than any other in his life.

He checked out the bank on a daily basis. It had become an obsession; he needed to get even with it. It was time. Tomorrow he would become a modern-day David and Goliath would finally go down.

Eddie woke up early and rolled over, feeling a little knot in his stomach. Lying back in the bed, he lit a cigarette and began to think about the fiasco five years earlier. He went over every point and his heart attack was the only problem he could think of. He kenw that if he didn't get another one he could take that bank in a flash. He smiled as he wondered what the employees would say when he entered the building. Probably they would all just line up and march back into the employee kitchen. He stopped grinning. That kitchen was the last place he wanted to go on this trip.

He jumped out of bed and began dressing. He would not wear any disguise on this job. He wanted everyone to know who he was. He checked his gun, making sure it was fully loaded before shoving it into his belt. He put on his hat, took a quick glance in the mirror and headed out of the room.

The ride down to the Society National was only a few minutes but to Eddie it felt like hours. Finally he was positioned where he could see everything he needed to. It was before nine o'clock and he watched as the employees filed into the bank. Something looked wrong, though he could not tell what. Finally he noticed that there were more employees than the bank had had before. He knew they could not have added any more space, so what was this—a stakeout? Did they know that Eddie would be trying to nail this one down for old time's sake. He kept watching as more people arrived. "The sons of bitches," Eddie mumbled to himself, "they got the joint staked out." He cranked up the car and slowly drove into the traffic. He did not want to stir up any trouble. Looking toward the bank, he saw nothing. Clever.

Eddie kept moving and suddenly realized he was in front of the Cleveland National Bank. He laughed. "Two blocks away and they probably don't even have a cruiser near this one. What a surprise this would be." Eddie began to laugh. He pulled the car carefully into a lot across from the bank and watched for a few moments, then pulled the pistol from his belt and rechecked it. Everything looked good. Making sure the keys were left in the ignition, he moved to the front door. Walking into the bank, he quickly covered every angle. In seconds he was aware of where everyone was positioned. He spotted the manager's desk and walked over to him.

"How are you today, sir?" The manager smiled and Eddie smiled too.

"I'm fine." Eddie reached inside his sport coat and pulled the revolver. The manager began to shake. Again a smile crossed Eddie's face, as the manager crouched back in the chair as if he had seen a ghost.

Eddie said, "I'm Fast Eddie Watkins and I'm going to rob this bank. You understand?" The manager slowly shook his head. "Now you stand up." The man quickly obliged, putting his hands in the air.

Eddie waved the gun. "Get your hands down."

"Yes, Mr. Watson." The manager quickly slid his hands to his sides.

"The name is not Watson, it's Watkins. Write it down." The bank manager used a pad and pencil. "You got it now—Watkins." Eddie spelled it out.

"Now let's get on with it. You be sure you stay calm, and advise your people to do the same. I want all the fifties and hundreds you have, and tell them to move fast." The manager headed for the tellers' cages with Eddie a step behind him. The manager announced what was taking place and the tellers reacted quickly. Eddie handed him a paper bag and followed as he walked along, collecting from each girl, with the manager practically running from cage to cage. The bag, now full, was handed to Eddie and he pulled the manager aside and walked him toward the door.

Suddenly Eddie turned and faced the man. "Listen, you. Tell the F.B.I. and the rest of the law that I couldn't take the Society National because they had it staked out, and Eddie Watkins doesn't fall into the same trap twice. So you tell them I may be reckless but I'm no fool. You also tell them I'll be seeing them again." Eddie tipped his hat; the bank manager looked at him in disbelief. "Now get the hell back in the corner or I'll blow your fucking head off."

As the manager ran toward the back, Eddie quickly made his exit. He was into his car and gone, not hearing a siren nor even seeing a police cruiser in the area. He smiled as he put his hand in the bag and felt his newfound wealth.

Back at the hotel room, Eddie counted out the loot. It was not as big as in the old days, but fifteen grand is nothing to sneeze at for a two-minute work day. He picked up the phone and ordered breakfast. Reaching for the paper, he lay back on the bed. The money was secure in his suitcase, and he knew that by now the entire city of Cleveland, the F.B.I. and the banking community were probably in shock.

THIRTY THREE

The morning papers were full of Fast Eddie, with news stories and sidebars. He was a celebrity again. However, knowing that he was fair game for every law-enforcement agency within two hundred miles, he stayed close to his room and wandered out only a night, always being careful not to attract attention.

Each day he would watch Channel 3 and get the reports on his latest escapades as the papers reported his possible tie-in to the robberies in Los Angeles. The scene was getting to be a bit too hot and he knew that it would be just days before someone in the hotel noticed the quiet man in Room 307. He had come to town to enhance his reputation and bust the Society National. On the latter, he had come close—just two blocks away. But he had certainly increased his fame. He had only been out of jail approximately six weeks and already he had the attention of the whole nation. He needed to be on his way. There was about thirty thousand dollars in his suitcase and that would hold him for a while. California would be his best bet. It was big enough for him to get lost in, at least until some of the heavy heat was off. But Eddie had one more thing to do before leaving the city: he needed to find out about Karen. She had a cousin living close by, and Eddie figured he would stop on his way out of town and get some information on her. He quickly packed his suitcases and again checked his gun. Checking the room carefully, he made sure no one would find out he had stayed there.

He paid his bill at the cashier's desk and carried his bags out to the Mercury Cougar parked in the hotel lot. Carefully putting the bags in the trunk, he climbed behind the wheel. For a while he watched the city passing by. He was leaving home again, still not the success he had wanted to be.

The drive over to Karen's cousin's house took about twenty minutes. Pulling into the driveway of the old frame house, he rang the bell and waited. Suddenly he heard footsteps and the door opened. John Morris stood there in a T-shirt, rubbing his eyes.

It had been a long time since Eddie had met John. On that occasion the meeting had happened by accident when Eddie and Karen dined out while she was still married. Eddie really did not want to stop by the house but his curiosity about where Karen was and how she was doing overwhelmed his common sense. Besides, John's wife Helen was a good looker and Eddie had always sort of had a fancy for the big-busted blonde. Karen and Helen had been close during his first few months of dating Karen.

"Eddie, how the hell are you?"

"I would be much better if I came inside. I hate to be standing out here too long." Eddie walked into the living room.

"Yeah, I've read about you. You sure shocked the hell out of this city." Eddie laughed and dropped down on the sofa.

"I read about your bust-out at Atlanta, too. You sure pulled off a fast one." John walked toward the kitchen. "Cold beer?" He turned to Eddie.

"No, I really can't stick around long. I was just headed out of town and figured I would stop by and see you."

John walked to the window. "That yours?" He was looking at the car.

"Yeah."

"You were always one for those big cars." John pulled the curtain closed. "Where you heading?" He popped the can of beer and held it out to Eddie but Eddie waved it off.

"Heading back to the coast. Too hot around here for me." Eddie lit a cigarette and reached for the ash tray.

"You seen Karen lately? I thought maybe I would look her up while I was in town. I didn't find her listed in the phone book, and her folks aren't listed either."

"You haven't heard?"

He squashed out the cigarette. "What's happened to her?"

"Nothing to Karen, Eddie, but her folks both

died a few years back."

"Where is she now?"

"She's remarried and lives over on the other side of town. She has a kid now and she's doing great."

Eddie rose from the sofa. "That's real swell." He put out his hand.

"You leaving so quick?"

"Yeah, I really can't stay. Just thought I'd stop by. If you talk to Karen, tell her Eddie said hello."

John walked Eddie out to the car and said a final goodby. He watched as the Mercury headed down the street; then he raced into his house, picked up a card by the phone, looked it over carefully and dialed a number.

"Hello. Agent Ferris? This is John Morris. You gave me your card and said if I heard from Eddie Watkins you would help me." Nervously he turned toward the door.

"Now do we still have a deal on that marijuana-dealing charge against me?" He smiled. "Okay. I just talked to Eddie Watkins."

Ferris was excited. "Morris, this better not be any bullshit."

"No, honest, he just left my house. He's cut off all his hair and he's driving a white Mercury Cougar. I think it's either a 1979 or 1980, and I even have the plate number."

"What is it?" The agent was calm now.

"MDC-118, California."

"Do you know where he's headed?"

John reached for a cigarette. His hands were

shaking. "He said he was headed back to California."

"Okay, Morris we'll follow up on this, and if everything is on the square we'll be getting back in touch with you." The agent put down the phone.

Eddie looked in the rear-view mirror and waited for traffic to pass him by before pulling onto the interstate. If anyone were following him he wanted to know now. Waiting, he looked over to the freight-yard and remembered the trips he had made from the coast into that yard. Now they were all gone—his mother, his father, Aunt Belle and even his brother. He thought for a second about Karen but didn't linger on that long. She had caused him a lot of trouble in the past and he sure as hell wasn't going looking for any more.

On the interstate he kept watching the rear-view mirror, and suddenly he noticed a white Ford that he sensed had been there for a while.

"You're getting nervous," he said to himself. He kept on watching the car and noticed it stayed behind him on the highway. Suddenly he spotted another vehicle moving up quickly and then almost coming to a halt when it approached his car.

Eddie began to speed up, still watching the mirror. The cars behind him speeded up too. Eddie reached over and opened the glove compartment, pulled out his revolver and put it on the seat next to him. He took another look in the mirror and jammed his foot down on the accelerator.

Now he could hear the sirens of the cars. Traffic cleared in front of him and he quickly pulled to the right and off on the Lodi exit. He almost lost control on the curve but pulled out straight and hauled ass along the road. Suddenly he spotted a dirt road and whipped the Mercury to the right, almost causing the pursuing police to pass him. But they got under control and Eddie started panicking. He wondered how the hell this had happened. His car was spitting up dust and stones. Opening the window, he could hear sirens coming from all directions.

He looked to the left and saw marked sheriffs' cars, red lights flashing, coming straight at him. They were trying to cut him off. Eddie quickly surveyed the fields around him and decided to try and make a new road in a breakout across the rural area.

"Here we go," he yelled wildly and swung the speeding vehicle toward the field. "Oh shit!" The car began a skid and Eddie hands on the wheel, knew he was either going to flip or get his ass stuck. All of a sudden he was jolted and found himself in a ditch. He couldn't see anything, with the dust and dirt still ringing the car. He jammed his foot on the accelerator—nothing but a whining sound. He was stuck.

Police and Federal cars skidded to stops around him. Officers jumped out of their cars and assumed firing position. Eddie hit the accelerator again. The dust flew and all of a sudden he heard pops; he was being shot at. Eddie ducked in the front seat. The

344

bullets ripped into the tires and he could feel the car float down as the air escaped. The car had had it.

"What do I do now?" he wondered, crouched down on the seat. He reached for his gun. "Can't shoot it out with all of them." He sat up slowly and looked around, saw figures darting from car to car. He put his head up farther. Nobody was shooting. Slowly Eddie opened the door of his car and stepped out, with his gun to his head.

Eddie smiled as the police officers looked at him in disbelief. He was his own hostage.

THIRTY-FOUR

Lodi, Ohio . . . The Final Hour

For nearly thirteen hours now the F.B.I., the highway patrol and various other police agencies have been stalled by a 62-year-old, balding, affable bank robber who has held himself hostage. It was a real sideshow, as he would sometimes wave to the crowd and the police, blow kisses to pretty girls in the large crowd of onlookers, and throw money to the hordes, trying to divert the attention of the law so he could possibly get one more chance to run. Eddie was creating a media spectacle.

The police saw in him a man who was a menace, a threat, a danger, a pest, a public enemy and an escaped inmate from a Federal prison. The people in the crowd see in that same man a flaky character who has provided them with thirteen hours of human drama, something they can tell their children and their grandchildren about for years to come. Some of them see him as a legend, the romantic figure of the lone bandit, a mysterious highwayman, a media star whom they had read about in bold headlines. In an antisocial way, he was like a *Star Trek* character in that he boldly ventured where few men dared . . . into the banks to steal dreams that he had been denied.

The media, of course, saw him as a colorful news story.

Eddie Watkins was, in a way, all of the above and yet none of them. He was not simply a public enemy, a menace or a pest; and, although he was indeed a fugitive from the Federal prison system, he was also a human being, the sum total of everything they thought he was, everything he thought he was and much, much more.

Eddie was also a beaten-down, tired old rebel who had had to swim upstream all his life. And where had it gotten him? To a field in Lodi where he was a spectacle for all to gawk at. In spite of all his bank robberies and daring criminal deeds, he had spent more than half his life locked up in prisons; always wishing he could get out.

From the beginning, when Eddie Watkins decided to take on the world, he really hadn't had a chance; the odds were too great against him. And finally, when he had his opportunities to swim downstream, where the going was easy, he just couldn't or wouldn't handle the change.

For all he had done, and in spite of the fact that high-powered rifles and magnum-loaded shotguns were pointed at him now—ready to take him out of it all in less than an instant—and in spite of the fact that he had his own loaded gun pointed at his own head, he was still a living human being with a big heart and soul.

In spite of all that Eddie had done in his life of crime, even most of those who had hunted him had few bad things to say about him. In his own strange way he had tried to establish his own morality.

Now the day had passed and the situation had grown more hopeless, Eddie had inched his finger toward the trigger. For a moment he expected that finger to jerk by itself and squeeze off an explosion that would send his brains splattering across the top of his car and into the ditch, where they would become part of the earth. And his last thought would be something like a movie projector when the film gets jammed and flickers violently.

But Eddie was a stubborn old bandit who knew that if he did squeeze that trigger, there would be that unmeasurable fraction of an instant, as the bullet came through the barrel, when he would think about that one last woman who was out there to love, that one last chance for escape, that one last faint hope of parole. Then he would want to change his mind, but it would be too late.

During the last thirteen hours Eddie had been cheered by the crowd, he had seen people from his past—people who had always meant something to him—and he had provided entertainment to the citizens in whose name he had been incarcerated. Now the battered old fish was out of the water and he was making his last stand.

The S.W.A.T. sharpshooters were itchy to open fire. It made not one bit of difference to them that Eddie Watkins, though operating outside of the law for all those years and stealing almost two million dollars, had never once hurt anyone. The sharpshooters were stoic; waiting for the word, waiting for the kill. They were tired of it all, they wanted to show their stuff. They wanted to bag one of the biggest trophies, they wanted to see the juice fly . . . they really wanted this man who could make J. Edgar Hoover go into cardiac arrest at the sound of his name.

But Agent Burke had kept the S.W.A.T. guns silent.

Now a decision had to be made. The nation had seen this standoff through the eyes of NBC, CBS and ABC. Newpaper reporters and photographers kept the lines hot, feeding the wires with the hostage story. Burke had to make the decision.

Finally it came down. Burke decided the only way to take Eddie was to let a trained attack dog, with its swiftness, make the approach. One final time Burke called for Eddie to surrender. His answer was a wave of the hand.

It was decided that while someone tried to talk with Eddie over the bullhorn and keep him distracted, the handler and the dog would move into position. It was nearly dark. Brent walked over to Burke, and they talked. Brent told Burke that S.W.A.T. guns would be trained on Eddie, and that if he made a move with his gun in the direction of the police, the sharpshooters would open fire. They both agreed to the plan.

Eddie stood with his hand on the roof of the car. He noticed nothing happening and looked around. At that moment the handler already in position pulled the German Shepherd to him and whispered the command. The dog bounded forward just as Eddie turned around. Suddenly the dog stopped and looked at Eddie. Eddie looked at the dog. The dog sat down and wagged its tail. The crowd went crazy. The newsmen stared in awe.

"Go, go," the handler began to scream.

The dog didn't move. Finally, in desperation, the handler dived from behind Eddie's car at the dog. The dog responded and leaped at Eddie. Eddie swung his gun arm outward to ward off the leaping dog; then he stumbled back and fell through the open door and into the door and into the front seat of the car. The dog leaped onto and over the roof and slid off on the other side.

At that moment the police opened fire. Guns blazed and bullets slammed into the car, the windows, the doors and hood. Shotgun pellets rained on the car and metal from the vehicle began to fly off. Burke was waving his arms and trying to yell over the roar of gunfire. Finally he grabbed the bullhorn and screamed into it to hold fire.

The gunfire stopped. The car was riddled, smoking, practically demolished by the gunshots. The crowd was completely quiet, some returning to the closer position where they had stood prior to the shooting. Nothing inside the car moved. Karen was still among the crowd and they could hear her sobbing as an F.B.I. agent comforted her.

The young agent held her arm to support her. "We gave him every opportunity to surrender."

"I know. But my God, what a horrible way for him to go." She wiped her eyes.

Slowly the agents approached the car. Burke raced up to the side window, saw blood on the seat and holstered his gun. He leaned into the car and suddenly backed away. Eddie sat up.

Burke heard the click of hammers behind him. He waved back signaling not to shoot. Eddie pulled himself to the edge of the front seat, grinning and holding up his hand. He pointed to his bleeding pinky finger.

"You know, Burke, your guys can't shoot worth a shit." Eddie pulled out a handkerchief.

"Eddie."

"Yeah, Burke, it's me. You're not looking at a ghost. They got me in the damn finger."

Burke shook his head in disbelief.

Eddie began to laugh.

"Eddie, what am I going to do with you?"

"Well, for starters, how about getting me a cigarette?" Burke turned and a lit butt was handed to him. He motioned to Brent to bring over the ambulance.

"You know, Eddie, I don't believe this." The ambulance pulled up near the car and the stretcher was pulled out of the back. Eddie puffed on the cigarette and watched Burke closely. Finally, as he was led to the stretcher, he took a long drag on the cigarette and defiantly blew smoke into Burke's face.

"You know, Burke," Eddie said, "if I knew those bastards of yours couldn't shoot any straighter than that, I would have been gone from here thirteen hours ago." Then he laid back down on the stretcher, flipping the cigarette out the door.

Eddie Watkins, in chains, was taken to Cleveland to face trail. It seemed almost fitting that on his way to the jail the Fedral marshal's car carried him down Euclid Avenue. His eyes focused on the May Company sign and as he stared at it his eyes grew bright with tears and he turned his head away.

Edward Owens Watkins was returned to a Federal maximum-security prison in Wisconsin, where he is currently serving a 295-year sentence. With good behavior he will be eligible for parole when he is 139 years old. The prison is allegedly escape proof.